UNCUFFED

Uncuffed
An Anthology
From Paul Anthony Associates

This is an anthology of work written, edited, published and promoted exclusively by police writers from the United Kingdom and the United States of America. Some of the writers are published authors in their own right and others have never been published before.

~

Proceeds from the sale of this work will be donated to COPS: A charity registered in England and Wales (1101478) and in Scotland (SCO038541) which is
'Dedicated to the Care of Police Survivors.'
http://www.ukcops.org/about-cops.html

~

Rights to individual works reside with the artists themselves. Each author is attributed to their work and is listed herein. This collection contains work submitted to the publisher by individual authors who confirm that the work is their original creation. All rights are reserved under international copyright conventions.

~

Cover Image © Ian McCrone Photography
Edited by Meg Johnston.

~

Published by
Paul Anthony Associates
http://www.independentauthornetwork.com/paul-anthony.html

~

http://paulanthonys.blogspot.co.uk/

~

www.ianmccronephotography.co.uk/

I am sure you will enjoy the varied contributions in this book. It is nice to see that cynicism within the service is not dead! That helps to keep some senior feet "on the ground".

When you have finished it, remember that it was a book written by police officers for police officers, and their families. Just remember the ones, many of whom we have known personally, who cannot be here to enjoy it and salute every one of them.

G.M.McCrone (MBE)
Penrith 1st July 2014

*

Foreword

~

Having served for 30 years as a police officer, I have the greatest admiration for those men and women who serve to care for their fellow citizens, without fear or favour and, more often than not, without appreciation. My first real contact with the police was when I left the Merchant Navy, having served for 10 years as a navigating officer. I knew as soon as I joined as a probationer constable that it was probably the best day's work I ever did. The men and women I met and worked with in every department of the service were some of the best people I have ever known, good team members, trustworthy and good to have beside you in a crisis. During my final years in Carlisle, as superintendent, the teams of officers policing the city were superb, dedicated to their public and always positive.

The Police Service has always been a "can do" organisation and this anthology of stories, poems, comments and observations written by officers, many of whom I have known personally, proves that this philosophy is true. Their talent is obvious and I wish them all well in their writing ambitions.

We were the lucky ones who lived to complete our service and moved, unscathed (more or less), into retirement to enjoy our latter years comfortably with our families and friends. Unfortunately, many who served were not so lucky and suffered death or serious injury serving their communities. The proceeds of this book are in aid of COPS (Care of Police Survivors), a registered charity which provides care and support for the families of police officers who have lost their lives whilst on duty. It was a great privilege to be asked to write this foreword – as it was to serve with many dedicated officers throughout the years. In retirement there is nothing more enjoyable than getting together with ex-colleagues and recounting old times!

REVIEW

~

UNCUFFED
An Anthology
From Paul Anthony Associates.

Paul Anthony is an established writer of crime thrillers who draws from his many years of policing experience to add colour and flavour to his work.

However, in this Anthology he has pulled together written works from a number of ex and serving police officers from the UK and US whose collective experiences are almost too many to count.

This has resulted in an eclectic mixture of short stories, poems, rhyming narrative and other short works which stretch from fantasy and young adult, to romantic through to satire and gritty crime thrillers. There is something for everyone.

From literary prose to contemporary procedurals, there is a wonderful depth and array of reading pleasures here waiting to be consumed. Showcasing writers from both sides of the Atlantic – some already published, and some soon to be so – this only whets my appetite of what is still to come.

With proceeds going to a fine charity – as in COPS – which tirelessly help survivors of officers who have lost their lives protecting us all; the purchase of this Anthology is the least we can all do. It serves as a reminder of the daily dangers facing our boys and girls in blue – some of which are touched on in these stories.

This is a well-crafted mixture of written works, none of which take more than ten minutes to read, so it is a joy to pick up and put down as busy schedules allow; an ideal companion on the commute to work or at the end of the day.

Not only will you come away from this Anthology sated with your every emotion involved, you will feel informed on many levels.

I thoroughly enjoyed reading the Anthology and congratulate everyone who contributed to the various different pieces.

Excellent, informative, emotional and just fun to read.

'An eclectic mix of great stories to please everyone.'

Roger A Price, Author of 'By Their Rules' and 'A new Menace'.

*

Publisher's Note

~

On behalf of the writers of 'Uncuffed' we would like to place on record our thanks to the following who have given up their time and expertise in the creation of this anthology by editing, reviewing or consulting with us regarding the work, and providing a cover in order that we might showcase our book.

With thanks to Meg Johnston, Roger Price, Simon Hepworth, George McCrone and Ian McCrone Photography.

Additionally, we offer a special word of thanks to our retired American police colleagues Mike McNeff and Wayne Zurl as well as our 'special guest author' Scott Whitmore: A retired US Navy officer. They have all contributed to this work and supported our endeavours without reservation.

This anthology was created, written, edited, published and promoted by a collection of retired police officers working in co-operation with each other across our homeland and across a pond that divides us yet also unites us.

Thank you…

*

CONTENTS

~ ~ ~

1) On The Joys of Retirement by Meg Johnston
2) Peelers by Paul Anthony
3) Writing the Wrongs by Station Sergeant
4) An Appeal For Information by The Boss's Snout
5) Another Shout by Ray Gregory
6) A Collection of Flowers by Ian Bruce
7) Dying For a Chat by Dave Miller
8) Meg, Liz and The Fairy Glen by Meg Johnston
9) Return Trip by Simon Hepworth
10) The Rainbow Tree by Meg Johnston
11) Life In Numbers by Dave Miller
12) The Last Three Months by Dave Miller
13) Risk – 90's Style by Ray Gregory
14) The Quick 'n' Easy Guide To Gardening by Simon Hepworth
15) Loneliness by Dave Miller
16) Black Dog by Dave Miller
17) A Childhood Dream Come True by Edward Lightfoot
18) The RIP by Mike McNeff
19) Street Justice by Wayne Zurl
20) The Visit by Dave Miller
21) The Christmas Table by Dave Miller
22) Welcome Aboard Chavair by Simon Hepworth
23) The Rider by Ray Gregory
24) Mother Nature by Dave Miller
25) Grass, The Green Stuff by Dave Miller
26) By Their Rules by Roger Price
27) The Fragile Peace by Paul Anthony
28) Moonlight Shadows by Paul Anthony
29) Luguvalium's Story by Paul Anthony
30) Paper Trail by Wayne Zurl
31) Carpathia by Scott Whitmore

32) Nights by Ray Gregory
33) Breakwater by Paul Anthony
34) The Door's Ajar by Ray Gregory

*

35) Meet the Authors – An introduction to the authors via a short biography.

*

'On The Joys of Retirement'
When I am Older
By Meg Johnston
~

When I am older
I shall wear purple,
And a red fascinator that doesn't go,
And looks ridiculous.
I shall spend my pension
On Port, Brandy, and holidays,
And say we've no money for cheese.
I shall sit down on the pavement when I'm tired
And gobble up samples in shops
And press alarm bells,
And use my stick as a battering ram,
And make up for the sobriety of my youth.
I shall go out in my slippers in the rain
And pick flowers in other peoples gardens
And learn to swear.

You can wear terrible tops and grow fatter
And eat three pounds of chocolate at one go
Or only bread and jam for a week,
And hoard pens and pencils
And candles and things in boxes.
But now we must have clothes that keep us warm
And pay our mortgage
And not swear in the street,
And set a good example for the children.
We must have friends to dinner
And listen to the news.
But maybe I ought to practice a little now?
So people who know me
Are not too shocked and surprised
When suddenly I am older
And start to wear purple.
~

The above has been adapted from the poem
'WARNING'
By the English poet
'Jenny Joseph'
*

'Peelers'
By Paul Anthony
~

'Peelers' is a term not regularly heard on the streets of the United Kingdom in the twenty first century. But it doesn't seem that long ago that the shout 'Peelers about' echoed through the towns and cities of our great nation. The term, as many a British beat Bobbie will tell you, is used to describe a uniformed beat officer: what we often call – a Constable.

And so, for the benefit of our American cousins, let me explain the term 'Peeler' and its origins.

Sir Robert Peel (1788 - 1850) was a British Conservative statesman who served as prime minister of the United Kingdom from 1834 to 1835, and also from 1841 to1846. Whilst Home Secretary Peel helped create the modern concept of the police force leading to officers being known as 'bobbies' (particularly in England) and 'peelers' (often in Northern Ireland).

Peel was born in Bury, Lancashire. His father was one of the richest textile manufacturers of the early Industrial Revolution. Peel was educated at Bury Grammar School, Hipperholme Grammar School, Harrow School and finally Christ Church, Oxford, where he took a double first in classics and mathematics.

Peel entered politics in 1809 at the age of 21, as MP for the Irish rotten borough of Cashel, Tipperary. With a scant 24 electors on the rolls, he was elected unopposed. His sponsor for the election was the Chief Secretary for Ireland, Sir Arthur Wellesley, the future Duke of Wellington, with whom Peel's political career would be entwined for the next 25 years. Peel made his maiden speech in 1810. His speech was a sensation, famously described by the Speaker, Charles Abbot, as 'the best first speech since that of William Pitt.'

As chief secretary in Dublin in 1813, he proposed the setting up of a specialist police force, later called 'peelers'. In 1814 the Royal Irish Constabulary was founded under Peel.

Peel first entered the cabinet in 1822 as Home Secretary. As Home Secretary, he introduced a number of important reforms of British criminal law: most memorably establishing the Metropolitan Police Force (Metropolitan Police Act 1829). He also reformed the criminal law, reducing the number of crimes punishable by death, and simplified it by repealing a large number of criminal statutes and consolidating their provisions into what are known as Peel's Acts. He reformed the gaol system, introducing payment for gaolers and education for the inmates.

He resigned as Home Secretary after the Prime Minister Lord Liverpool, became incapacitated and was replaced by George Canning. Canning favoured Catholic Emancipation while Peel had been one of its most outspoken opponents (earning the nickname "Orange Peel"). George Canning himself died less than four months later and Peel subsequently returned to the post of Home Secretary under the premiership of his long-time ally the Duke of Wellington.

However, the pressure on the new ministry from advocates of Catholic Emancipation was too great and an Emancipation Bill was passed the next year. Peel felt compelled to resign his seat as MP representing the graduates of Oxford University (many of whom were Anglican clergymen), as he had stood on a platform of opposition to Catholic Emancipation (in 1815 he had, in fact, challenged to a duel the man most associated with emancipation, Daniel O'Connell). Peel instead moved to a rotten borough, Westbury, retaining his Cabinet position.

In the years that followed Daniel O'Connell became the icon of Irish Republican History. His statue stands at the end of O'Connell Street, close to O'Connell Bridge, in Dublin.

Indeed, O'Connell Bridge, and the seedlings of Irish Republican History, forms the backdrop of the early part of my novel – Moonlight Shadows – but I digress.

In 1829 Peel established the Metropolitan Police Force for London based at Scotland Yard. The 1,000 constables employed were affectionately nicknamed 'Bobbies' or, somewhat less affectionately, 'Peelers'. Although unpopular at first they proved very successful in cutting crime in London, and by 1857 all cities in the UK were obliged to form their own police forces. Known as the father of modern policing, Peel developed the Peelian Principles which defined the ethical requirements police officers must follow to be effective.

The Middle and Working Classes in England at that time, however, were clamouring for reform, and Catholic Emancipation was only one of the ideas in the air. The Tory ministry refused to bend on other issues and were swept out of office in 1830 in favour of the Whigs. The following few years were extremely turbulent, but eventually enough reforms were passed that King William IV felt confident enough to invite the Tories to form a ministry again in succession to those of Lord Grey and Lord Melbourne in 1834. Peel was selected as prime minister but was in Italy at the time, so Wellington acted as a caretaker for the three weeks until Peel's return.

This new Tory Ministry was a minority government, however, and depended on Whig goodwill for its continued existence. As his statement of policy at the general election of January 1835, Peel issued the Tamworth Manifesto. The issuing of this document is often seen as one of the most crucial points at which the Tories became the Conservative Party. In it he pledged that the Conservatives would endorse modest reform, but the Whigs instead formed a compact with Daniel O'Connell's Irish Radical members to repeatedly defeat the government on various bills. Eventually Peel's ministry resigned out of frustration and the Whigs under Lord Melbourne returned to power.

Peel was thrown from his horse while riding up Constitution Hill in London on 29 June 1850, the horse stumbled on top of him and he died three days later on 2 July at the age of 62. His Peelite followers, led by Lord Aberdeen and William Gladstone, went on to fuse with the Whigs as the Liberal Party.

Peel married Julia, youngest daughter of General Sir John Floyd, 1st Baronet, in 1820. They had five sons and two daughters. Four of his sons gained distinction in their own right. His eldest son Sir Robert Peel, 3rd Baronet, served as Chief Secretary for Ireland from 1861 to 1865. His second son Sir Frederick Peel was a politician and railway commissioner. His third son Sir William Peel was a naval commander and recipient of the Victoria Cross. His fifth son Arthur Wellesley Peel was Speaker of the House of Commons and created Viscount Peel in 1895. His daughter Julia married the 6th Earl of Jersey. Julia, Lady Peel, died in 1859. Some of his direct descendants now reside in South Africa, the Australian states of New South Wales, Queensland, Victoria and Tasmania, and in various parts of the United States and Canada.

They might even be reading this explanation and tribute to the character most associated with the formation of the British Police Force. Indeed, the content of this anthology is written by both American and English 'Peelers'.

*

Writing the Wrongs
By 'Station Sergeant'
~

To paraphrase Kermit the Frog, which is not something I do very often, it isn't easy being a police writer. It's great, I imagine, when you retire and your wealth of experience and steady flow of anecdotes pour effortlessly on to the page, your credibility as a crime writer enhanced by your ability to assert 'I was there...' Until that time comes a serving officer, affected as much as any other author by the need to write, faces a stark choice: to set down what they really want to say, but anonymously, or to water down their message into the inevitable stream of lukewarm platitudes and 'on message' drivel in their own name that will pass the scrutiny of the force Press Office?

We have, you see, fewer rights than most, we scribes within the law enforcement community. Anything we say can be taken at face value by our readers; we mustn't talk about operations, investigations or identifiable people lest we inadvertently scupper a case, out an informant or, worst of all, offend the sensibilities of some scrote. The lawyers would be all over us, swiftly followed by Professional Standards Department: the latter-day Gestapo as we fondly think of PSD. All that is, of course, something akin to common sense. The powers-that-be, however, don't encourage any free thinking. The police are a disciplined organisation, and there is no room for independent thought, unless you are independently coming up with the same sort of thoughts that they would have if they weren't so busy. Above all, they really hate satire, because that implies ridicule and our glorious leaders can never be seen as ridiculous.

Fortunately, for the standing of the higher echelons, police humour has been abolished. The New Puritans, so entrenched in the public service, rightly identified a number of years ago that we were making the most of our frequently unpleasant, often risky and sometimes downright dangerous vocation. As we all know, if you've just faced down a crowd of drunken yobs, dealt with a festering body (alive or dead) or simply just acted as the ringmaster in the never-ending circus of disputes between neighbours, you have to get it off your chest. Since time immemorial the way to cope with such stress is to laugh it off, poke fun at the situation with gallows humour, and bounce the experience off your mates, who all understand, because they've all been there. Naturally, that no longer sits comfortably with the *bien pensants* of the social tree-hugging fraternity. They would prefer that we submit to counselling, taking the chance to sit down and talk through it with some well-meaning wet blanket who hasn't been there and wouldn't know how to cope if they did. My plan for coping with police counsellors, by the way, is to visit them on every conceivable occasion and frighten them rigid with stories of death and mayhem. Those who survive can always become special constables.

In the good old days, which staggered on until the late Nineties by my reckoning, police humour was accepted, even tacitly encouraged. It was a rite of passage, as a probationer, that you endured at least one practical joke intended to test your mettle. My first sergeant had a shop dummy which he would dress in a variety of clothing borrowed from a handy skip. New PCs on their first night shift would inevitably get a shout to attend the multi-story car park where, it was reported, there was a potential suicide. As they turned up and took stock of the situation, the suicide would shout "Oh no, it's PC Smith. That's the last thing I need!" and plummet from the fourth floor. I am pleased to report that many PCs survived the experience and, indeed, went on to follow illustrious careers. Nowadays I expect they would go off sick with stress and look for someone to sue.

So humour is out, officially at least. We have been harangued and chastened into accepting that humour is inappropriate, because inevitably it is at someone else's expense. The fact that the supposed victim hasn't got the faintest idea that they are making our day is neither here nor there. Just the very fact that we are not grieving for their plight makes us bad people, unworthy of our calling.

The same thought process holds true even amongst our leaders. If we lampoon their latest, invariably ludicrous, visions and mission statements, we are part of the problem rather than the solution. Even if we stifle our mirth, it does not mean that their hair-brained schemes to make the public love us are in any way sensible. We just have to express it quietly and surreptitiously. How much better it would be, perhaps, were we allowed to express our views and opinions away from the gaze of the public. I have long advocated a 'humour board', perhaps in the refreshments room, where memos can be defaced, mission statements altered and caption competitions held. Then, the pressure released, we can all move on and get on with our jobs knowing that we have had our say, even if no one is actually going to take any notice.

With discipline comes hierarchy, and the capacity for bruised egos that accompanies the scaling of the promotion pyramid. The bosses can hand out copious helpings from the dish of vengeance, whether it is served hot or cold. So any truly independent writing by serving officers must be carefully crafted and, essentially, published under a cloak of anonymity. A few years ago one such cop, using the pseudonym PC David Copperfield, wrote a book called 'Wasting Police Time'. Its key message being the reality of policing a provincial town with depleted resources, massively wasteful bureaucracy and the dead hand of political correctness snuffing out any attempts to point out that the Emperor's New Clothes were somewhat lacking in substance. The establishment hated it. It was a best seller and was emulated by other officers including 'Inspector Gadget'. There was, I felt, a gap in the market there for an anonymous sergeant which I was only too happy to fill. I had written a number of articles for Police Review, now sadly no more, and the Editor thought there was scope for a weekly column penned by a cynical, sarcastic dinosaur of a sergeant for whom everything was too much trouble. For some reason he had me in mind. We thought it would run for a month or so, but in the event it outlasted the magazine and, at the time of writing at least, the column now appears in the Federation's monthly magazine Police. Now the Home Office is gunning for the Federation so perhaps my days are numbered.

Writing a weekly column proved more fruitful than I had originally anticipated. I decided not to highlight operational and resourcing concerns, in part because these had been so adequately covered by Messrs Copperfield and Gadget. Plus I valued my career; Professional Standards were, I considered, more likely to hunt down and eradicate, if only metaphorically, those who frightened the public by exposing their vulnerability. Abject cowardice has always been the better part of valour in my book. Besides, there was so much comic potential in the weekly news pages of Police Review, even if that was not as intended by the force Press Offices conjuring up the snowstorm of drivel that the editorial team had to sift through. And, boy was there some rubbish churned out across the country. Prior to 2010 when we went out of fashion, the police service was on one long New Labour-ordained charm offensive. Pink and fluffy policing was the order of the day as we sought to build confidence and satisfaction amongst the public by dressing up as furry animals and holding interminable open days at police stations. And the public lapped it all up; just over fifty percent of them thought we were actually rather nice. The rest, I imagine, were too busy demanding to see their brief, ranting about speeding tickets or had their heads buried in the Daily Mail and were less effusive in their love and respect for us. Now that we don't worry about whether the public gives two statistical hoots about us, and we are getting on with the serious business of trying to convince them that we can still afford to put some uniforms on the streets, I notice that just over fifty percent of them still think we are actually rather nice. This tells me that pink and fluffy policing was a complete and utter waste of time and effort, but I won't say 'I told you so'. Whilst we are on the subject of statistics, our current Home Secretary criticises us, pointing out that one third of the population don't trust us. Interestingly, whilst 65% of respondents in the 2013 poll trust us to tell the truth, only 18% trust politicians to do so. So I would suggest that, before she tells us to remove the splinter from our eye, she remove the scaffolding pole from her own.

Of course, we didn't have it all our own way. The obsequious kowtowing of our bosses to political correctness saw some spectacular own goals; an East Midlands force investigated TV puppet Basil Brush for making disparaging comments about gypsies until, presumably, someone pointed out that he wasn't real. Another force, further up the A1, banned ham sandwiches from its buffets in case they offended those scrounging a free lunch. You couldn't make it up but fortunately I didn't have to.

Even the Home Secretary at the time pitched in with her spectacular impression that it was too dangerous for her to go out after dark to get a kebab without an armed escort. Jacqui Smith was henceforth dubbed 'The Princess of Darkness' in my column although I did relent on one occasion and put in a spoof column from the Station Home Secretary. This singular honour was only afforded otherwise to a Victorian Station Sergeant, an anonymous Superintendent and Arthur Scargill. Don't ask.

With the benefit of hindsight I wish I hadn't been so awful to our Jacqui. She probably wasn't as bad as all that and, if ever there was a case of being careful what I wished for, the change of regime was it. There is no potential for humour with the present incumbent of the Home Office.

Of one thing I have always been aware: the bosses generally do not approve of my column. Perhaps they didn't appreciate my rants about their unfathomable mission statements and ceaseless torrents of 'ACPO-drivel' along with the suggestion that some of their more insane ideas were due to them sleeping with their heads too close to the radiator. That sort of thing doesn't generally go down well. Amongst the comments passed to my editor were the assertion by a current Chief Constable that 'There is no place in the modern police service for the Station Sergeant', whilst the Superintendents' Association, which I have otherwise regarded as a rare voice of sanity in the higher echelons, described me as 'Out of touch with today's police officers.' Not to be outdone by those further down the food chain, the ACPO Press Office suggested that giving me a column in Police Review was like letting Richard Littlejohn edit The Guardian. Can't win them all, I suppose. I even managed to outrage a reader in Switzerland by referring to 'Urban Hillbillies and banjo players', this being in the context of Dewsbury Moor and the ludicrously-planned mock kidnap of Shannon Matthews, rather than picking on hill dwellers and rural musicians everywhere. On the other hand, Hugh Muir in The Guardian itself, untroubled by Mr. Littlejohn, once described my column as '...painting the truest picture of modern policing.' Good old Hugh.

ACPO did occasionally conjure up some real characters, though few can compare with Richard Brunstrom, sometime Chief Constable of North Wales Police. Not content with establishing a speed enforcement minefield along the local roads, including placing speed cameras in horse boxes, Mr. Brunstrom sought to highlight security issues at his own headquarters by clambering up some scaffolding and entering his top floor office via an open window. This giant amongst Chief Officers crowned a glorious career by taking his community engagement responsibilities to a new height by becoming a Druid. I suspect we will not see his like again, so I honoured Mr. Brunstrom by writing a pantomime for him.

Most of the time, though, I tried to celebrate and honour the unsung heroes of the police service; the ordinary cops. This comes far more naturally as I am an ordinary cop and I've never been a senior officer, a situation that will not change. The ordinary criminals, for the most part inadequate, pathetic excuses for human beings, make life easy for us by generally being pretty stupid, which has given me plenty of mileage. Even amongst the more law-abiding section of the community we have our work cut out with a preponderance of loonies (I think I will use that phrase as the title of my autobiography, should I ever write one). The loonies who pop up in the column from time to time are all too real, as any cop will verify. There really are people out there who are convinced that the government is scrambling their brains with thought-rays. Come to think of it, after Winsor, they might have a point.

Every so often a nugget of news would gleam in the pile of dross we endure. One piece that still shines brightly in my memory is the fact that a police dog in Derbyshire was named after Herr Flick, the Gestapo man in 'Allo Allo'. This was a better name by far than my mate's dog Florence who got binned off the force for running after a burglar and then sitting down and wagging her tail when she caught up with him. It also confirmed to me that resistance to the politically correct commissars was still alive and well which, I hardly need add, pleased me immensely.

It then dawned on me that, whilst there were many awards and accolades for pink and fluffy policing, cuddling communities and generally ticking the boxes set by politicians for our senior officers to fill, there was nothing that encouraged or rewarded the ordinary bobby for cracking on with their job, or in support of Common Sense Policing, my new ethos. This resulted in the annual Police Review awards extravaganza being followed, as the man with the shovel follows The Lord Mayor's Parade, by the Grumpy Awards. There was no evening out in the West End, nor even a prize, but winners of the Grumpies were, temporarily at least, immortalised in the annals of the magazine. Not only did these include stars such as the afore-mentioned Richard Brunstrom and Herr Flick the Dog but, in a spirit of inclusivity that would have made a diversity trainer swoon, they also embraced spectacularly inept villains, such as the two Australian half-wits who tried to rob a pub when it was hosting a Hells Angels convention. They received the annual 'Not Wasting Police Time' award, as no arrests were apparently necessary following an out-of-court resolution. Hospital treatment for them was a different matter entirely.

My columns range between the extremes of satire and downright anger; a column that is based on personal opinion affords me the freedom to reflect whatever emotion a snippet of news, or middle-of-the-night germ of an idea inspires my next column. Ranting about criminals and senior officers or simply haranguing politicians has been my trade. I never have concerned myself with a devising a creative yet credible plot, inventing fascinating characters or crafting exquisite dialogue. I have the utmost respect for the other authors featured in this anthology, as their writing will endure long after my columns fade into history, and I wish them the very best of luck. There's an insatiable hunger for murder mysteries and crime thrillers, far more than there is for police satire. You can't beat a bit of blood and gore after all.

If I tried to write a sensible detective story, I suspect it would fall at the first hurdle, as I would struggle to imagine how a sensible detective would speak or act. A slightly deranged custody sergeant, forever plotting ways to make incarcerated scrotes suffer for their misdemeanours, would certainly feature, and I do fear that my ingrained cynicism would permeate the entire novel. I expect that the suspect would be refused charge by the Crown Prosecution Service and walk out of custody flicking the hero a V-sign. So I would have to engineer, somehow, an unpleasant demise for the wrongdoers. The serial killer cop idea has been tried, of course, but I'm not sure that anyone managed to explain away a high body count in a cell block before. I couldn't possibly make the hero of the story a Senior Investigating Officer from Professional Standards or, worse still, some glamorous Jane Tennyson type from the Independent Police Complaints Commission. It would be too much to bear. So I shall continue, if the fates allow, to keep churning out my exhortations to give up pink and fluffy policing and get back to kicking in doors and locking up villains.

*

An Appeal for Information
By the Boss's Snout

~

They seek him here; they seek him there.
That masterful rogue driving us to despair

~

Indeed, ladies and gentlemen, I wish to make an appeal on behalf of those who think they are running the so-called police family. You'll know them. They are vociferous when the going is good and 'heads down' when the going is bad. I speak of the 'bosses'; Moreover, they are top 'bobbies' and senior politicians of various shapes, sizes, gender, colour and belief.

Some of these individuals wear suits, some wear dresses, some wear uniform, and some of them are just….. The Bosses.

Basically, my friends…. You can trust me. I have a very close affiliation to the boss. Your boss!

Yes, you reading this! Your boss!

I'm on the tail of a miscreant police officer. Well, we think he's a police officer. Or is it a she? We don't know you see.

Who is the station sergeant? Where is the station sergeant? Are they male or female?

But not to worry, I'm after them. He or she is a rogue writer of ridicule and satire who has penned their way across a thousand magazine pages in recent years. Oh yes, you've had a chuckle at those articles I bet but it's time to call a stop to this 'writer of wrongs'.

We need a detection!

We need a positive result!

We need to please the bosses!

They like to tick all the boxes.

So who is the Station Sergeant? Where are they? And what will they write next?

Time is up. No more satire; no more jokes, no more twisting the words and upsetting the status quo. It just won't do.

It's just not good enough to pretend to be 'onside' when actually all the Station Sergeant is doing is taking the mickey out of the job and all of us in it. The Station Sergeant is upsetting the status quo don't you know. And the bosses are upset that whilst the rank and file are laughing their heads off – they – the bosses - are often the target of such banter and buffoonery.

Now listen up. You can trust me. I'm the boss's best friend. What I tell the boss stays strictly between us and would never be mentioned outside these four walls. You can trust me. I can help you in return for information leading to the identity of …. The 'Station Sergeant'….

Now I know some of you know who it is, some of you think you know who it is, and some of you haven't a clue who it is. My problem is we don't know who on earth it is either and so far 254 people have been falsely accused of being 'The Station Sergeant'.

BUT THE BOSS WANTS TO KNOW….. AND NOW.

So, for a limited time only, information leading to the identification of the Station Sergeant will be looked upon favourably. There will be no more night shifts and no more early mornings for the lucky person who turns the satirical miscreant in. Time off for darts, dominoes and pool in the pub will be granted without reservation. Tickets for the 'Policeman's Ball' will be made available, or for your favourite show if need be. And the main prize is a 'must have' - Tea with Theresa? Perhaps a quiet move to somewhere warm and cosy, like an office, is on the cards for the person who can cosy up to me and quietly divulge the real name of 'The Station Sergeant'.

Now I have the boss's ear – between you and me – so tell me. Who the hell is Station Sergeant and where can I find them? Come on, ladies and gents….

You know you can trust the boss's snout.

*

Another Shout
By Ray Gregory

~

Blue lights flash, sirens wail. Another shout to some sorry tale. Broken bones, broken homes, drunken yobs, maybe druggies too. Does anyone care? Could it just be you?

Kit in the van, food left to get cold. It often gets left so we are always told as I rush out to something being ever so bold. I never say 'No' or hold back you see because sometimes more often it is only me.

I never look back and never do shirk; I always go to it as it's my job to see to the weak or the obnoxious yob.

I'm spat at and sworn at every which way I turn, but I try to keep smiling 'cause I ain't gonna squirm. My job is to serve and protect so look out you bad guys 'cause you're gonna learn.

Body in the cage, 'good lock up' we say. So back to the shack tis the end of the day. Cold tea and bacon, left on the plate, kit cold and sweaty the usual way, that's how it is until the next shout.

No rest for the Blue Line, here comes the next shout.

*

The Collection of Flowers
(An excerpt from chapter seven)
By Ian Bruce
~

Mac shut his eyes and then clamped them tight against the onslaught of rain that nailed itself into the ground at his feet and then pushed him hard against the trunk of an old and lonely looking Rowan tree. It was obvious that this piece of living wood, flowing up against that great empty backdrop, had grown in defiance of all of the horrible conditions that had been thrown over it since it had sprung out of that poor and unhelpful ground. It rose up against the clouds like a lost and forgotten member of one of those great ghostly gatherings at the granite pillars put up by an ancient host at the nearby circle of stones. If there had ever been another of these Rowans here then it must surely have given up some time ago and slipped back under the grass, melting from sight, surrendering itself to leave no trace or any signs of its lost struggle.

That solitary Rowan, having been spared in its younger days from the attentions of the many clans of hungry red deer that trawled their way round these soulless emptied lands, stood there on borrowed time. That sheltering tree, decorated only by fungus and moss, had now become the last of its kind hereabouts. It would become a matter of when and not if the elements forced it down, soon maybe but not today. Mac thought it was all the more surprising to find this stubborn Rowan to shelter under as he would have expected it to have already fallen prey to the blade of some hawk-eyed crofter who in eking out his thin living could always find a good use for a solid piece of wood, be it crooked and spent as this one was, or straight and true.

The Rowan had clung stubbornly to its task, unwilling to give up its hard won place. The knoll upon which it perched rose up between the fields of cold grey time shattered rock that spread like a rash across the contours on the lower reaches of the hillside. To the other side of the Rowan lay the long broad bog which trailed off to a point at the other end of this hidden glen. On occasions what had once been a large cleft in the land was overfilled with snow melt and rain. This surplus water eventually filled and bloated this vast and usually ever thirsty sponge which was then woken from its damp slumber. Slowly it crept up and reaching out it touched the very stones that sat at the base of the knoll. It then advanced on them and then on again into the tangled weave of bleached tree roots that netted the weighty boulders beneath. It came up filling like an agonisingly slow rising tide against the shore, dragging itself up to its new found elevation then… finding its height and halting. The gentle ripple which had been stroked up by the breeze at the edge of this new volume then gently reached out and lapped playfully against the sun-bleached weave of the Rowans roots looking for the entire world as if it were some old crone come to dip her ancient gnarly toes into its margins.

This black walled bog ran deep. The constant inflow of water that filtered into it came leaching through the ancient layers of peat which then carefully stained each and every drop of the cold sweet waters as they tumbled recklessly down from their lofty reservoir making them gleam like amber tea as they forced their descent. The disorganised warp of burns and trickles rarely failed to complete the journey to its ungrateful mossy recipient. This slow sustaining melt of ice tearfully gave itself up from the deep jagged, sun-famine corries that reluctantly took a season to empty the harvest of snow from their elevated mass. These generous lofty, sustaining lumps of rock were drenched in their turn by a constant parade of mists and clouds that gathered in the helm of those summits and paraded over them like hurried processions of gloom throughout those sometimes too short months of summer.

The bog gave out the impression of being a flat and seemingly solid area; it prospered and gave the whole place the air of a cultivated formal garden. In fact it was made up of millions of those ancient pastel coloured, acid loving sedges and grasses that platted and poured themselves into place between the sphagnum mosses that tripped and spangled their way across the living bog forming its fragile mantle. These little mosses did their best to hide the bottomless morass beneath the surface. The bog acted as a great barrier and potential trap for the unwary that were unfortunate enough to stumble across it.

Mac became momentarily distracted as he clung onto his share of that little piece of wilderness. He had a thing or two in common with that awkward Rowan tree. Both he and it were born out of this wild place, both shaped by the same harshness and qualified as undoubted survivors in their own right. The difference between them both was that, unlike that special tree, Mac was intent on doing better than just surviving the place; he had reason for his presence out there that day. The thought of the task ahead steeled him against the unstoppable chilling blast that accelerated down on them both. That blast streamed the cold rain over his face, down to his red stubble chin and then whipped a few drops up and away before pouring the rest down showering it over his streamlined coat. As he readied himself for the undertaking ahead he found consolation in the knowledge that there was a better than average chance that this weather would pass away quickly and that it would then torment its next victims in some other place very soon, he smiled. This he thought was perfect cover and after all it was better that he arrived at his destination without notice. He would certainly avoid anything that would give his presence away after all if he had wanted a welcoming committee then he wouldn't have spent the best part of a day and a half walking over the mountains to get here.

In kinder times around this area the visiting gaggles of tweed clad stalkers and fishers, all strangers to this place, may have been surprised to find that what had begun as a rather cheerful, if not reluctant, spring day had later been transformed in what seemed like a few moments, into this resentful and bad tempered frothing beast of a squall. It would have fallen amongst them all forcing them off the hill and from the water toward whatever shelter they could steal. Over time this need for quick shelter had led to the construction of various little huts and bothy's that stood alone and frightened in the most isolated and lonely of places. Mac would make a point of avoiding these warm dry and perhaps more importantly, well stocked sanctuaries despite the inclement welcome that the place had given him and in turn avoid any sharp eyes on the lookout for any things that did not meet the daily norm.

This day had started well enough, light and keen, gone the heavy concrete laden skies and drizzle that had tested the week to be replaced by a joyous clear blue sky which brought out the buntings and other wee birds who then chirped and called out their proclamation of the promise of better things to come. The weak rays of this benign spring sun had even brought the cruellest of all the birds to visit and for it to call out at them all with its mean, cheating call "Cuckoo, Cuckoo". This thin filtered sun had slowly grown into a warming glow. This glow seemed intent on waking up the mass of begrudging, sleeping flora and did its upmost to breathe the life back into this cold and reluctant countryside still holding out against and resisting its subtle prompt. The clumps and strings of that proud plant the gorse that rode across the hill took their respective cue and had all burst as one onto the scene with a ready flush of golden yellow flowers. The gorse bushes offered up these rich translucent offerings to the day, they shone out like lights against the dark unhappy wall of weather that had growled its way south over the corries and ridges to the north. That dark wall of mean weather had rolled all the way down from the Artic seas. It had been sent as a stark reminder, like the echo of some dark promise delivered from a bad tempered Norse God, that nature not man dictated the pace of life in this place.

Life, Mac had found out to his cost, just like the weather, could be fickle, very fickle and it was bound to steer a man in wherever direction and in whatever manner it pleased. Some things, like the certainty of spring and summer, were never quite as sure here as they were elsewhere. Winter could return whenever it desired, if only for the day, or there again for a week or so if it chose. That recent event of nature was by then already in the process of covering the near mountain tops with a thick hissing rain and a cold, cold wind that pressed itself to Macs face, it was better that than the hail he thought, hoping that he had not given that callous weather any other ideas by which to further test his battered patience.

The Rowan tree, or at least the spirit that lay within it, had seemed troubled by Mac's sudden and unwelcome arrival and having been duly offended by his presence in that ancient and perhaps special place, decided that it would with every blast of the squall, do its best to unseat Mac from its bosom, to push him out into the storm, away so that it may continue its time honoured fight with that sullen, relentless and unswerving enemy, the wind. He felt the tree push into his back as if it was trying to shake him off. As it pushed back against him it then sprung suddenly the other way as if to confront and face another enemy. The new enemy, that sudden squall, speared in hard across the knoll announcing its arrival from the open ground to the north.

As he crouched there, his heart still pounding as he fought hard to catch his breath, Mac desperately tried to convince himself that there had been a time when he had actually enjoyed the feeling of that cold Highland rain stinging into his face and that he had always revelled in it. The reality was however that it blew so hard into him that it numbed him and reached deep into him as if it was picking at his very soul. He fell out of that numbness, that short trance and opened both his eyes and leant into that onslaught. He quickly stood up straight against the tree and looked around digging his boots into the soft and soggy carpet of moss and mud at his feet as he did so. Mac had taken the appearance of some wild bedraggled animal that was being hunted down by a dangerous unseen foe. This however did not do the man justice as he was just careful; careful because he did not want to risk disclosing his presence and then because if he wasn't quite careful enough, he would risk meeting someone rather like himself and what's more that other self may have brought a column of his friends with him. That may become both messy and distracting. He would make sure that he did offer himself up as prey as he had come way too far for that to happen. He then peered across the hills into the tumbling mists that danced and poured their way forward, he paused, searching every ledge and crag for any sign of movement. He squinted at the expanse behind him just one more time before slumping back down as sharply as he had sprung up. As he dropped a bellow of air rose up from inside his jacket and eased into his face, he had started to enjoy himself!

No living thing moved about the place, the wind no longer carried sounds from the birds or the bleating of those flocks of sturdy hefted sheep, just the blast of the sodden wind as it carried over the slippery moss. He was sure that he was, for the time being anyway, alone. Mac then ran hard, head down stooping as he scampered across the ancient lichen covered rocks. As he flitted over the last few yards of open ground, he dived down and belly crawled the remaining few feet moving carefully to a vantage point that gave him a view over the crofting hamlet of Laxdale, its bay and more importantly off into the open sea to the West. The loch was strewn with dozens of rocks and islands that gave the impression of their having been thrown out there into the great sea loch deliberately in order to make life that little more difficult for those hardy long suffering crofters that fished the herring and lobsters from that motley collection of small black painted boats that they had roped so carefully to the side of the irregularly shaped old jetty. This for now he thought would do nicely.

*

Dying For a Chat
By Dave Miller

~

Jane was flying!! How did this happen?

Jane was at a loose end again. She seemed to have been sitting staring at her laptop screen for hours.

A widow at an early age, children all grown up and flown the nest however they did keep in touch, albeit by phone.

They had suggested SKYPE but she didn't feel she wanted her offspring to see the state of her house. Jane suffered from a new phenomenon: CBA. In fact her friends addressed her with the letters after her surname like a CBE or an OBE. However is stood for, "can't be arsed".

She was her own person, do or don't do? Get dressed or stay in PJ's all day? Her kids never did have any say in her life so why she should she worry now?

Today though, she had more positive thoughts. She went through her emails and then went on her dating website. She didn't think she would ever look as this as a way to meet people but after a friend had met and got engaged to a lovely man, Jane changed her mind, and she did because she could!

When she opened her mail box on the dating site there was a nice surprise waiting for her: three replies and therefore three possible dates?

After her heart slowed down from the onset of palpitations she thought this was going to be a real problem. Why? She couldn't remember what she had written about herself.

That's the problem with lying you have to have a very good memory and unfortunately Jane's was poor. "I've put I'm a blonde and also a red head quite tall and curvy but how did I put these ideas together on my site?"

Jane went back to her site and put all her website descriptions together and selected the one she would answer to these possible suitors today.

She had her description in mind but needed to see which one she would answer first?

She scrolled down the possible dates and decided to accept one more local to where she lived.

Paul, that's the one she selected, wanted to meet her at Wetheral, a small village just outside Carlisle where she lived. She knew the area well as she used to work in a local hotel and she used the train to travel to and from work. The hotel was just up the hill from the station. It was the main line to Newcastle and she has often spent weekends there, on her own, looking for love.

So that was it then, Paul was going to the lucky man to meet up with Jane and make her day!!

She got her file up on the screen and sent her profile as she remembered it and arranged to meet Paul.

She sat and waited what seemed ages. However Paul acknowledged her reply and it was on. One pm in two days' time, and "come casual" he said. 'We can go for a walk and chat and maybe go to the pub for lunch, there's a pub at the other end of viaduct.'

Jane couldn't hide her excitement and put a rather raucous tune on and danced around her unkempt flat. This could be it she thought time will tell.

Jane decided, on the day, to attend earlier and see if there was going to be any future with this Paul.

She caught the train from Carlisle station. It left at 12.28 and it was only an eight minute journey. The train was busy with groupies making their way to the Newcastle Arena. Some boy group were playing there today and iPod's were playing their music loudly into young ears that would suffer in years to come.

Jane had dressed casual and had worn her anorak today as there was a chill in the air and if she was going to have a walk to the pub she wanted to keep warm. Her red anorak was rather loud and she could be seen from the orbiting space station, no fear that she would not be seen by Paul.

The train pulled in and she fought her way off the train through throngs of more youngsters getting on. Relax, she thought to herself, this could be the day her life would change.

There was a man stood on the platform looking at the faces of other people getting off the train but he couldn't see the person he was supposed to be meeting from the description given.

Jane looked up and down the platform and she couldn't see the man she was supposed to be meeting. There was a rather large man, wide as he was tall, looking like a poor excuse for a train spotter. This one had greasy lank hair and was dressed in poor taste.

Six miles away, hidden eyes in the cavernous bowels of Carlisle citadel railway station looked at a bank of CCTV screens when all of a sudden a flash of red brought the eyes attention to that screen.

PC Bertram, of the British Railway Police, was monitoring these screens on all platforms in the Cumbria area and on trains to and from Newcastle when the red flash caught his eye. He closed in onto the coat and watched the encounter of red coat and lank greasy haired individual.

Jane was approached by the unkempt man who introduced himself as Paul. Jane pointed out he didn't fit his online profile and he responded with the same.

Paul pointed out that you can't judge a book by its cover and perhaps a walk and talk might help.

"This was built in 1830 by William Dalton and is six hundred and sixty feet long," Paul droned on.' "It's over one hundred foot high over the River Eden, which is one of the best salmon rivers in Britain and where Fiona Armstrong from the television news fished." Still, he went on with more points that Jane thought the most boring one way conversation she had ever had. "It's also called the Wetheral Bridge, the Eden Bridge and Wetheral Viaduct."

"Are we going for a bar meal or a lesson on bloody viaducts?!" asked Jane agitated, wishing she had not bothered to agree to this.

They set off again, this time without a commentary and slowly making their way across the bridge, still being watched from six miles away.

As they approached the end of the bridge Jane stopped to look over at the river below, running fast and brown from the last downpour, making its way down from the hills into the flowing river. She had to stand on her tiptoes to see over the side. All of a sudden Paul dropped to his knees, it looked like he was tying his lace when, without warning, he grabbed Jane's ankles and with a heave pushed her up and over the side of the bridge.

PC Bertram shouted over the radio as to what he had just witnessed and sent cars speeding to the scene. He contacted Police Headquarters for back up and called for medical attendance as well. He hoped they would get there quickly.

Jane could hear voices, it sounded like the voices were at the end of a tunnel, sort of echoing but quiet, "Jane, Jane open your eyes," said the voice.

Jane gave a cough and felt the feeling of a retch coming from her throat. She tried to open her eyes. They felt heavy and she wanted to be left alone. "Jane, open your eyes." Then she saw a strong light in her eyes. Someone was lifting her eyelid and shining the light; this made her eyes open alright, she became very much aware of her surroundings with some trepidation. Why are my legs up in stirrups? Have I just given birth? The last time she was in this compromising position she had.

"Hello sleepy head," said the voice, "I'm nurse Nightly and you're in hospital and have been for three weeks."

"Three weeks," croaked Jane, "Three weeks?"

"We had to put you into an induced coma," replied Nurse Nightly. "You had a very nasty fall from a height and your injuries needed you to rest to repair them."

"What injuries?" asked Jane. "I thought I had given birth by the way my legs are up here"?

Nurse Nightly laughed, "No, you had a bad pelvic injury and this has helped it heal. You had a nasty injury to your head as well that's why you've been in the coma but welcome back."

"There's a police officer here to see you, just to update you about your injuries and how it came about but we have told him to come back this afternoon so you can sort your own mind out."

"Thank you," said Jane. "But I'm not sure what happened."

"The officer will let you know later, now rest."

Later that day PC Bertram called in to the ward and sat next to Jane. He looks nice, thought Jane; I hope he knows what's going on and why so long.

"Hello, Jane, are you okay to speak to me?"

"I'm okay but I can't remember much about what happened."

"I can tell you exactly what happened. I was watching a CCTV monitor because we had word there was a man using web sites to encourage women to meet up with him. He had previous offences that ended in serious assaults. It was your red anorak that drew me to keep an eye on you. I watched your trek across the bridge and as you stopped to look over the side he bent down and lifted you over. I saw you struggling to get your hands out of your pocket but as you opened your coat it acted as a parachute and the wind caught you and threw you into the trees. This allowed to fall slower than free fall and you fell about eighty feet through the trees and landed on the river bank. You were unconscious when we found you and I got you airlifted into hospital."

"What happened to the man then?" she enquired.

"Well, he obviously didn't have a guardian angel like you. He looked over the side to look for you and a goods train making its way over the bridge caused quite a draught and blew him over the top. In fact he hit the riverbank before you did but his injuries were fatal," said PC Bertram. "Someone up there was looking after you that day," he said as he looked to the sky.

The police had raided the home of the deceased. There were walls of photographs of women and their profiles and Jane's profile was highlighted with the word "BITCH" in bold letters. The man called Paul seemed to have had a vendetta against Jane but the police were unable to find a link that ended the life of one of them and caused major injuries to the other.

Jane never bothered with websites again but she did go for an evening out with PC Bertram and they were looking forward to another date soon.

*

Meg, Liz and the Fairy Glen
By Meg Johnston
~

Meg and Liz were best friends. They lived next door, went to the same school, and liked to do identical things.

What they enjoyed doing most was riding their bicycles. As soon as they got home from school the girls quickly changed out of their school uniforms, took bicycles out of the sheds, and rode around the village. A favourite place to cycle was along the riverbank close to their homes.

On a hot sunny day during the school holidays, Meg and Liz begged their parents to allow them to take a picnic and go for a bike ride. Excitedly, the girls explained that they wanted to go to their favourite place by the river and promised to be very careful, not going close to the water. To their great delight both sets of parents agreed.

Meg's Mum provided sandwiches, biscuits and juice whilst Liz's Mum packed cake, fruit and sausage rolls. Carefully stowing the food in rucksacks and chattering like magpies they set off on their adventure. The friends peddled very quickly through the village, waving to people as they sped along. Riding down a narrow lane they passed fields of golden corn whilst sheep and cattle lazily watched as Meg and Liz cycled by. Leaving the lane the girls dismounted, pushing their bikes over a very narrow, bumpy path which ran around a field. Liz made sure the gates were closed after they entered and left the field.

At last the river could be seen ahead. Here the friends stopped to watch a kingfisher diving from a tree into the water. The bird was trying to catch fish. As they watched the kingfisher reappeared out of the water with a gleaming fish in its beak. The bird's bright blue and orange feathers shed water as it flew onto a tree branch to eat its prize.

'Wow! Did you see that?' exclaimed Liz.

'Yes,' replied Meg. 'It was so quick.'

'I just love being here by the river,' Liz announced as she propped her bicycle under a tree.

'Me too,' declared Meg. 'It always feels magical here. Where should we have our picnic?'

'Just along here where the little stream runs into the river and those little blue flowers grow,' decided Liz.

'Good idea,' agreed Meg putting her cycle beside Liz's and collecting their picnic.

Together they walked to the grassy dell which was shaded by overhanging branches.

'I think those little blue flowers are forget-me-knots,' said Meg. 'My nana has some in her garden.'

The girls sat down on the grass and began to unpack their picnic. Looking around they could see other flowers, daisies, buttercups, dandelions and tall foxgloves. Beautiful butterflies decked in blue, orange, red and white flitted from flower to flower and bees buzzed lazily overhead. Because they were talking quietly Meg and Liz could see and hear birds singing in the trees and frogs croaking at the waterside. A family of ducks swam past the dell. Swifts and swallows skimmed the river to drink then flew high above to search for insects. Sitting happily side by side munching sausage rolls and sandwiches and drinking juice, the friends felt the magic of the dell.

'Do you think those little fish would like my crusts?' Liz asked Meg.

'I'm sure they would and the ducks,' Meg replied. 'I'm not sharing my crusts though. It's the best part of the sandwich'.

Laughing at her friend Liz threw crusts into the stream and watched the fish nibbling them. Some of the crusts floated away towards the main river where the girls hoped the ducks would be waiting for a tasty snack. Deciding to save some food for later the girls lay on their backs looking skyward. Small fluffy white clouds floated high overhead resembling balls of cotton wool.

'That cloud looks like a white kitten,' Liz told her friend pointing towards one of the clouds. 'What can you see?'

Meg looked at the sky for a few minutes, shading her eyes as she did.

'I can see a dragon chasing a flying pig,' giggled Meg. 'It must be snack time for sky dragons.'

They watched the clouds for a while pointing out the different shapes and patterns to each other. Rolling onto their tummies, the two girls discussed plans for the remainder of the holidays. Abruptly, Liz sat up, peering into the shade under a tree.

'What's the matter?' asked Meg looking a little alarmed. 'Did you see something?'

'I thought I saw 1 tiny light beside that fallen log,' replied Liz. 'But it must have been the sunlight, I can't see it now.'

Both girls looked towards the log but no light was visible.

'Let's have some cake and biscuits,' suggested Liz.

'You do have some good ideas,' laughed Meg reaching for the bag that contained cake. 'Is there any juice left?'

'Plenty,' said Liz shaking the juice container.

As Meg was turning back towards Liz she suddenly froze mid turn.

'There is a tiny light by that log, I've just seen it,' Meg whispered.

Slowly the friends moved towards the log; all thoughts of cake forgotten. They crawled carefully on their hands and knees, hardly daring to breathe. As the girls approached the shaded log another flash of light appeared, then a second, third, fourth. Then nothing.

'Did you see that?' They said together, carefully peering into shade.

For long few seconds, nothing moved within the shaded space by the fallen log. Holding their breath, Meg and Liz watched and waited; for what, they weren't sure. Light showed again but this time it didn't vanish, it glowed steadily. The girls looked at each other in amazement, not able to say a word then returned their astonished gaze back to the log. Hovering above it was a shimmering, floating 'person' with beautiful long brown hair, a short red dress, crystal wings and about 9 inches high!

'Hello,' said an astounded Liz. 'Are you really here?' Then she laughed.

'That was a stupid thing to say, I'm sorry, of course you're here.'

Meg said nothing, just looked at the small person in front of them. Liz stopped talking and watched her friend. The small person regarded them solemnly from above the log.

'I think we have just found a fairy dell,' Meg told Liz. 'And we need to introduce ourselves before she can speak to us.'

'How do you know that?' an astonished Liz asked her friend.

'I remember reading it in a book at my nanas,' Meg replied. 'Hello, my name is Meg and this is my best friend Liz. Can you speak to us?'

The shimmering person nodded her small head and beckoned the friends forward with tiny hands. Moving slowly, with great care the girls realised there was more than one small shimmering person beside the log. On reaching the log Meg and Liz realised they had indeed discovered a fairy dell as there appeared to be at least ten different, shimmering individuals.

'Wow! This is beautiful,' Liz said to her friend. 'Are we dreaming or is this real?'

'If it's a dream we must be having the same one,' replied Meg.

'You aren't dreaming,' said a small tinkling voice. 'Welcome to our picnic. My name is Scarlet'.

'Hello Scarlet,' the girls replied together 'Thank you for your invitation.'

'We were just about to have something to eat and drink. Would you like to share it with us?' Meg invited.

This invitation resulted in a chorus of tinkling sounds, the girls couldn't quite understand but found fascinating to listen to. Within a few minutes Scarlet floated over to them. With her were three other tiny fairies dressed in beautiful, shimmering clothes of the brightest hues and sparkling hair. One wore shimmering blue, another emerald green and the third shining white.

'These are my friends, Sapphire, Emerald and Mist,' Scarlet announced. 'And we would love to share a picnic with you. We have been watching you since you arrived and enjoying your cloud game.'

Sharing a delighted look, the friends unpacked the remainder of their picnic, cake, biscuits, sausage rolls and juice. They had eaten all the sandwiches. Their new fairy friends joined them bringing yet more friends with them.

'Do you all live here?' Liz asked as they were eating cake.

'Only during the summer,' Scarlet told her. 'It's too cold during the winter. We are summer fairies and fly south with the Swallows and House Martins in autumn.'

'Where do you go?' Meg asked.

'We don't always go to the same place,' Scarlet replied. 'It depends on which bird we get a lift with and where we've been before. Some of our friends prefer to go to the same place every year but we like to see different places. It's exciting when you go somewhere you haven't seen before.'

'Have you decided where you will be going this year?' Liz asked.

'We haven't decided yet,' Sapphire told her. 'We won't do that 'til the day before we go. It's more interesting that way.'

'Anyway, there is more than enough work to keep everyone busy during the summer. It would be a waste of summer days thinking of autumn and winter,' Scarlet added

'You have to work! I thought you were having a holiday,' Liz said sounding surprised.

'Fairies love to work and we love to play,' Scarlet replied. 'Looking after flowers, birds, insects and baby animals is a wonderful thing to do. It doesn't really seem like work. Then we get to have picnics and sometimes meet big people like you.'

'Have you stayed in this dell before?' Meg enquired. 'It's one of our favourite places but we've never seen fairies here.'

'This is our first time but it won't be the last,' Scarlet told the girls 'We think it will become one of our favourite places too.'

'Wonderful!' The girls cried together. 'Then we might see you again before the end of summer.'

'I think my friends and I would like that very much,' Scarlet said looking around at the gathered fairies.

There was a tinkling sound and much nodding of heads as all the other fairies agreed with Scarlet.

Reluctantly the girls checked their watches and sadly agreed it was time for them to return home. They had made a promise to their parents not to be late so they gathered up their picnic boxes and packed them away.

'Thank you all for a lovely afternoon,' they said together.

'We will try to come back at the end of the week,' Meg told the hovering fairies.

'We'll know when you are here and will come to see you,' Scarlet assured her.

Waving their tiny hands, the fairies rose into the air in a blaze of coloured lights and vanished.

Meg and Liz blinked their eyes, looked at each other in amazement, laughed delightedly then set off to collect their cycles. It had been a very exciting picnic and they couldn't wait for the next one.

However, the friends decided to keep their new fairy friends a secret as they didn't want anyone disturbing the magic of their very own fairy dell.

Return Trip
By Simon Hepworth

~

'Wake up, you lazy Pommy bastard.'

The words of my Australian room-mate were, as ever, accompanied by the soft thud of a rolled up pair of flying socks colliding with my head. Garry had, for the past few days, taken to waking me in that rather inconsiderate manner, just as he now always told me his plans for the evening, even though they never seemed to come to fruition any more.

'If we're not on tonight, I'm off to the Bull's Head. I'm dying for a pint and that Sheila behind the bar has got the hots for me mate.' I had to admire his optimism.

'That's a big 'If' and you bloody know it, you daft Ocker. We'll be on ops. We're always on bloody ops and it'll be sodding Berlin again.'

'Yeah, well, I can always live in hope I suppose. They've got to give us a break some time. I mean, how often do they expect us to visit the damned place? We went there yesterday and the day before. There can't be much of it left to bomb. We're just moving the bloody rubble from one pile to another.'

Garry was sounding more despondent now, and I wished I hadn't spoiled his pipe dream. We were in this together, along with the other lads in our crew, and the half a hundred other crews in our squadron, all of whom shared our lot.

'I dunno, old chap. It seems we've been going there and back since the dawn of time and for all I know they might keep sending us there till doomsday. Have you checked the board to see if we're on?'

By way of an answer Garry informed me, in tones no doubt befitting a Sydney docker, that he had not so far seen fit to do so. I looked at the alarm clock on the shelf by my bed. Half past one. Great. I'd slept through half the day and the battle order, if there was one, would be posted by now.

We must have got back about 0400 hours that morning and after the debrief, breakfast and winding down, I expect I went to bed about seven. These days, though, I could never remember the details. I seemed to have developed some form of amnesia as nothing came back to me after we'd bombed and left the target. I hoped to God that I'd been more aware of my surroundings for the trip home, even if my mind was blank now. I'm the navigator, responsible for getting us all out there, delivering a few tons of HE and incendiaries, and getting us safely home. We had at least made it so it must just be my powers of recollection. By now, with all our recent trips to the Big City, Douggie, our pilot, probably knew the way himself. Hell, I expect our aircraft knew the way. There was an idea. Next time, if it was Berlin, she could just do the trip herself and let us go to the boozer.

I sat upright, shifted round and got out of bed. My battle dress uniform was hanging in the wardrobe. No slinging discarded clothing on a bedside chair for those of us actively serving His Majesty. As an officer, albeit at the lower end of the hierarchy, there were some privileges: one of which was that an erk usually saw fit to polish my shoes, which I appreciated. They were waiting for me outside the door, as usual. A quick shave at the sink, a wash and brush up, and I resigned myself to what I foresaw as the inevitable: another night out over the capital of the Third Reich.

After the recent series of raids I had started to be troubled by a recurring nightmare. It was always vivid and always the same. I was sitting at the nav table, plotting the latest wind estimates for the return route and deciding whether to risk a cup from my flask of coffee as we left the target area. Suddenly there would be the clatter of six Browning machine guns as both turrets opened fire, a desperate shout from one of the gunners: 'FIGHTER!! CORKSCREW PORT, GO!!' followed by a scream which ended, chillingly, as suddenly as it started. It was accompanied by the racket of exploding cannon shells, my vacuum flask shattering as it was struck by passing ammunition and then a feeling of falling in the dark. Then, invariably, I would wake up. I suppose I ought to be grateful to Garry for the comedy sock routine as that interrupted my headlong plummet towards oblivion. Coupled with my repeated bouts of homeward-bound amnesia, I was beginning to worry if my sanity would last until the end of my tour.

I faced a bit of a dilemma; if I went to see the quack he might tell me to get a grip, maybe muttering darkly about the unendurable stigma of 'LMF', Lack of Moral Fibre, the official term for cowardice. Alternatively he might be sympathetic and diagnose sinusitis which would ground me for a few days as I wouldn't be fit to fly. It happened occasionally and there was a chance that he would give me that respite rather than see me go round the bend. The downside would be that my crew would carry on with their tour, albeit with another navigator, and they'd finish before me. If, that is, my replacement knew which way the pilot should point the Lancaster so it got to the target. And then, on my return, I would probably be inserted into a sprog crew and the odds of me living to tell the tale would plummet faster than the plane in my bad dream.

Along with the dreams came an increasing sense of foreboding, a growing sense of conviction that I wasn't going to make it. So far we had had a quiet tour, with little to rattle us, though of course we had seen other aircraft explode or go down in flames along the route and the demented inferno of flak all around us over target. But we had, whisper it quietly, so far been lucky and had outlived many of our contemporaries. None of us kept score and we never knew the bigger picture. The senior ranks at Group, Bomber Command HQ and the Air Ministry didn't seem too keen to share the figures for raid numbers and losses with us. I don't know why they didn't treat us like adults as I was hardly likely to ask the station telephonist to patch me through to Reichsmarschall Herman Goering so I could share the joy with him. Privately I figured that our losses each time out seemed to average about one aircraft missing from every twenty or so despatched. They might not share the figures with us but we weren't blind and every empty dispersal pan told its own story.

We didn't talk about it, of course. It was considered a frightfully bad show to mention The Chop. Faces came and went, but we never knew the other lads. They might easily not have existed. So we would have a good few beers in the Officer's Mess, or clear off as a crew to the more relaxed atmosphere of the Bull's Head where we could let our hair down a bit more.

We were a mixed crew, as were so many. Douggie, from York, was a Flying Officer along with Garry, who was the Bomb Aimer, and I. The other chaps were Sergeants. Alan, the Flight Engineer, was a soft-spoken lad from Merthyr Tydfil whilst the Wireless Operator, Joe, was a strident South African. His real name, he once confided, was Johannes which he felt was a tad German for comfort. Half-Afrikaner, he was one hundred percent behind the war effort, as evidenced by his sticking his neck on the line every time we headed out over the North Sea. Our backs were watched by the two gunners, Tweedle Dum and Tweedle Dee. Not their real names, of course, but both were short, dark-haired and slight in stature and might conceivably have been brothers. They were really called Bill and Ben, and they shared an intense mutual interest in gardening. Ben had been trying to persuade the Station Commander to allow an allotment to be set up behind one of the hangars where there was a piece of rough land that might do more, he argued, to contribute to the war effort. The Station Commander had yet to reach a decision.

We had been together since the Operational Conversion Unit, apart from Alan who joined us a few weeks later. We'd been training on Wellington aircraft, retired bombers, and they didn't need a Flight Engineer. Once we got onto heavies, the spanner monkeys were suddenly needed and Alan joined our merry throng, having decided he would rather fly ops than stay down the mines. I thought his choice was academic as both jobs involved not inconsiderable danger and precious little daylight.

Since our posting to RAF Elmsford in the East Anglian fen country, my log book showed twenty four ops. We should have done twenty six but had to turn back twice due to engine problems and a knackered intercom. Both were no-go items, though this didn't stop some of the 'press-on-regardless' chaps. There weren't many of those, but that might just be because, for them, the attitude had proved suicidal. I remembered then that my own logbook was in the Navigation Leader's office as he checked and signed it every month. It would by now be a few trips behind. Updating it would wait. Again, the bureaucratic tail wagged the dog. He was probably checking to see if I'd been taking shortcuts on the route to Berlin; not that there was much chance of that. For the past few trips the big wigs had stuck to the same cunning plan which saw us taking a direct route to Berlin with no discernible deviation. That would outwit Jerry, I thought. He'll never believe we would keep that up so would most likely send his night fighters to Munich just in case in we were really planning to go there instead. Funny how he hadn't yet thought of that though. Every bloody night they were waiting for us in the same place. It saved petrol for both sides, at least that was something.

All in all, I decided I would be better off keeping my mouth shut about my personal concerns and just getting on with the job. Twenty-four completed ops from our tour of thirty meant we were eighty percent of the way to a period of calm, at least for six months. Screening off ops did not actually mean we were safe; there was still a war on and a posting to training school to look after the new boys would place us in the hands of the chronically inexperienced. In our world, if you learned from experience your odds of survival improved dramatically, from non-existent to merely woeful. By my reckoning we could, at the start of our tour, expect to survive twenty ops and we had done that and more. We only had to survive another six to have a chance of a long break, and who knows when the war might end? It was January 1944 and there was an expectation that Allied boots would be on European soil before too long. It might all be over by Christmas.

It wasn't too late for lunch, as long as we didn't hang about, but our plans for the rest of the day, possibly the remainder of our lives, hinged on the answers to a two-part question. One: was there an ops battle order posted? And two: was our crew on it? Based on the past few days' experience it would be a quiet but firm 'Yes' to both of those, but I felt we were due for a bit of good luck. We didn't often fly more than three nights running. The weather usually saw to that, and even the chair-borne warriors at Group felt that it was useful for us to have a breather every so often. Battle fatigue was expensive on aircraft; they seemed to have an endless supply of crews however.

Garry and I sauntered over to the 'A' Flight office. There were a few people coming and going, some of the other crews greeted us in passing but most just ignored us, almost looking straight through us. There was a constant stream of new faces turning up to replace those who were lost and, to them, we were probably just a couple of old lags who wouldn't be around much longer, in all probability.

The board was adorned with a fresh piece of paper listing those of us lucky enough to be blessed with the chance of getting ourselves wiped out this very evening. Sure enough, there we were, listed under our aircraft designator, a simple 'L'. L-Love was her call sign. She had a serial number, as did we all, and that would stay with her for as long as she stayed 'on charge' in the Royal Air Force. Her squadron code might change occasionally but, since we'd been assigned to her, she had always been A6-L. The chaps thought L-Love was a bit soft, so Douggie called her L-Lass and arranged for the name 'Top Lass' to be painted on her nose, along with a suitable portrait of a well-endowed female gleefully throwing bombs at a cowering Nazi with a toothbrush moustache. I wondered how many beers that had cost him to bribe an artistic fitter. Douggie told us that the female was an accurate caricature of his wife back in Yorkshire. Garry had told him to dream on.

Briefing was at 1600 hours for navigators, so that we could plot the route on a nice large, flat, table before taking off. It made life so much easier. Main briefing was at 1700 hours so, I presumed, we would take off around 2000 hours. That had been the pattern recently and it would give us an hour or so to grab something to eat before festivities commenced. That was unless Douggie fancied a trip round the block by way of a Night Flying Test.

We went to give our pilot a shout, not wanting him to miss the fun. He was, as usual, lying in his bed gradually adjusting to being awake. 'We're on, mate,' Garry told him. 'Briefing's in a couple of hours. Are we taking the old bird out for a flap round the countryside or getting some nosh? The choice is yours, cobber.'

'She was fine when we parked her so we'll take a chance, as long as the ground crew haven't lent her to some other lot in the mean time to take her out for a spin. Give me give minutes and I'll be with you. I'll see you in the Mess.'

It wasn't far from the Officers' Accommodation block to the Mess; in that respect we had it easier than the Sergeants who had hike half a mile from their Nissen huts to their own mess. The riff-raff weren't allowed to eat with the officers, even though we depended on each other for our lives. We couldn't socialise on the station either so the seven of us routinely cleared off to neutral territory whenever we could. We were close-knit, and sod the class distinction inherent to the RAF.

By the time our driver had stirred from his pit and joined us in the entrance to the Dining Hall, there were a few others hanging around waiting for a table. We had WAAF waitresses to cater for our every reasonable need; unfortunately it was left to them to decide what was reasonable. Garry's earthier needs had long-since been categorised as not strictly desirable, let alone reasonable, by many of the young ladies he had made them to. As before, we

55

chatted with some of the more familiar crews, some of whom I couldn't remember having seen for quite a while. In fact, I was surprised to see some of those present at all as I could have sworn blind they had been reported missing. They had, it would seem, evaded capture, or had simply landed their damaged aircraft elsewhere, whilst perhaps some had been away on leave. One of the navigators, who I thought had failed to return a couple of weeks earlier, told me he hadn't been away and put it down to us just not being on the same ops. I wondered if it was yet another symptom of my crumbling mental faculties. However, at least it gave me some hope; if these lads we had thought lost had eventually turned up safe and sound, maybe the chop figures weren't as bad as I'd reckoned. I mentioned this to Garry, who just looked out of the window at the leaden sky and said 'When your ticket's called, mate, you go for the ride,' before changing the subject to a reasoned discourse on the menu.

My feeling of gloom and despondency had been suppressed by the company of my mates, especially the irrepressible Garry, but I have to confess it was still there, gnawing away at me. My mouth was drier than normal, my stomach unsettled, neither of which boded well for the forthcoming trip. In particular, stomach problems would be a complete and utter disaster; encumbered by layers of thick flying clothing I would be lucky to make it to the aircraft's chemical toilet in time to meet a sudden need. That would also mean I was away from my post for the duration of my personal emergency, so I would then have to play catch up with our position when I was fit to continue. I toyed briefly, once again, with going to the Sick Bay but just couldn't bring myself to do it. Maybe Garry was right, I considered; if it's your turn there's nothing you can do about it. Then I comforted myself with the thought, as ever, that we would be OK. It was always another crew that bought it. Twenty-four down, six to go.

Bacon and egg was a rare luxury for most people but, for us fearless fliers at least, it was a regular repast, just so long as we were on ops. We always had it before a sortie; it was something of a ritual. Just recently, though, the meal had become tasteless. It was a treat for us, the RAF seemed to think. Those who are about to die, we salute you. For me, though, the meal was tarnished by association. Imagine being locked in a room, given a tray of thirty eggs and told that to be let out, you must eat one at a time, but every time you pick one out and eat it, the lights go out and you know that there'll be a bogeyman somewhere there, lurking in the dark, waiting with a nasty weapon to bludgeon you. It's like a kid's worst nightmare. But this bogeyman is very real, and he's got a radar operator, and they can see you on his screen, and the pilot can see the flames of your exhaust, and if that's not enough they've got fighter flares, or else the searchlights illuminate the clouds beneath you, or the fires you have worked so hard to ignite show up your aircraft so you are exposed to their searching gaze. If you use a device to try and see him before he sees you, he can detect that and follow its beam and it will lead him right to you. And when the bogeyman sees you, he hasn't got a cudgel, but instead he's got some 20 mm cannon and he is going to blow you to hell. You know what's coming, but you just don't know when. So that's why now I don't like eggs and it's why I'm shit-scared of the dark.

It might appear that, by this time, I was on the point of breaking down, collapsing on the table with my head in my hands, blubbering like a terrified child. It wasn't quite like that. This was fear, not abject, screaming terror. Outwardly I remained calm. We all did, it was what was expected of us. We would have been stark raving mad not to feel scared, though. Terror, leading to panic, was entirely different. The fear I felt was kept inside, locked in by the unspoken support of my pals who were all, I had no doubt, sharing the same emotion, and by the rigid hierarchy within which we existed. I could still function as a normal human being, even if normality for me entailed navigating a heavy bomber across half of Europe and bombing its cities.

'Are you going to eat your breakfast or just sit there staring at it? Some poor bloody chook has given up her offspring to feed you, not to mention the porker whose number came up to supply the bacon.' Garry had obviously retained his appetite despite the growing tension ahead of briefing.

It would have sent out the wrong signals if I had handed over my breakfast to my crew mate, so I overcame my reluctance and finished the plateful. A cup of tea also helped, but then again, I had never known a brew to fail in this respect.

I hated having to kill time before the briefings. There were a thousand things I would prefer to do on what might be my last day on Earth; top of the list was a range of activities with a host of obliging young ladies, but these are best left to the imagination. After that, a concert, hiking in some of England's magnificent scenery, and an evening in the pub would do the job. Unfortunately, as the station was sealed before ops, none of these were on offer. No one got in or out without a chit and telephone calls were prohibited. There was no point, when all's said and done, in giving Jerry advanced warning that we were going to do exactly the same thing that we had done for the last few nights. He would find out soon enough. So I joined Douggie and Garry in cycling out to dispersal to make sure our aeroplane was fit for the job ahead.

Top Lass was sitting where we had left her earlier this morning, no doubt brooding over the coming night. If machines have feelings I expect hers were no different from ours; she rarely showed it apart from the occasional technical hiccup when she really didn't want to play. Lass was ahead of us in experience having survived thirty-seven trips over enemy territory. Each was celebrated by a bomb painted above her name and caricature. Our squadron, unlike some, tended to allocate crews a specific aircraft. They probably thought it inspired a sense of ownership and hence we would be more likely to bring the plane back. Every so often a crew whose own steed was playing up or damaged would borrow a

Lanc if her own crew wasn't on the battle order. All too frequently neither aircraft nor crew were ever heard from again, so we preferred to stick with our own.

Douggie chatted to the ground crew chief, a Flight Sergeant who answered, simply, to 'Chiefy'. Chiefy believed that Lass was his personal property and had been known to chide Douggie and the rest of us if we brought her back with holes in. For the most part we had, thus far, looked after her. In the absence of the rest of the crew, Douggie was resolute in his decision not to air-test Lass before the op. 'She was sweet as a bird again last night, Chiefy. Not a flicker on the instruments.'

'That's Rolls-Royce for you, sir. Nothing but the best for King and Country.' Chiefy's tone suggested a hint of irony; God only knew how many cold, wet hours he and his team worked to keep Lass airworthy. 'She's knocking on a bit, this old girl. You sure you don't want to trade her in for a younger model?'

'I don't think the RAF would let us do that. There's no second-hand market for a used Lanc. One careless owner isn't much of a selling point. No, thanks Chiefy; we'll stick with her for as long as she'll let us.'

Douggie and the Flight Sergeant wandered off to stare at Top Lass's nether regions and give her a poke or a prod as they saw fit. I wasn't one of those navigators who had failed pilot training, so it was all a black art to me. I was happy to work out where we were now, how to get to where we needed to be and how long it would take us. It was far less grief.

The navigators' briefing was a civilised, almost perfunctory, affair. There was absolutely no surprise when the target was revealed as Berlin once more. As I had cynically predicted, the route was identical. I mentioned this to the bod next to me, whom I recognised having sat next to him the previous night.

'It's always the same now,' he confirmed. 'They seem to think it's easier to manage, or something. I'm sure Butch knows what he's doing.' I wished I shared his confidence in the C-in-C of

Bomber Command, but it was good to know it wasn't just me who had picked up on this seemingly bizarre, if not potentially lethal, tactic. At the end of the day, though, it was not my place to question these things. HQ at High Wycombe decided these things and my role was to do what I was told, when I was told to do it. Butch, or Air Chief Marshall Sir Arthur Harris as he was more properly titled, certainly knew his own mind, but whether this was synonymous with knowing what he was doing was always open for quiet debate. At least we knew where we stood with the man, even if we never actually got to see him. He seemed to support us, even as he sent us out every night to carry death and destruction to the enemy, whilst facing our own demise along with it.

    There was more of the same at the main briefing, a sense of *déjà vu* that continued to move remorselessly to the forefront of my mind. The feeling of foreboding grew with it, something that I had never truly experienced before. I had heard of other bods experiencing a premonition of their own impending loss, but I had never truly believed in its stark reality. What happened, I wondered, to all those who had such a conviction but who survived? How did they talk their way out of their insistence that they wouldn't come back, when they'd been proved wrong? Once again, premonitions were rarely spoken of amongst our number.

    The squadron CO, a Wing Commander with two tours behind him, led the briefing, it being his show after all. He was respected by us as a good leader, who was prepared to stick his neck out as far as he expected us to. Tonight, he told us, he would be joining us with a sprog crew, rather than send them out as inexperienced lambs to almost inevitable slaughter. He didn't phrase it quite like that, however. I remembered he'd done the same on the past few ops, and in doing so must have known the huge risk he was taking. We had our twenty-four ops under our belts; the Wingco had twice that number and more.

    Much of what followed the briefing was routine, borne out of necessity. The RAF had its processes, its rituals and its rules. If there's a routine you don't need to worry about what to do next, it becomes second nature. Of course, after a while you get to depend on the routine and eventually it morphs into superstition, at least if you're facing death every time you go through the process. It's human nature to want the same kit, the order, the same lorry and driver to take you to dispersal. It worked last time and the time before so if you're going to come back safely this time, everything needs to be just so. Irrational obsession was a secondary consideration compared with stacking the odds in your favour. On this occasion, everything was as it should be, no one stirred up my personal demons by upsetting the order of things, and for this I was truly grateful.

Our crew traditions continued when we reached the dispersal pan and waddled over to Top Lass, weighed down with kit. This we stowed; flasks, rations, parachutes, pigeons and the equipment specific to our role. In my case it was a nav bag, chart and pencils. Then we clambered back out as we still had time to kill. A few last cigarettes, the orange tips glowing bright against the darkness of this far-flung outpost of the airfield, though they would be as nothing against the inferno of light we knew we might well see before long. Searchlights, tracer, exploding flak and perhaps, if the cloud was sufficiently thin, the fire bed of a burning city. If our mates were unlucky there would be the bright multi-hued conflagration of a bomber exploding as petrol, rubber, aluminium, amatol and human bodies combined in a brief but diabolical firework display. Awesome, it was, and terrible too, and repeated far too many times but, to our private shame, each fireball was shared by a sense of relief that it was somebody other than us. They couldn't get us all, so every time it was their bomber rather than ours, the chances of us making it home seemed to rise.

It was nearly time to board, so we gathered round Lass's tail wheel, unzipped our flying suits and gave it a soaking for good luck. The old girl never seemed to mind. Then we took our places. I was luckier than most, especially those of a sensitive disposition, as

I had a curtain to shut me off from the hellish reality outside, unless I needed to shoot the stars through the astrodome. I could at least pretend I was somewhere else. The other chaps were paid to look out of the window, though Joe was technically employed to listen. He did double up as spare gunner though so had to do his share of staring out at the proceedings.

'Southwold,' I told Douggie over the intercom when we were settled. 'For a change.' That much, at least, was to be expected. We had almost always used that coastal town as a mustering point as we set out over the North Sea. To get there at our assigned altitude of 21,000 feet we would head for Birmingham and then double back. A Lancaster with five tons of bombs and sufficient fuel for a return trip to Berlin would not exactly climb like a homesick angel. I'd got Gee equipment to plot our position, at least as far as the German border, possibly further if the enemy didn't manage to jam it. After that we were dependent on my skill as a navigator to get us to the target and back.

The peace and tranquility of my work space was suddenly disturbed by the roar as the first of Lass's four Merlin engines started up. I wasn't actually privy to that procedure as Douggie and Alan tended to run through the start-up check list without using the intercom. This involved speaking civilly at first, the necessary volume increasing in proportion to the number of Lass's engines that were up and running. When all four were running they had to shout to make themselves heard, even though they were a matter of inches apart. According to Garry, who was usually not too far from the action, it was because they liked to listen to the engines to make sure they were functioning correctly. I wondered how they could tell over the racket.

'Pilot to Navigator.' We were formal now, and would remain so for most of the trip, unless something unusual happened. Intercom discipline bred crew discipline, and a disciplined crew was professional and might, just might, live longer. So we cut the banter when we were flying.

'Navigator to pilot, go ahead.'

'Pilot to Navigator, all set?'

'Navigator to pilot, all set.' Douggie then repeated his call to our colleagues, ensuring that the intercom was working and that no one raised any last minute objections to the idea of stirring up the hornets' nest that was the Luftwaffe's night fighter defences. The noise from the engines increased as Lass edged forward then I felt a familiar lurch as Douggie applied the brakes. We stopped for quite a while, seemingly held up by some unseen problem, unseen by me, at least, sitting down in the cheap seats next to Joe. After a couple of minutes I stuck my head around the bulkhead and looked up to the flight deck. Douggie and Alan were seemingly waiting for a gap in the line of Lancasters rolling past us.

'Problems, gentlemen?' I enquired.

'No bugger's letting us in,' Garry drawled laconically, doubtless from his unofficial take off position in the nose. 'That's fine by me. You carry on chaps.'

'Someone normally backs off a bit, as we're none of us in any rush. But not, it would appear, tonight,' Douggie informed the rest of us. Eventually, Lass roared again and we moved forward.

'Right at the back of the taxi rank,' said Bill from his seat in the rear turret. Along with Ben, who sat tonight in the mid-upper position, he would spend virtually the whole trip facing backwards. I wondered if they got disorientated when they got on a bus, unless of course it was reversing at speed, in which case they would feel quite at home.

'Pilot to crew, going on green,' said Douggie as we paused again, evidently waiting for the green lamp to shine from the control caravan at the end of the runway.

For a while nothing happened, and then Alan broke in. 'The bastards are going home! Can't they see us sitting here?'

Douggie must have looked past Alan as he joined in. 'What the hell are they doing? Is the caravan on fire or something?'

'No. They've just packed up and got out of the van for a leg stretch.' Looking up at the flight deck I saw him slide back the panel in the window and heard him shout something. If they couldn't see the Lanc and hear the Merlins, I thought they were hardly likely to respond to a bloke shouting out of a window twenty feet off the ground. And so it proved, as they took no notice whatsoever.

Douggie had clearly lost patience, and probably his sense of humour. 'Pilot to Rear Gunner. Clear above and behind?'

'Rear Gunner here, clear above and behind skipper,' Bill replied. Once more the engines roared and Lass edged forward, then began to accelerate as her props bit the cold night air. I wasn't entirely sure that this was proper procedure, but then again the airfield control staff clearing off with a fully-laden Lancaster parked next to them probably didn't feature in the Airfield Procedures Manual, or whatever rules they ran by, either. I figured Douggie probably knew what he was doing; he was quite likely as hyped up as the rest of us and had probably decided to argue the toss if and when we got back. If they were out of the caravan then they obviously weren't expecting any imminent arrivals so the runway should be clear. We had more to worry about for the next eight hours than a breach of procedure, and as long as we didn't crash or collide with another aircraft whilst still in the vicinity of the runway, Douggie would probably tell them he saw a green. Alan would back him up; we all would. It was, for now, us against the world.

And so we went to war, seven men amongst a few thousand, opposed by several million Germans, many of whom were in possession of seriously offensive weapons. We droned through the cloud layers, occasional turbulence causing Lass to buck and sway, sometimes to lurch and drop but the altimeter by my desk slowly wound its way upwards. I focused on taking Gee readings and plotting these on my map, then comparing forecast winds with actuals. For once, the Met. people had been reasonably accurate and I had no cause for complaint. We crossed the North

Sea and, when my Gee plots showed that we were a couple of minutes from crossing the Dutch coast, I advised my colleagues, 'Enemy coast ahead,' as countless navigators have done before and, I have no doubt, since.

With dense cloud beneath us, several thousand feet thick, there was no way the searchlights could have any effect whatsoever. They didn't even light the clouds to provide a backdrop for us to crawl across. So far, so good.

It couldn't last, and it didn't. Halfway across Holland, the duck shoot started. The Wing Commander was the first to go, by our reckoning at least. He'd signalled to us by lamp as we crossed the English coastline and we had then flown in parallel, separated by a few hundred feet laterally. That was safe enough; we each knew where the other was. In the starlight we could occasionally make out other bombers but, to mind at least, there were far fewer of them than I'd expected. Normally there would have been ten or fifteen bombers for every one we saw tonight. Maybe this was a diversionary raid, and our squadron, along with possibly one or two others had been sent to Berlin whilst the Main Force went off somewhere else. If that was the case, I hoped the night fighters didn't fall for the ruse. Better that someone else should bear the brunt.

'Jeezus...' That was from Garry. 'The Wingco's just blown up.'

Looking up to the front I could see the fading glow of the explosion reflected on the inside of the cockpit Perspex. That was it; no more shepherding and nurse-maiding sprog crews from our fearless leader. He'd been a good type, and that would probably have to serve as his epitaph. As for the lads with him we neither knew nor could we get too worked up. We'd lost too many friends to grieve for those we didn't even know.

A flamer, a short while later, a bomber burning as it fell, showed us that the bogeymen were still with us and in numbers, then another explosion took a third crew to meet their Maker.

When the fourth fell, as we crossed into German territory, my bad feeling returned with a vengeance. Ten percent of the force destroyed, by my count, and we were not even half way to the target. The diversion must be working as the night fighters were definitely amongst us.

The carnage continued as explosions and flames periodically reminded us of our own mortality. It was usual practice for the navigator to log these, to help with accounting for missing crews on our return. I kept adding to my list, which was twenty entries long by the time we reached Berlin. The target focused our minds on our task, despite the local flak barrage adding to the nastiness surrounding us.

'Steady, steady…. Bombs gone.' Lass leapt for the heavens as Garry pressed the bomb release button and unleashed our contribution the redevelopment of Berlin. An agonising wait for the photoflash, to prove we'd actually gone to Berlin as opposed to carpet-bombing Grimsby, and we turned for home.

I went through my wind calculations and thought about a cup of coffee. Maybe, just maybe, I'd overreacted, I thought, mentally cursing myself for going soft. Then my nightmare moved from dream to reality. Bill and Ben opening fire on something simultaneously, the truncated scream in the intercom, my flask shattering and it all going dark. My parachute was stowed next to my table but it might have been on the moon for all the use it was. Lass was plummeting earthwards, spinning now. Far from the darkness I had imagined in my dream there was an orange glow in the flight deck, probably from one or more engines blazing merrily away.

I knew that this was no dream. I couldn't move, my body weight massively increased by the g-forces caused by Lass's death roll. The old girl wouldn't make the end of the war and neither would we. Somehow I felt calm. There was, after all, nothing I could do to escape so no point at all in panicking.

I closed my eyes, thought of my family, and waited for the end.

'Wake up, you lazy Pommy bastard.'

The thud of Garry's socks against my forehead disturbed my personal peace, as was his intention. 'If we're not on tonight, I'm off to the Bull's Head. I'm dying for a pint and that Sheila behind the bar has got the hots for me mate.'

Here we go again, I thought. Something was not quite right. My dream was too vivid, far too real. And my day was staring in exactly the same way as the last few had done.

'Garry,' I asked. 'Do you ever get a feeling that we've been here before?'

'Course we've been here before, you drongo. We bloody live here.' But there was an evasiveness that I hadn't noticed previously, almost defensive.

'You feel it too, mate, don't you?' I wanted Garry to tell me I was wrong, but this time his silence was no reassurance. 'We're just doing exactly the same thing day in, day out.'

Garry paused; standing at the window, contemplating God alone knew what. He turned to look at me. 'I hoped I was wrong, mate. I sincerely thought I was going round the bend and I certainly wanted that to be the case, but I know you've cottoned on too. We are on ops every night, and it's always to Berlin. The same times and route too. We never used to do that; in fact it's bloody suicide.

'The food is always the same and it's tasteless. We're not really eating it; it's just that we remember eating it. Those people who ignore us are nothing to do with us now, they can't see us and they don't know we are here. Same with those Lancs that wouldn't let us in, and the control people pissing off while we are waiting to go. It's like we're invisible, because we are bloody invisible.

'Do you get it now, mate? We're ghosts. We got the chop the other night, or last week, or it might be last year for all I know. The only people who see us and talk to us are the other bods who bought it, either before or since. They didn't miraculously come back; we've joined them, not the other way round.

'Every night the Wingco comes with us and he's always the first to get the chop. Then they all fall in the same order. I see it from the flight deck, you can't from back there. There's only about forty planes with us and it's the same forty, night after night. Then we get hit by the same fighter, at the same time in the same place; Ben gets it first then we are going down, spinning. None of us get out, which is why we're all here. For all I know, we are going to spend eternity doing the same trip time and again, always hoping to finish it but never getting home. Long after the war is over, and all we see around us has been abandoned, we will still set off for Berlin every night, us and the other forty-odd aircraft that bought it the same night. Every night we will fail to return. Better get used to it. But like I say I'm dying for a pint…'

*

The Rainbow Tree
By Meg Johnston

~

Twin sisters Beverley and Jayne were spending their first day in the family's new home. They had moved to the country with their Mum, Dad and little brother Jamie. The girls were unhappy because they hadn't wanted to move. All their friends lived in the city and that's where they had wanted to stay. Nevertheless here they were; in a place they didn't want to be, with no friends and no idea what their new school would be like.

Jamie was very excited by the move and was running all over the house, exploring all the rooms and the garden.

'Come and see what I've discovered,' he called to his sisters.

With a sigh Beverley and Jayne followed the sound of Jamie's excited shouts and found him in the garden pointing up into a tree. In the tree was a house - a tree house!

'I've always wanted one of these,' declared an excited Jamie as he scrambled up the rope ladder.

'Hey! It's got my name on the door,' he shouted. 'Come up and have a look.'

The girls climbed up and sure enough there on the door to the tree house was Jamie's name, in blue wooden letters.

'I wonder who left this for me?' he asked his sisters with a puzzled frown.

Jayne laughed saying, 'I think you need to ask Dad that question, I'm sure he had something to do with all this.'

'It is great Jamie,' said Beverley.' 'Now you will have to bring all your treasures up here.'

Whooping with glee Jamie climbed back down the ladder and went in search of his parents and his treasures.

With another big sigh the twins clambered down to the ground and walked towards the house. They knew their parents had been working on the house before they had all moved in. The removal men had just finished bringing all the family's belongings into the house and there were boxes everywhere. Nana and Granddad were arriving later to help everyone unpack. They lived not very far away and the one good thing about moving was that the children would see much more of their grandparents.

'Hello you pair,' Mum greeted them, 'are you going to help unpack?'

'Yes,' they replied together but with no enthusiasm in their voices.

'You could begin with your bedrooms,' Mum suggested. 'Dad has just finished putting your beds in there.'

With another big sigh they nodded to Mum and set off.

'Have you been upstairs yet?' Mum called after them.

'No,' replied Beverley, 'Are we having that room we saw when we looked around the house?'

'Come on you pair, we'll go and find your rooms together.' Laughing, Mum slid an arm around each of her daughters and guided them into the house.

Reluctantly the twins allowed themselves to be taken into the house and up the stairs.

'This isn't how I remember the upstairs,' Beverley mentioned to Mum as they reached the landing.

'Me neither,' Jayne agreed with a puzzled look at Mum.

Mum smiled, shook her head and said, 'We told you we were going to make a few changes, come and see.'

Following Mum along the landing they passed the room they thought was going to belong to them. Mum walked to a second flight of stairs the girls were sure hadn't been there the last time they had visited the house.

'Are these new?' Jayne asked Mum.

'Yes,' Mum replied. 'Up you go.'

Beverley and Jayne climbed the stairs together wondering what they would find. At the stop of the stairs was another landing with a window and two white doors. One door had Beverley's name written in red on a white plaque, the other had Jayne's name in pink on a white plaque.

'Are we not sharing a bedroom?' The girls asked together, looking at their Mum.

'Why don't you go in and see,' she replied giving each child a small push towards the doors.

Beverley walked towards the door with her name on and very slowly pushed open the door. Jayne was doing exactly the same with the other door. Dad had joined Mum on the landing and they were watching their daughters with some apprehension.

'Wow,' the twins called out together. 'Come here and look at this.' Then they started to laugh.

As Beverley walked into her new bedroom she began to really smile for the first time that day. Mum and Dad had decorated the bedroom in her favourite colours: red and white. There was red and white love heart wallpaper on one wall with matching curtains and bedding, and a white wardrobe and chest of drawers for her clothes. The small white cabinet by her bed held a red lamp with a love heart shade and all the furniture had heart shaped handles.

Jayne's bedroom had also been decorated in her favourite colours of white, black and pink. One wall had pink and black striped wallpaper with matching curtains and bedding. Her white furniture had pink and black butterfly handles and the lamp was black with a pink butterfly shade.

There was another door in each room which both girls opened at the same time. They stepped into a bathroom decorated to suit them both. Laughing they hugged each other, ran to find their parents to say thank you, then spent the rest of the day unpacking and arranging their possessions. When their grandparents arrived the twins couldn't wait to show off their new rooms, which they promised to keep very tidy!

Over the next few days all the children were very busy, arranging their new bedrooms, unpacking clothes and toys, and helping to sort out Jamie's tree house. They were so busy they forgot to be sad!

Late one afternoon Beverley and Jayne were sitting in the window seat on the landing between their bedrooms reading and watching raindrops race each other down the glass pane. It was one of their favourite places in the house. It looked out over the garden and fields to the hills beyond. They pretended it was the tower of their very own magic castle. The rain became heavier and the clouds darker, then suddenly there was a loud bang and a bright flash of light lit up the garden and fields - showing a lonely tree standing in the field beyond the garden. The girls jumped and let out a scream of fright. Grabbing each other they started to laugh.

'Wow! Did you see that?' Jayne asked her sister.

'Yes, that old tree looked magical. When it stops raining I want to go and see it.'

'Me too,' remarked Jayne quickly.

However it rained and rained for the next three days, so the twins forgot all about the tree for a while.

One morning they woke up to discover the rain had finally stopped. Although there were still dark clouds in the sky, as they looked out of their window the sun began to shine. Arcing over the tree the girls saw a beautiful rainbow. Looking at each other in wonder they held their breath and gazed at the tree and its colourful rainbow. Running down the stairs the girls found Mum and quickly asked if they could go to the tree in the field.

'Not before you have your breakfast,' Mum replied. 'And you'll need to find your wellington boots. That field will be muddy after all the rain.'

'Did you see the rainbow over the tree?' They asked together.

'It was magical,' Jayne added with her eyes sparkling.

Mum smiled saying, 'No! I missed that. Eat up before you go looking for adventures.'

'Do we have any neighbours?' asked Jayne.

'We haven't seen anyone next door,' replied Beverley.

'We do but they are on holiday. They are due back soon,' Mum told them.

Having eaten, Beverley and Jayne found their wellington boots and went outside. The sun was shining as they set off through the gate and into the field. The rainbow was no longer there but the tree stood tall and proud in the middle of the field.

'I wonder what Mum and Dad are going to do with this field,' Beverley remarked to Jayne as they walked towards the tree.

'No idea,' Jayne replied. 'I don't think I've heard them talking about it.'

'Well, I'm pleased it's ours because I'm sure that's a magical tree,' her sister said.

'We didn't have any magical trees in our old house, did we? At least I never found any,' Jayne replied.

'Did we ever look for any?' Beverley asked her twin.

Jayne thought for a moment then replied with a shrug of her shoulders.

'No, I don't think we did either,' remarked Beverley.

'That tree is huge,' declared Jayne stopping to look up into the branches. 'Do you think it's an oak tree, Beverley?'

'Yes it is, and yes I do,' replied Beverley.

'It looks quite dry underneath those branches,' Jayne observed. 'Let's go and see.'

Together they walked under the spreading branches of the old oak tree.

'Look at the trunk,' Beverley told Jayne as she examined the tree.

'It looks as though there are lots of small doors and windows in it,' Jayne said, as she too looked closely at the large tree trunk.

'I think we could climb onto that big branch,' Beverley suggested pointing to a branch above their heads.

Beverley then proved her words by doing just that, leaving her wellingtons under the tree. 'Come on, slowcoach,' she called down to her twin. 'It's a great place to sit. We could hide up here and no-one would know we were here.'

'I'm coming,' Jayne called as she too scrambled up and onto the branch. 'There are more doors and windows up here look,' Jayne added as she settled herself on the branch beside Beverley.

'There's also something hanging on that branch above our heads,' Beverley told her pointing to something colourful.

Holding onto a branch above their heads, the girls stood and walked towards the mystery object.

'It's a bracelet!' exclaimed Beverley. 'And it's got a name on it.'

Jayne looked very carefully and then declared, 'Patricia! That's Mum's name. How did a bracelet with Mum's name on it get into this tree?'

'Don't know,' answered Beverley, looking as astounded as her sister. 'Let's go and ask her. We could get some sandwiches at the same time and bring them back here to eat.'

'Great idea! Come on, race you home,' Jayne replied climbing quickly down to the ground.

The twins raced home across the muddy field calling for their Mum as they took off their muddy boots.

'What's the matter?' asked Mum from the kitchen. 'You haven't hurt yourselves?'

'No!' They chorused. 'You'll never guess what we've just found.'

They excitedly told their Mum about climbing the tree and finding the bracelet with her name on.

Mum smiled wistfully and looked out of the window towards the tree saying, 'This house used to belong to my gran and I often stayed here when I was little. I put that bracelet there when I was about your age. I'm surprised it's still there.'

'We didn't know that,' remarked Beverley.

'Is that why we moved, Mum?' Jayne asked.

'Yes,' Mum replied. 'My gran left this house to me. I loved coming here. I always thought that tree was the most magical tree in the world.'

'We do too,' the twins said together.

'Can we take some sandwiches there for lunch please?' Beverley asked.

'I don't see why not,' Mum responded.

Half an hour later the girls were walking back over the field carrying their lunch and a pair of trainers each.

'It will be much easier to climb with trainers on,' Jayne declared as they sat underneath the tee to remove their wellingtons.

They climbed back into the tree, settled themselves onto a strong branch, and began to eat.

'Imagine Mum climbing this tree,' said Beverley as she munched on a sandwich.

'Didn't know Mum could climb,' Jayne replied with a giggle.

They both leaned against the tree trunk and finished their lunch. The sunlight filtered down beneath the branches and made patterns on their arms, legs and faces.

Watching the sunlight, Beverley suddenly held her breath and shaded her eyes with her hands.

Jayne opened her mouth to speak but Beverley put her finger over her lips and slowly shook her head.

Jayne followed her sister's gaze not knowing what she was looking at. There was nothing there!

'What?' queried Jayne in a hushed voice.

'I thought I saw something really colourful by that leaf there,' said Beverley in a whisper.

'It must have been the sun shining through a raindrop,' said Jayne. 'Some leaves are still wet.'

'Yes, it must have been,' agreed Beverley looking at her sister with a smile. The she relaxed back against the tree trunk.

Sitting quietly, the twins looked across the fields towards their new home.

'I do like this house,' suggested Jayne after a few minutes.

'Me too, and I love our new bedrooms. I don't have to put up with pink,' declared Beverley.

Jayne chuckled and offered, 'And I don't have to see red everywhere,' She gasped. 'Except in this tree! I've just seen a small red - Something!'

'Where?' queried Beverley.

Jayne pointed above their heads to the branch where their Mum's bracelet hung.

Beverley looked carefully but there was nothing to be seen.

'That's something colourful and something red we've seen. I'm sure this is a magic tree,' suggested Jayne.

'You are right,' a soft quiet voice remarked in Jayne's ear. 'What did you say?' Jayne asked Beverley.

'I didn't say anything,' she replied.

'I did,' repeated the same soft voice. 'Look up a little.'

Jayne slowly raised her head a little and then let out a gasp of surprise.

Beverley followed her sister's gaze and held her breath.

Sat on a branch close by was the smallest person either of them had ever seen. She was dressed all in red. She wore a red dress and had red shoes, red hair and red wings.

Rubbing their eyes in disbelief, the twins looked at each other and then looked again at the branch.

'Hello,' said the small person. 'Who are you and what are you doing in our tree?'

The girls stared at the small person in astonishment.

'H..H..Hello,' stammered Beverley awkwardly. 'My name is Beverley and this is my sister, Jayne. We've just moved here and thought this tree was magical and came to look at it.'

'Why do you both look the same?' the small person enquired.

'We are twins,' Jayne informed her. 'But we aren't really alike when you get to know us. Who are you?'

'I'm Roxy. I'm a red rainbow fairy. My friends and I live in this tree and we put the colours in all the rainbows around here.' Roxy told them proudly.

'You made that beautiful rainbow over the tree this morning?' queried Beverley.

'Not on my own, silly. We all did,' declared Roxy.

'Are all your friends here?' asked Jayne. 'Will they come and talk to us?'

'They are already here. You just have to look carefully and believe.'

The twins did as was suggested and looked carefully, and believed.

Standing or sitting close to Roxy were seven other small people. They smiled and waved at the twins and then, one by one, introduced themselves.

'I'm Olivia, an orange rainbow fairy.'

'My name is Yasmin and I'm a yellow rainbow fairy.'

'They call me Greta the green rainbow fairy.'

'Hi! You can call me Bella, the blue rainbow fairy.'

'Me? I'm Iona an indigo rainbow fairy.'

'And my name is Vieda. I'm a violet rainbow fairy.

Then Roxy told the girls, 'This is Crystal. She is a white rainbow fairy, very shy, and rarely speaks to people.'

When the eight fairies moved together, a miniature rainbow formed over their heads. Like Roxy, each fairy was dressed head to toe in their own particular rainbow colour.

'We are very pleased to meet you,' the girls said together, smiling at the sight of the lovely fairies.

'Do you all live here in this tree?' Beverley asked Roxy.

'Not just us, all of our families live here too. You saw our doors and windows as you climbed up our tree,' revealed Roxy.

'What a beautiful place to live,' said Jayne. 'Is this where you make rainbows?'

'Yes,' Bella replied. 'Then we send them into the sky.'

'How do you make a rainbow?' asked Beverley. 'Could we learn how to make one?'

'Making rainbows is easy,' replied Roxy.

'If you're a rainbow fairy,' added Yasmin.

'People can't make rainbows,' Olivia told the girls.

'Not on their own,' suggested Greta.

'They can with help.' Iona and Vieda pronounced together, giggling.

'Would you like to learn?' Bella asked.

'Yes please,' the twins replied.

'How?' asked Beverley, her eyes shining.

'Follow us,' Roxy told them as she flew into the air and then down towards the ground. A moment later, her friends followed.

Beverley and Jayne looked at each other in astonishment then scrambled quickly to the ground.

'In here,' Roxy said, indicating a small door shape in the tree's bark.

'We won't fit through there,' Jayne remarked.

'We definitely won't fit through there,' agreed Beverley looking at the small door.

'Of course you will. Come on!' said Bella taking hold of each of the sister's hands and pulling them towards the door.

The girls thought she was very strong for such a small person and felt themselves walking forward.

How it happened they could never say, but one second both girls were standing beside the tree trunk and the next - they were somewhere else!

'What happened?'

'Where are we?'

The girls asked the questions at the same time.

'You wanted to learn to make a rainbow,' suggested Yasmin.

'So here you are; where we make rainbows,' Greta added.

'Is this Fairyland?' asked Beverley.

'That's what you call it. Yes!' admitted Roxy. 'Come on! We've no time to waste.'

'This is beautiful,' Jayne told their new fairy friends. 'All the colours are clear and bright.'

'Thank you!' chorused the fairies when they flew ahead of the girls. 'We think it's beautiful too.'

The sisters followed looking around in wonder at everything. Fairy folk of all kinds were working and playing, dancing and singing, laughing and waving.

'It seems such a happy place to live,' Beverley said very quietly to Jayne.

'It is most of the time,' Bella told the girls. 'Sometimes it can be a little sad, but not often.'

'What makes a fairy sad?' asked a concerned Jayne.

'When people don't believe in us,' Olivia replied.

'But most people do so that's why we aren't sad often or for very long,' Vieda assured the twins.

'Come on, you lot. We've a rainbow to make. Hurry up!' Roxy called.

Smiling with delight, they followed Roxy passing fairy houses, sweet smelling colourful flowers, tall trees in every shade of green and silver streams.

Soon they arrived at a building that was larger than the others they had passed, but still looked beautiful. Lots of fairies in rainbow colours were flying in and out and the building itself seemed to change colour as the girls looked at it.

It went from red to orange to yellow to green to blue to indigo to violet and back again so quickly the twins were dazzled.

'Wow!' They said together. 'That's fantastic!'

Then they followed the fairies inside where an even more amazing sight awaited them. Everywhere they looked, the colours of the rainbow glowed - From the walls; the floor, the ceiling, the windows, the doors, and the fairies. It was like walking inside a rainbow. It was just unbelievable! It was breath-taking.

Beverley and Jayne couldn't believe what they were seeing.

'How do you do all this?' asked Beverley in wonder.

'We couldn't do it without the special stones,' Roxy told her.

'Or the dwarves who get them for us,' added Iona. 'They dig underground for them. I would hate to be underground but they love it.

'What special stones?' asked Jayne.

'These bright sparkly ones,' Roxy revealed pointing to a large mound of stones.

'They don't look sparkly,' suggested Jayne.

'Not when the dwarves first bring them to us,' Bella said. 'We have to find the magic inside.'

'Oh!' said Beverley. 'How do you do that?'

'Watch!' Roxy told the twins as she flew towards the stones. 'Not all of them are magic.'

Bella interrupted with, 'Most of the ones without magic are given back to the dwarves. They use them to decorate the things they make. We use the others ourselves. They are very useful and pretty.'

The stones didn't look very pretty but the girls didn't think it would be polite to say this so they just watched the fairies.

Roxy chose one of the stones, picked up a cloth and some special dust, and began to rub the dust into the stone saying, 'This one's not magic. But it will be pretty and useful.'

Roxy set it aside then selected another one. 'This is a good one,' she cried put happily. 'Come and see!' As she said this, she was rubbing the stone with the cloth and her dust.

Suddenly the stone began to shine with a beautiful red glow. The more Roxy rubbed, the brighter the stone glowed.

'How did that happen?' Beverley asked her voice full of wonder.

'This is a Ruby,' Roxy told her. 'We rubbed it with diamond dust. The ones with magic have a special glow. I can only do this with rubies because I'm a red rainbow fairy.'

'What about your friends?' asked Jayne?

'They all have their own special stones,' replied Roxy. 'They will tell you.'

Smiling, Roxy continued, 'Red rainbow fairies find magic rubies.'

'Orange rainbow fairies find magic Topaz,' said Olivia.

'Yellow rainbow fairies find Amethyst,' added Yasmin.

'Green rainbow fairies find Emeralds,' informed Greta.

'Blue rainbow fairies find Sapphires,' announced Bella.

'Indigo rainbow fairies use magic from the sky at dusk,' Iona told the twins.

'Violet rainbow fairies use magic from the sky at dawn,' said Vieda.

'White rainbow fairies help to bring it all together,' declared Roxy as Crystal nodded and smiled shyly.

'Crystal likes you two,' Bella added. 'She would have hidden if she didn't.'

'How do you get the magic out and turn it into a rainbow?' asked Beverley.

'That's what rainbow fairies do. It's our gift to the world,' Roxy told her. 'We don't question how. We just can.'

Beverley and Jayne looked very confused.

'Every fairy, or group of fairies, has a special talent. Flower fairies look after flowers. Dawn fairies make each new day bright. Rainbow fairies make rainbows. Understand?'

'Not really,' said Jayne still a little confused.

'Perhaps if we show you,' said Roxy.

The fairies disappeared and each returned with a glowing stone. The seven stones were the colours of the rainbow! Red, orange, yellow, green, blue, indigo, violet, and one was very clear.

'Our stones were clear,' Iona said to the twins pointing to Vieda and her glowing stones. 'But we can take our colours from dusk and dawn skies and keep them in these diamonds.'

'We can make small rainbows without stones,' said Roxy. 'Large ones take more magic so we use these.'

The eight fairies stood in a circle and held up their stones. Crystal floated in the centre of the circle holding her stone high above her head. The fairies began to sing. The song sounded beautiful to the girls although they couldn't understand the words. From each of the seven stones came a bright beam of light. Each beam went into Crystal's diamond. The diamond shone brighter and brighter without changing colour. Then from the bright stone came a circle of seven colours: red, orange, yellow, green, blue, indigo and violet: the colours of the rainbow!

Beverley and Jayne clapped their hands, jumping up and down cheering.

'That is fantastic,' yelled Beverley.

'The most magical thing we've ever seen,' cried Jayne enthusiastically.

'Except I've never seen a rainbow that was a circle,' added Beverley.

Roxy laughed and said, 'That's because you've never seen a rainbow from the sky. If you are standing on the ground all rainbows look like arcs.'

'Oh,' replied Beverley. 'They always look magical though.'

'Now I understand,' said Jayne suddenly. 'You can't help making rainbows when you're altogether. You are happiest when you are making rainbows, just as we are happiest when we are with Mum, Dad and Jamie.'

'Yes!' Beverley said. 'You are right, Jayne.'

Beverley turned to the eight fairies saying, 'Thank you for showing us your special magic. I wish we could make rainbows but I know we can't. We will remember you all whenever we see one and know you are all happy.'

'Yes, thank you all,' added Jayne. 'Is there anything we can do for you?'

'Please come to visit us in our tree as often as you can,' suggested Bella.

'Would you leave us something?' asked Roxy.

'Of course,' replied Beverley. 'What would you like?'

'You have to decide that yourselves,' Roxy told her. 'We love surprises.'

'It's time to leave us,' Yasmin said flying towards the twins. 'Follow us and we will show you the way.'

As the twins turned to go they felt a little tug on their hands. Crystal was pulling on their right hands and as the girls looked at her she placed a clear stone in each of their hands.

'These are crystals,' she told the surprised girls. 'They will help you make your own rainbow when the sun shines.'

'They are lovely, thank you,' said the astonished twins.

They were still looking at the brilliantly bright crystals when they suddenly found themselves sitting under the oak tree. Of the fairies, there was no sign but the girls still held a crystal in each of their right hands.

'That was brilliant,' enthused Jayne.

'It was,' agreed Beverley. 'And I know what our present should be.'

The next day, the girls returned to their rainbow tree, climbed to their special branch, and tied gifts to the tree. Each girl had made a lovely bracelet from beads that were all the colours of the rainbow. One bracelet had Beverley's name on it whilst the other bore Jayne's name. Both bracelets were similar to the one that had previously hung there. They remembered when they returned home after their visit to the rainbow fairies that Mum also had a crystal she kept in her bedroom. Mum had told them once that it had been a present from some very special friends.

As Beverley and Jayne sat happily in their tree they saw a car pull into the drive of the house next door to their new home. Four children tumbled noisily out asking if they could go and play.

'Codie, Leah, Jacque, Peter! You can play when you've helped unpack the car.'

It looked like the girl's neighbours had arrived home.

Beverley looked at Jayne and grinned.

'You know, although I miss our friends, perhaps our new home won't be so bad after all. We have a magical rainbow tree, fairy friends and a chance to make lots of other new friends.'

They climbed down from the tree and headed for home.

The crystals they held gave of a glowing light as they walked across the grass.

Eight small people watched them go and as a rainbow appeared over the tree accompanied by fairy laughter.

Life in Numbers
By Dave Miller

~

When I was born there were three,
My Dad, my Mum and little old me.
Four years later, a knock on the door.
A few years later, up our drive,
My little sister came, then there were five.
A few years later I met my wife.
So then she became family and my life
Instead of me it became we,
Six years later we became three.
Daughter born brought hope and joy
Perhaps next time we'll have a boy!!
Six years later there was a change
Another daughter we wouldn't exchange
So there we were a family of four
As poor health cancelled anymore.
We became foster parents, made us alive
Then the family became five.
Soon our baby John left the front door
He went to his new family, then there were four
But then our Ben, he did arrive
And once again we were back up to five.
He went to his family that wasn't a chore
Back once again to our family of four.
Then our daughter met her beau
Then guess what? You'll want to know
Between them out of the mix
Our family grew to six!
Grandson and son in law in a flash.
Although we were happy it wasn't a hash!!

Our daughter again was with child
We were happy, we all smiled.
Soon we were all in heaven
As our family grew to seven
Another boy added to our crew
As together we all grew.
In a few months some more good news
Maternity hospital in the queues.
Granddaughter joined us now it was great.
Our family had swollen to eight!!
Not all in the same house I hasten to add
But we saw them all daily that made us glad.
Moving on, our first born got wed
Away from our home her husband he led
A few years passed the weather was mild
When we heard she was having a child
A scan explained it would be a girl
But when it was born it was without a curl!!
So there we were now up to ten
Ladies outnumbered by men
But, as in most families, the nest they have flown
So wife and I are now on our own
Family keep in touch almost every day
But we don't take part or have any say.
They will start counting their own families soon
Across the country they may get strewn.
So what started as a family of three
My Mum and Dad and little ole me
I grew and made my own family
But now we're back from us
To we.

*

The Last Three Months
By Dave Miller

~

Every day I sit and stare,
Across the room at your empty chair.
You're now in another room
Whilst I sit under a cloud of gloom.
The doctors decided in their wisdom
To have made our life just pure bedlam.
Removing tablets that were your support
Not realising how your mind would distort.
A tablet you've taken for forty years,
They weaned you off and left you in tears.
Withdrawal symptoms, a living hell,
Family and friends they can tell
Without warning or telling you the effect
We felt this was going to be incorrect.
We think in the end we were right
Because you have now gone out of sight.
Taken to your bed as you've done before
Mixing with friends, not any more.
Panic, sweating, crying aloud
Your head covered by the dark cloud.
This has had an effect on me too,
Because I don't know what I can do!
These last three months have changed our life
As forty seven years as man and wife.
I'm on tablets for my peace of mind
Family and friends are really kind
But how much longer will this nightmare take?
A decision from doctors we still await.
We thought a crisis would be more prompt
On our heads we feel we feel we've been stomped.
Me, talking to a long lost friend

Has helped my mind to mend.
Back to my writing is also helping
My dark clouds I want to sling.
Throw them off to ease my mind
But to you I ask, please rewind.
Back to days when you were well
Get away from this living hell.
So that you come back to your lovely chair
And I have a reason to sit and stare.

*

Risk 90s style
By Ray Gregory
~

It was just another day at the office. Winter had arrived so the town was quiet. The weather was, as usual, dull and damp, most folk staying inside taking in the telly soaps for a bit of escapism.

It was early evening when a call was received that a domestic incident was in progress at one of the houses not far from the Police Station. The two officers on duty at the time decided to attend on foot, being that it was just around the corner. They had no details of the occupants and no background information. Intelligence was pretty sketchy in those days of the 90's and the words 'risk assessment' were one of those new-fangled corporate management terms that was trying to get into fashion. The only information the officers had was that raised voices had been heard by neighbours interspersed with loud banging and crashing coming from inside the house.

On arrival they found one of the neighbours standing outside. A front door was wide open and every light must have been on in the house. They could hear loud banging coming from inside. The neighbour assured the police that the only persons she knew to be inside were the husband and wife, both in their early fifties, no children. The couple were well known in the street and neighbours told police that they had not seen the couple that day but that the noise was highly unusual.

The officers entered the hallway and noticed immediately that the floor was covered in glass from the inner door and a number of pictures lay broken on the carpet. They called out and a female voice shouted, "In here."

The duo turned and went into the front room. What they saw is best described as a scene from a blitzed house.

The television was smashed in half as were a dining table and several pictures. Sitting in amongst the chaos was a very distressed female in her Fifties being comforted by a female friend.

She informed us that her husband had come home and accused her of having an affair, something that she denied but he didn't believe her. He told her he wanted a divorce and wanted half of what was his in the house. Literally half that is, so he went out to the shed and got an axe! Coming back into the house he began to half everything, first the television followed by the dining table, several photographs, a chair, then into the kitchen taking out the microwave and toaster. The officers could hear banging coming from upstairs so they called out from the foot of the stairs. It went quiet so they went up. At the top of the stairs was the bathroom and they could see a male inside with his back to them. He turned round and the officers realised he was armed with an axe.

He made no threat towards the two officers but said, "It's nowt to do you with you lads. I'm only halving what's mine."

He then raised the axe and was about to smash it into the bath when one of the officers called out, something daft like, "You won't get much of a bath in that cut in half will you, which bit you going to keep?"

He stopped, looked at the police and began to recount how his wife was having an affair. It was clear he was in some distress over this but as the conversation developed it was clear he had no evidence. His wife in the meantime had been confiding that her husband had been suffering from depression for some time and was taking medication, which he sometimes forgot to take. He was not violent towards her nor had he made any threats to harm her on this occasion. The local doctor was called and together the officers managed to calm the man down. He handed over the axe and then sat on the stairs talking to the police whilst arrangements were made for him to go to hospital for treatment re his mental condition.

Years later, in the twenty-first century, the two officers might recount the story and agree that the situation was resolved without resorting to overzealous tactics but with calm negotiation. They had no means other than that to deal with it, no Taser, pepper spray etc. Maybe things have changed today. Would today's police have disarmed the man, thrown him to the ground, and arrested and detained him having first stunned or sprayed him?

Maybe they'd carry out one of those old fashioned things – a risk assessment.

*

The Quick 'n' Easy Guide to Gardening
By Simon Hepworth
~

Many of us have gardens but are a bit too busy to really do them justice. You work all week then at the weekend remember you have family matters to deal with or, if you are young and single, you are either out clubbing or generally too hung over to get out of bed. Meanwhile, however much time and effort you actually manage to put into it your garden swiftly returns to its natural state. There comes a point where you realise something has to be done. Usually this is about the time that you can't see out of the front window because of the dense foliage. Alternatively you get home and wonder where your house has gone.

There are several ways of avoiding this state of affairs:

Retirement: You will spend months pottering around getting backache until you look up and suddenly find that you have an immaculate garden with fine, close-cropped grass lined with white bricks. You will then discover that a greenhouse has materialised in the middle of your lawn and that you have become an expert on begonias or dahlias. You also notice that you get extremely annoyed with next door's kids for playing football with reckless disregard to your greenhouse. The drawback with retirement is that you have to stop earning money and start living off your pension so you might not actually be able to afford a lawn mower. You could buy a goat to nibble the grass and but the kids when they trespass in your garden to fetch their football from amidst the shattered remnants of your greenhouse, but be mindful that goats like nothing more than chomping away on your begonias and dahlias, or indeed anything else that will kill them or incur massive vet bills.

Hire a gardener: This might lead some people to think of romantic trysts as in Lady Chatterley's Lover, and construct themselves a handy potting shed hidden in the shrubbery. The reality, however, is that, rather than some eye candy of the gender of your preference, you will get some chav who's just been kicked off the dole or else a banjo-playing yokel who will speak incomprehensible rustic drivel about ripping out the chrysanthemums and planting mangel-wurzel's. You could take advantage of European integration and subsidies of course, strike a deal with an organised crime group and avail yourself of imported cheap labour but this constitutes Human Trafficking so is illegal and immoral, so is best avoided.

Pave over your garden: To many people this seems an ideal solution, and would appear to get round the upkeep and maintenance problems. For the same reason, it occurred to me to ask my dentist about pulling all my teeth out and replacing them with false ones so that I wouldn't have to have any more fillings. He talked me out of this course of action, probably because it would ultimately be less of an earner for the dental industry. Tarmac isn't cheap and you need to find a reputable contractor to lay the stuff smoothly. Whilst European organised crime groups do not yet specialise in tarmacking gardens, a quick trip to an unofficial roadside caravan site might provide a useful lead. Do remember, however, that tarmac is best laid over a substantial underlay of crushed rubble rather than simply dumped on top of the grass and you should point this out to the tarmacking gang when they arrive. The good thing about lawns, though, is that your children can fall over all day without coming to grief, which cannot be said for playing football on tarmac.

For those of you who don't have a horticultural bent, the money to employ gardening staff or the inclination to take early retirement I have written a handy guide to effort-free gardening. It is actually very easy if you follow a few simple rules, most of which are common sense. It need not be difficult, or expensive

Lawns: Left to their own devices grass grow everywhere. If you look at fields, as you drive past them, you will notice that this is true. No one planted the grass; it has always been there. Just try leaving a flowerbed for a few months and you will see that it sprouts grass without any effort on your part. This will also be the case if you forget to put any rubble underneath you newly-laid tarmac. This is the secret to happy gardening. Leave your lawn to its own devices and it will be fine. Lawns don't need any food or a complicated sprinkler system. They might go a bit brown occasionally, in which case you spend the summer pretending you have emigrated but come the rainy season (July to June) the grass will come back OK. So all you need is a lawn mower and a pair of edge cutters. Once a week is great for very short grass; if you prefer the lusher look, give yourself every other weekend off. Other plants thrive on your lawn amongst the grass stalks but as they are green as well you won't notice them.

Weeding: This is one of the most tedious parts of gardening but you can benefit from the decades of research into chemical warfare by buying selective weed killers. Agent Orange, for example, had an excellent reputation for enabling you to see the wood for the trees, although most of the wood itself was permanently incapacitated. Personally I don't recommend them as you never know what carnage they might wreak, especially as you will usually have too much, not want to waste it and wind up storing the surplus in a lemonade bottle, which your child will probably want to drink. So it's a case of falling back on physical effort and removing the herbaceous interlopers by hand. Once again the Quick 'n' Easy Gardener will employ some basic decision making and act decisively. The golden rule is that it is your garden and you can leave or remove whatever you want. If you like the natural look, you can rest assured that you will soon play host to a wide range of native plants. Many of these will sprout colourful bits in summer and actually look quite pleasant. The exception to this is the dandelion, which is the pigeon or rat of the weed world and deserves no less than total extermination. You can recognise dandelions by the fact that they are yellow, and everywhere. They have deep roots as well, which means that you have to dig them out with a spade or similar implement. For everything else, just take a good look and remove anything that looks like it shouldn't be there. Remember, the choice is yours.

Plants: The golden rule for plants is 'Keep It Simple, Stupid'. There are lots of decent native plants that evolved here over millions of years and these will survive your best efforts to kill them. These include things like roses, for example, which you can leave unpruned so that they soon form an impenetrable barrier for burglars or next door's kids. Daffodils are quite straightforward, if somewhat transient whilst heather is also hard to get rid of. Problems usually start when you get adventurous and plant something exotic, such as anything from a garden centre in a little pot. These come with a limited life expectancy, usually measured in days rather than weeks. The exception to this is the Nasturtium. I bought one of those at my old house and very shortly my garden was a vision of orange foliage. It is possible to have fun with some plants, especially if you are planning on moving house. Before you move, simply stick some crocus bulbs in your lawn to spell out a cheery message to the new owners, especially if they drove a hard bargain when negotiating the purchase. Come Spring they will be delighted to read your good wishes in blue, yellow and orange as the crocuses wake up. This is an eco-friendly alternative to the alternative surprise for difficult purchasers when they rip up the carpets on arrival to find that you have painted pentangles and satanic symbols on the bedroom floor.

Trees: A tree is for life, not just for Christmas. Trees are great and you can never have too many, except that as they grow their roots will make your house fall down. However by the time this happen, you will probably have moved so it won't be your problem. Of course, you can always warn the new owners through the medium of crocus. The other thing you need to know about trees and their smaller relatives, bushes, is that they need pruning from time to time. Again, it is possible to be too pedantic and worry unnecessarily about chopping the wrong bits off. I can reassure you that this is not possible. I've spent years pruning trees and have never found one that didn't grow back all its missing bits within a few short years. Just lop off anything you don't think should be there. A word of caution though - do this from ground level. Don't do what my neighbour once did and sit on the branch you are sawing off.

Happy gardening.

*

Loneliness
By Dave Miller
~

There are twenty fours in every day,
But what happens when you can't play?
Sitting with thoughts all alone
No one calls not even a phone
Room full of people noise all around
But sitting alone hearing no sound.
Sitting watching TV
No idea what I see?
Over my head the programmes go
What was it about? I don't know
Reading a book is a drag
My Heart it seems to sag
When this dark descends
It's time like this you need your friends
But that's easier said than done
Especially when you don't have one!
No one to talk to for a chat
Nothing in particular just chit and chat.
Friends, later in your life
Don't want to hear of your strife
They have their own lives to live
So your attention they can't give
"He should have asked", is what is said
When at your funeral and you're dead
Wonder if you're lonely then
As into heaven you ascend
Or do you meet your friends who've passed
Who for my help they never asked
Or are you still going be alone?
Because your friends have now all flown?

*

Black Dog
By David Miller

~

I've had quite a few days of real hard slog,
Walking around with Churchill's black dog,
I'm not saying this to make an impression
It's what the great man called depression.

Depression, the curse of the strong,
Whoever said that wasn't wrong.
Depression is devious, it is also said,
Quietly and quickly gets into your head.

Once in, it makes itself at home,
Round and around anywhere to roam
Making himself comfortable and lying down
His scratching and noise gives you a frown.

"Pull yourself together," I've heard people say
As if it's that easy I say, "No way"
It's an illness, a curse of the strong
So no one can hurry you along.

But there is help from a little pill
It's not a disease it's because you are ill
The doctor is there to make you feel better
Get rid of Black Dog and get a Red Setter.

Something that is so full of life
A kindly animal not giving you strife
With Black Dog you don't have to walk
Just meet a friend; it's so good to talk.
After a while then better you'll feel
When you have Black Dog bought to heel

Walking behind you at heel instead
Of roaming and sleeping and messing your head.

If you remember Churchill and his cause
What he achieved would bring applause
So depression can be defeated, now you know
So don't let that big Black Dog show.

*

A Childhood Dream Come True
By Edward Lightfoot
~

I was just about to finish work for the day, when my Warrant Officer told me, "Thank you for all your hard work and service and we're sorry to see you leaving. But as a 'Thank you' I've arranged for you to have a 'back-seater' tomorrow with 31 Squadron. You've to make sure you see the Senior Medical Officer tonight."

I didn't know what to say. I was overcome with emotion; this was something I'd wanted to do since I was a child.

Growing up in Cumbria, I've spent many a time with my parents visiting local towns and villages in the Lake District: a patch of Gods Garden I consider to be 'home'. I can't think of anywhere else I'd rather be: the Lakes, the scenery, the people. Spending as much time in the Lake District, it's inevitable that you will have at some point, heard the roar of a jet engine. If you glanced across to see where the roar was coming from the chances are you would have missed the culprit when it passed overhead travelling faster than the speed of sound. If by chance you were quick enough you would catch a glimpse of the skills of some of the finest pilots in the world at the controls of some of the most expensive military aircraft enjoying the scenery themselves.

As a child I so much wished that I could do that one day. Now that day was soon to become a reality - a childhood dream brought to life.

I was coming to the end of my career in the Royal Air Force after nine years, to spend more time with my family, and carve a career as a Police Officer.... one uniform for another.

That evening I went to the Medical Centre to see the SMO who was slightly older than me. He sat me down and asked a series of questions regarding my health followed by a full physical check: eyesight, hearing, manual dexterity, and respiration. His final piece of advice, "Make sure you have a hearty breakfast in the morning, something substantial," with a slight smirk on his face and a glint in his eye.

I hardly slept that night. I phoned my ever so proud parents Mary and Eddie, and they were just as excited as me at my news. No matter what I've chosen to do in life, my parents have been there for me, supporting me in everything that I have achieved in my life so far.

I phoned my partner Sharron. She was pleased for me but I don't think she was excited at the prospect of me hurtling around the sky at stupid miles an hour. The RAF report that the Tornado GR4 aircraft has a maximum speed of Mach 2.2 equivalent to 1,442 mph.

I was too excited the following morning to even think about having breakfast. I raced over to the squadron buildings anticipating the day's events. My friend Ian, one of the station photographers, was there when I arrived to record my day. We were led through to the Flying kit room where I was measured up for my flight coveralls, Anti-Gravity Suit (G-Suit), gloves and most importantly - my helmet. Having never worn such items before the Safety Equipment fitters (also known as Squippers) dressed me up and ensured everything was adjusted to a perfect fit.

A few lunges and rolling of the arms in the flight suit ensured that I didn't have any restricted movement. I was advised that this was a necessity as I was to be strapped securely into the cockpit and I may have to stretch and reach the ejector seat handle. The lump in my throat at the point suggested as to how nervous I was at hearing that.

We moved from the kit room round to flight planning where I was escorted into a side room and made to watch a twenty minute VHS video. It had been recorded sometime in the 1970's and explained what would happen should the aircraft have to ditch into the sea and how the ejector seat operated. All of these things combined yet it still didn't deter me from what was waiting round the corner.

It was a lovely sunny day in Norfolk, not a cloud in the blue sky. You could see for miles around. I made my way from the hanger to the flight line; I felt like I was Tom Cruise from the Top Gun movie. The only thing I was missing was a pair of Aviator sunglasses - not supplied by the RAF. Out on the tarmac stood a long line of Tornado GR4 aircraft along with their maintenance crews preparing them for the day's sorties.

I was guided by ground crew up the steps and into the Navigator's seat, which was to be my office for the next few hours. The crew strapped me into the ejector seat and removed the safety pins from the small explosive devices. These devices were now capable of propelling the seat and myself from the cockpit through the canopy at about 20G's (1G is the force of earth's gravity). When the crew gave me an informal introduction as to what sensitive electrical equipment encompassed me in the rear cock-pit, I was handed four sick-bags to place within arms-reach. The standing joke on the squadron is for the ground crew to take bets as to how many of the four sick bags I will fill during my flight.

When I settled into the seat the next face I saw was that of my pilot Sqn. Ldr. Duncan Forbes. I had known Duncan for a year or so. What I didn't know was that he was formally a pilot with the Red Arrows aerobatics team and that he knew how far he could push an aircraft during such dynamic aerobatics.

The crew ensured that Duncan was secured into the front ejector seat in the cockpit and that we could safely communicate via the helmet microphones. Sitting in the cockpit I realised how confined the space was once the canopy was shut and secured. I watched from my elevated position when the steps were taken away and the ground crew retreated to a safe distance. The next thing I heard was the turbines of the twin turbofan Rolls Royce RB199 Mk 103 engines starting up. I felt my adrenaline levels increasing. There was a slight vibration within the cockpit when we moved slowly from the flight line, along the taxi-way, before turning and coming to a stop at the end of the runway. When I looked passed the pilot I could only see the runway disappear into the distance with the view slightly hazed due to the heat. Another Tornado pulled up alongside us on the runway as if it was going to race us to the end

I sat with anticipation and in trepidation of what was to happen next. I'd flown before commercially around the world but was not prepared for what happened next. As the whining of the engines built, the vibrations coursed through my body, and with 16,000 pounds of thrust I was firmly catapulted back into my seat when we accelerated down the runway. Our speed increased. I was sunk further and further into the seat before finally the aircraft pulled up and we left the ground.

With commercial flights, pilots head upwards towards the flight paths high in the sky. This is not the case with military pilots and we skimmed along the countryside surrounding the airfield. I had thankfully - at this stage - not been sick but my memorable journey had only just begun.

The two bits of advice that Duncan did gave me just after take-off, were:-

(1) If he told me to eject then I was just to pull the black and yellow handle situated between my legs. The canopy would shatter and the seat would pull my legs and arms back into the seat and I've leave the aircraft... rapidly. He added that if HE were to eject I would see the words written on the bottom of his boots "FOLLOW ME".

(2) If I was going to be sick then remember to switch off the microphone in my helmet. He didn't want to listen to me wretch.

Heading across the Norfolk countryside we headed out across the coast and above the North Sea. Duncan explained to me that, upon manoeuvring the aircraft, I would feel the G-suit I was wearing and it would constrict me. This was to combat the G-Force I would be subjected to and prevent the blood from rushing from my head and hopefully stop me from passing out... hopefully. We flew out to sea and Duncan banked the aircraft from side to side to prove how the G-suit operated, and, when he did so, I could feel the suit restrict around my legs forcing the blood upwards as the blood from my head attempted to vacate the cranium downwards.

When Duncan levelled off and I regained my composure. A slight jolt got my attention and as I looked out I could see the wings sweeping back into the fuselage. This allows the aircraft to operate at high-speed at low–level since it reduces the drag over the wing surface. The aircraft leaned over to the left when we travelled inland from the sea.

About forty minutes into the flight we entered Cumbrian airspace from the south. We passed over Grange-Over-Sands and entered a valley at Newby Bridge. I can only mention the names now having looked at a map since at the time of passing over we were travelling at an exhilarating speed. This exhilaration was increased when I realised that we were now flying below the level of the surrounding fells. On reaching Lake Windermere I jokingly commented to Duncan that I couldn't see the lake. The next thing I knew Duncan inverted the aircraft and so all I could see was the deep dark blue of Lake Windermere. When you are upside down your hands automatically come up to stop you falling. It was then I realised I was securely strapped into a thirty five million pound multi-capable aircraft. Looking out I was sure I caught glimpses of people in their boats and on the shoreline waving as we whizzed past. It reminded me of what I did as a child hoping that the pilot would acknowledge my presence.

And here I was waving back at them.

After a few moments of inverted flight we rolled back over and continued flying low-level up the valley towards Grasmere. When we flew through the valley, I heard a recorded message sounding in the cockpit, "WARNING – LOW GROUND." It repeated two or three times and I looked in horror towards Duncan who reassured me that the warning was normal and that there was nothing to worry about.

We climbed up and dived low, banking left, banking right, passing through the valleys I had driven down with my parents so many times before. Passing over Grasmere, Bassenthwaite, and out towards the Solway before we banked and rolled and headed in the direction of my home town of Carlisle.

Heading down Bowness-on-Solway, Duncan contacted the Air Traffic Control Tower at Carlisle Airport. To my amazement a male voice in the tower replied, "Roger, Confirm your Pax. His parents are here. His mother is wearing one of our hi-vis jackets and is waving her arms frantically next to the runway".

My colleagues back at camp had contacted my parents and informed them of my estimated time of arrival. My father later described to me that that when he heard our jet engines he turned in the general direction of the noise and saw two plumes of smoke when Duncan pushed the jet engines to their limit. I recall, as we approached the airfield, Duncan rolled us onto our left side. When we passed over I caught a glimpse of a figure stood in bright yellow waving. I held out my gloved hand onto the canopy in the hope that my proud parents could see their son had fulfilled his childhood dream. And within a blink of an eye we were gone.

Our journey continued south following the path of the M6, before turning left and heading east following the A66. It dawned on me that during my nine year RAF career it had taken me between four and five hours to drive from camp in Norfolk back to the Cumbrian Fells. Today it took us only forty minutes to fly there.

I recall that when we passed over the Hull estuary Duncan couldn't help himself and felt the need to go back down to low-level and buzz a Navy frigate which was on manoeuvres in the area. Again I had visions of the scene from Top-gun as Maverick does the same and captain spills his coffee. We both had a chuckle as we flew from the scene.

When we neared the end of our journey we passed into Lincolnshire and I had earlier mentioned to Duncan that my partner and children and I had been to Skegness recently. He must have kept this in mind. On reaching Skegness we again were low-level and Duncan pitched the aircraft vertically up and into a loop. The G-suit was squeezing me tightly as I watched the ground disappear from view, then reappear when we headed down and out of the loop and out into the North Sea again.

After about four hours of flying we returned to our base in Norfolk, but not before Duncan decided that I needed to try and fill the last of the four sick-bags I had been provided with and barrel rolled the aircraft down the full length of the runway. Thankfully, I had nothing left to give and after one last lap of the airfield we came into land.

We taxied back to the flight line. The engines were shut down and the stairs put back into place. The canopy opened and I could take a lung full of fresh air rather than recycled air through a mask. On reaching the bottom of the ladder, and reaching terra-firma, I shook Duncan's hand and thanked him for making a small child's dream come true.

To this day, I still stop and look up to the sky when I hear the noise of a jet engine racing by.

But now I don't dream of wanting.

I'm proud to say that I've achieved my dream.

*

The RIP
By Mike McNeff
~

Sgt Robin Marlette, supervisor of the Special Narcotics Enforcement Unit of the Arizona Department of Public Safety, was just signing off on the last report when his phone rang. He picked up before the second ring made it out.

"Marlette."

"Hey, Rob, it's Chucky." Charleston "Chucky" Ehrlander was a long time confidential informant; one of Robin's best CI's when it came down to it.

"What's up?"

"That five kilo heroin deal looks like it's finally going down?"

"It's about time. When?"

"This afternoon."

"What's the deal?"

"The guy needs another hundred grand to do the buy. He wants me to invest in the action. I figure you can give me the money, cover the transfer to him and then follow him to the deal."

"How 'bout we follow the both of you to the deal."

"Rob, I love ya man, but I'm just a lowly informant. You know dope is not my main thing. Dope deals are dangerous and I'm not nearly ready to die."

"Okay, are you home?"

"Yep."

"I'll call you back."

"I'll be here."

"Emmett!" Robin yelled before the receiver was down.

Emmett Franks appeared at the door. "What's up, Sarge?"

"That five kilo heroin deal Chucky's been working on is going down. Get everyone called in and ready to go."

"Roger, boss."

Robin picked up the phone again.

"Phoenix Police Special Investigations, Sgt Jackson."

"Ernie, it's Rob. You guys available for a five kilo heroin deal?"

"Absolutely! Where and when?"

"Have your team, raid van and tactical gear at our office ASAP."

"We're on our way!"

Robin hurried down to Captain Tom Pearle's office. He and Lt. Bob Hammel stopped talking when Robin came in.

"Tom, I need a hundred grand in the next thirty minutes."

Pearle's eye brows shot up so high Robin wouldn't have been surprised if they flew off his face.

"I got a five kilo heroin deal going down in the next couple hours."

"How'd you get on to this?"

"Chucky just called."

"I thought he worked money laundering."

"This just fell into his lap."

"You'll need more guys."

"Ernie's team is rolling."

"This is so typical of you, Rob. You waltz in expecting me to have a hundred grand on a moment's notice. I have bosses to get clearance from too, in case you forgot."

Robin just calmly looked at his former partner.

Tom let out a long breath. "Okay, I'll get you the money."

"When's the briefing?"

"As soon as everyone gets here."

"Lt. Hammel and I will sit in."

"Yes, sir." Robin saluted and walked back to his office and dialled Chucky.

" Charleston Ehrlander."

"It's Rob. We're a go. Who's your guy?"

"His name is Shawn Hill."

"What's he look like?"

"Blond hair. Late twenties. Skinny and a little taller than me."

"Okay, we'll meet at our usual spot in an hour."

"I'll be there."

Twenty minutes later, everyone was in the conference room. Robin conducted a quick briefing to make sure all officers knew what Chucky and his car looked like. He passed out a driver's license photo of the suspect, Shawn Hill and laid out the basic role of each officer. Nothing else could really be said. As with most dope deals, the situation promised to be fluid and challenging.

In the parking lot of Kelly's Deli, two blocks from Chucky's house, Robin sat in Chucky's car with a brief case containing one hundred thousand dollars. He handed Chucky a baseball cap containing a hidden transmitter, in the front of the cap.

"The bug is turned on, so you don't have to mess with it."

"That's good because I'd probably screw it up." Chucky's hands were shaky as he pulled the cap down on his head.

"Look Chucky, this is not so different than sinking a corrupt banker. You're not going to be near the dope or the sellers and you're going to give your guy the money, so he has no reason to hurt you. We'll be covering you all the way, but if you smell a rat, just get out. No bust is worth your life."

Chucky gave Robin a weak smile. "That's the nicest thing you've ever said to me. Does this mean I'm your favorite informant?"

"Yes, Chucky, you're my favorite informant."

Chucky stared out the windshield. "I have a bad feeling about this, Rob."

"You called us. You don't have to do it."

"I can't let five kilos of heroin hit the street."

"There's no guarantee they have any heroin. It could be a rip."

"I can't take that chance. If I heard someone overdosed on heroin after this, I couldn't live with myself."

"Well then, let's do it." Robin got out of the car. "We've got you covered."

Chucky waived and started his car. Robin got in the passenger seat of Burke Jamison's pickup truck.

"Bug's loud and clear, Rob."

"Good. Chucky's all assed up."

"Why? He's done busts with us before."

"I know, but for some reason dope scares him."

"Well, he ain't exactly wrong about that."

Robin didn't reply.

Chucky's car pulled out and the surveillance team set up around him; two cars behind him and two cars along the parallel streets on either side of him. Ernie's squad followed a half mile behind the moving surveillance in their van.

Chucky drove to Nineteenth Street and Glendale Avenue and pulled into the parking lot of a small restaurant.

"The guy I'm giving the money to is in that green Chevrolet Impala in the back corner," Chucky said over the hat bug.

Robin radioed the info to the other units on his portable. Everyone acknowledged the transmission.

Chucky got out of his car and got into the Impala. The bug crackled with his movements.

"Hey Charleston, I thought for a while you weren't coming."

"You should know better than that. I know a good investment when I see one. There's a hundred grand in there. Don't lose it."

"I won't. You wouldn't want to come with me, would you?"

"I'm just investing in this deal. Dope isn't my thing, man."

"Charleston, I'm a little nervous. I've never done this weight before. I'd appreciate it if you would come with me for moral support."

There was momentary silence over the bug. "Don't be stupid, Chucky," Robin murmured.

"Oh, alright let's go."

Robin hit the dashboard with his fist. "Dammit, Chucky!"

"We can take the other guy down for conspiracy now, Rob," Burke offered.

"No we can't. Chucky works for us, so he can't be a co-conspirator." Robin picked up the mic. "All units, our man is staying with the suspect. Keep a close watch for a rip."

The Impala drove to the Metro Centre shopping mall and parked near the Golf and Games attraction in the southeast corner. The mall sat next to the freeway. A few minutes later a black van pulled up next to the Impala. A Hispanic male got out of the front passenger seat and approached the driver's side of the Impala. The bug picked up the Hispanic male's broken English saying they were ready to do the deal. Chucky volunteered to get in the back so the other two could talk business.

One of the surveillance detectives, clicked the comm. "Two Nora Six-three we have possible counter-surveillance just north of Golf and Games—an older grey Pontiac with two Hispanic males."

"Two Nora Six, Two Nora Six-three, we copy. All units prepare to move in on my command." Robin reached into the back seat and retrieved blue raid jackets with the word POLICE in large yellow letters on the back and front. They hurried to pull the jackets on and just as they zipped them shut a scream came over the bug.

"Hey! No guns man, no guns!"

Robin picked up the mic. "All units MOVE IN! MOVE IN! IT'S A RIP!"

A shot sounded over the bug, then another.

Chucky screamed, "Rob, help me!"

"NINE, NINE, NINE—NINE, NINE, EIGHT! METRO CENTER!" Robin yelled the code for officer needs help, shots fired into the mic.

Burke accelerated then hit his brakes, skidding the truck towards the Impala. Robin jumped out in full stride, gun in hand.

The suspect jumped from the Impala carrying the brief case. . He fired a shot then headed for the van. .

Robin ducked as he made to Chucky's door. He opened it and pulled the informant out.

"Chucky are you hit?"

"I, I don't think so."

"Run to Burke."

Robin pushed Chucky towards Burke and at the same time saw the driver of the van pointing a gun at him through the front passenger window of the van. Robin fired at the middle of the window and the driver's head snapped back in a crimson spray. The other suspect turned and toward the mall.

Chucky was made it to Burke.

Robin keyed his portable. "Six-one, get our man out of here!"

"Six-one, ten four," Burke replied.

Robin could hear sirens as he followed the money man, who turned and fired another shot at him.

People in the parking lot were screaming and running.

"POLICE, GET DOWN! POLICE, GET DOWN!" Robin yelled. Radio traffic was non-stop and jumbled as officers talked over one another. Mike Collins and Ernie Jackson were reporting two more armed suspects running into the mall.

Emmett said something about three in custody. Robin focused on the one suspect and pushed his body to its maximum sprinting speed. The suspect went through the mall doors and Robin went to the right of the doors and stopped, looking through the glass for the suspect. He didn't see him and entered the mall.

His heart pounding, Robin saw everything in vivid color and crystal clarity. He moved along the wall and looked around the corner. He heard yelling and screaming further down the walkway.

Terrified people stared at him with wide eyes. "Police, stay down!" He said in a forceful voice. "Police, stay down!"

Robin moved along the right wall towards the yelling and screaming. He came to the next corner and did a quick look see and saw the suspect holding a gun to a screaming woman's head, his eyes wide with fear and yelling at the top of his lungs. It was Robin's worst nightmare. An innocent person's life was now in his hands.

He closed his eyes and took deep breaths to calm his pounding heart. The team had trained for this situation over and over. He knew he had the skills. He assumed a half crouch and raised his gun to eye level. He started around the corner.

Robin covered five yards before the suspect saw him. The agitated Hispanic turned the woman and faced Robin.

"Drop your gun or I'll kill her!" He yelled in a thick Spanish accent.

Robin did not stop. He focused on his sights, his trigger finger along the slide of his Colt .45. The suspect's head moved to the right, trying to get a better look at Robin. The front sight was clearly defined against the suspect's face, whose mouth was moving. Robin heard nothing. He put his finger on the trigger.

Robin put ever increasing pressure on the trigger and his .45 jumped in his hand. He brought the front sight down and saw no target. He came off his sights and quickly scanned the immediate area for threats. The last of the roar from his shot reverberated in the marble and glass mall and he began to hear people yelling and screaming. He smelled the acrid odour of burnt gunpowder.

Robin saw the suspect sitting against the opposite wall in front of a spray of blood and brains, his legs splayed out and a large part of the right side of his face gone.

The woman was on the floor and for a moment Robin's heart sank, but then he saw she braced herself on her knees and hands, shaking and retching. As Robin got closer he could see she

113

had lost control of her bladder. He wrapped his free arm around her chest and pulled her into an alcove.

A cold sweat covered her ashen face. Robin knew he couldn't leave her to look for the other suspects. He keyed his portable. "Two Nora Six, Phoenix, one suspect down approximately fifty yards north from the main entrance. I'm with a victim and need paramedics."

"Two Nora Six, ten four. Is that part of the mall clear?"

"Ten four, Phoenix. Medics can come through the main entrance."

"We'll get them to you Nora Six."

"Ten four."

Robin heard shouts of "Police, get down!" A Phoenix Police officer came around the corner.

Robin yelled, "DPS! I need medics!"

The officer yelled back, "Show me id!"

Robin slowly held up his badge.

"I'll get medics to you, DPS."

The woman shook uncontrollably. Robin took off his raid jacket and put it around her. "I'm a police officer. You're safe now," he said gently. "I won't let anyone hurt you." He laid her on her back and raised her knees, to keep the impending shock at bay.

The woman stammered, trying to say something. Finally she said, "I thought you were going to kill me."

"I'm sorry I scared you. I had to get close enough to get a good shot at him. I wouldn't have fired if I thought I might hit you. He was going to have to shoot me before I'd take a bad shot."

The woman looked at Robin, searching his eyes. She wrapped her arms around his neck and buried her face in his chest. Shots rang out down further in the mall. The woman jumped.

"It's alright. I'm here."

Robin's radio crackled. "Victor 32, one suspect down, one in custody. No officers hurt." It was Ernie's voice.

Phoenix Police, Glendale Police and Highway Patrol officers began to pour into the mall, some escorting medics to Robin and the woman. The medics worked on the woman for fifteen minutes and decided to transport her to hospital. When they raised the gurney, she held out her hand to Robin.

"Please don't leave me." Her voice was shaky and quiet.

"I'm here. I'll walk with you to the ambulance."

Robin walked with her holding her hand to the ambulance. When the medics started to put her in, she said, "Can't you come with me to the hospital?"

, "Where's Sgt Marlette?" someone called out.

Robin cocked his head towards the voice. "I'm being called. The shooting investigation will be underway shortly, so I have to stay here. You're in good hands, now."

"You saved my life. I won't forget you."

"What's your name?"

"Pam."

"What's your last name?"

"Snider."

"Well, Pam Snider, I think you'll be fine now. Maybe we can have a cup of coffee later on."

"I'd like that."

"We gotta go, Sarge," one of the medics said.

"So long, Pam."

"Bye, Sergeant."

The medics loaded Pam into the ambulance and Robin turned to find Tom Pearle calling him. "You okay?"

"Yeah. How's everyone else?"

"All officers are okay. Chucky is a basket case, but at least he didn't get shot."

"What about Shawn Hill?"

Pearle looked at Robin shook his head.

Robin looked down at the ground.

"Rob, you are going to take three days admin leave and you are going to see the psychologist."

"But—"

"No buts this time. We waived it last time because, things were moving too fast, but this time you killed two suspects. The new wiretap can wait three days and that's final. You understand?"

"I understand."

"Alright, let's get over to command."

The two men walked across the parking lot to the two mobile command posts set up near the Golf and Games. Pearle led Robin to the DPS command post.

Lt. Morrison from internal affairs greeted Robin. "You all right, Rob?"

"Yeah, I'm fine."

"I know you're familiar with the drill, but I have to go through the motions."

"I know."

Lt. Morrison proceeded to give Robin the pre-investigation admonitions including not talking about the incident with anyone until further notice.

"I assume that doesn't include my wife."

"It does not include your wife."

"Good because that's the next thing I have to do, before the investigation starts."

"You can use the one in the command van."

"That's okay; I'll use the pay phone over at the Golf and Games."

"All right, just don't be too long. We need to get started."

Robin walked over to the Golf and Games and called his wife, Karen.

"Hello."

"Hi, Babe."

"Oh, Rob, please tell me you're not involved in the Metro Centre shooting."

"I'd only be lying."
"Are you alright?"
"I am."
"And the guys?"
"We're all fine."
"Rob..."
"I know what you're going to say and I agree with you."
"Are you serious?"
"I am. As soon as this new case is over I'm going back to patrol. We'll get a rural duty station."
"Are you sure you can live with that?"
"I am. We'll talk about when I get home. I'm going to be on admin leave, so we'll have time. I gotta go now. They want to start the investigation."
"When will you be home?"
"It will be at least four hours or more."
"I love you, Rob. I'll be waiting."
"I love you, Karen."

Robin sat next to Ernie in the foyer outside the homicide division of the Phoenix Police. Ernie had shot the other suspect in the mall. They were waiting for their turn to be interviewed by homicide detectives and internal security investigators. They both wore jump suits as their clothes and weapons had been confiscated according to standard procedure.

Ernie shifted in his seat. "We've sure been to a lot of these interviews together."

"That we have."

"You call Karen yet?"

"Yes, she took it surprisingly well."

Ernie leaned back and took a deep breath. "Yeah, Mary too." Ernie looked out the window. "Rob, do you think we ought to chuck this shit and go back to patrol? We've been shot at so many times in the last couple of years, I think we've used up a helluva lot of our luck."

Robin looked at his friend. "I am going back…as soon as this new case is over."

"You serious?"

"Amen, brother. Karen can't take any more of this and I don't blame her. I've missed so much of the kids' lives that it hurts. It's time to get out of the dope business."

"SWAT too?"

"Yep."

"Damn! I never thought I'd ever hear you say that!"

"Now you have. I'd like us to be around when your son and my daughter have our grandchildren."

"I've been thinking about that my own self. You know I bet the grandkids will like me more than you." Ernie flashed a sly smile.

"It's a bet, old man."

A detective opened the conference room door and Burke came out. He looked at the two sergeants. "Boy, that was fun."

The detective said, "Sgt Marlette, we'd like to interview you now."

Robin saluted Ernie and patted Burke on the shoulder as he walked into the conference room.

Six hours later, Robin walked through his front door. It was ten o'clock, and the whole family was waiting for him. They all got up and hugged him.

"Thanks for the hugs, gang. I needed them."

"We were worried about you, Dad," Eddie said.

"I'm fine; son and none of the guys got hurt."

"What happened, Dad?" Laurie asked.

"I'm afraid it's the same old' story. I can't really tell you anything right now. I have to wait until the investigation is over."

"That's so stupid!" Laurie pouted.

"I know it seems that way, but there are good reasons for it. How 'bout you guys head off to bed. Mom and I have some things to talk about." Robin gave each of his children another hug and kiss before they went to their rooms.

He turned around and Karen handed him a Jack Daniels on the rocks. "It's a double. I thought you might need it tonight."

"Thanks." Robin sat down and put the drink on the coffee table. Karen sat down next to him. She was drinking wine and he figured it was at least her third glass.

She shifted her position so she was looking at him. "Are you going to tell me what happened?"

"If you want to know. You're exempt from the order."

"Did you shoot the man holding the hostage?"

"That was me."

"The news said medics took her to the hospital."

"She was in shock. She didn't have any serious physical injuries."

"Was he the only one you shot?"

"No, I shot the driver of the van too."

"Why?"

"He pointed a gun at me."

"And Ernie shot the other man?"

"Yes, how did you know?"

"Mary called. So, it was a good operation."

"No, it wasn't. The suspect we were originally following was shot to death and one of our informants was almost killed."

"Is that your fault?"

"I don't know if it's my fault, but it bothers me."

Karen fell silent for a moment and then said, "I'm a little concerned about what you told me this afternoon."

"What? About going back to patrol?"

"Yes. I'm not sure you can do that and I don't want you blaming me for the move."

"You're misunderstanding my motives."

"Okay, enlighten me."

"It's no secret that I enjoy this work. We're making a difference on the narcotics problem in the state and we've taken out some serious bad guys. But this problem will still be here after I retire. I have put in my time and more importantly, you and the kids have put in your time. We all need a change and I want to get us out of this big city." Robin looked at Karen. "I love you and I love the kids more than I love this work."

"I wish I could believe that."

"Well, if I were you, I'd believe it because I told Pearle this new case is my last. I also told him I wanted his support for a transfer."

"You did!" Karen threw her arms around Robin and kissed him deeply. "Oh, Rob, I love you!"

"Wow." Robin smiled and looked at his beautiful wife. "Maybe I'll transfer every year!"

*

Street Justice
By Wayne Zurl

~

Jamal Willie Walker raped and murdered a six-year-old girl in a cracker box home on the seven hundred block of Taylor Avenue.

We traced him from North Bellport in Suffolk where the crime occurred to the third floor of a six family tenement in the Brownsville section of Brooklyn.

I kicked in the door and my partner covered the room with his revolver. As the door snapped open and slammed against the wall, Walker grabbed an old "tuxedo Colt" automatic from the dinette table.

"Two against one, Jamal," I said. "Pull that trigger and no matter what, you're dead."

His eyes widened. He believed me. "Whoa, Man. No trouble here. Ain't my day to die." He raised his hands, still holding the pistol.

My Smith & Wesson stared at his chest and I looked down the barrel. "Paul," I said, "Go outside and make sure those uniforms cover the fire escape in case our friend bails out that open window."

"You gonna take his gun?"

"Close the door on your way out."

My partner left and I waited fifteen seconds. "You burned that girl with a cigarette before you raped and strangled her. Bad move. Sayonara, sport."

*

The Visit
By Dave Miller

~

The father lies,
The mother cries
The grandma sighs.
Social services as the door
Sees the filth upon the floor
A small child smiles no more.
And so they take him well away
Where to they will not say
But somewhere safe this very day.
A foster family will take him in
Where his new life can begin
Away from filth, drugs and sin.

His foster family have served him well
He's really thriving, they can tell
He's clean now he doesn't smell.
No soiled nappies on all day
Clean and happy in every way
Smiling, singing and enjoying play.
Part of a happy family now
Teddy bears and a cuddly cow,
He plays with all, they showed him how.
To mix together and take on love
He's cooing now like a turtle dove
And fitted in like a well-worn glove.

*

The Christmas Table
By Dave Miller

~

The turkey's cooked
The veggies are too
Now what is left to do?
Set the table, get it done
Although this year we'll miss someone.
Around others tables everywhere
This year there'll be an empty chair.
Family or friend, who this year went away
It hurts so much we cannot say
They went to a higher place up there
And so we look at their empty chair.
Memories and thoughts there'll always be
They'll be sitting at a table we can't see
They've met up with our families past
For an empty chair will never last.
Every year, without fail
Someone we love will to Heaven sail
But we know in our heart of hearts
That whenever a loved one departs
On the other side we'll meet again
Free of trouble free of pain,
And sit around the table fare
With us down here and them up there.

*

Welcome Aboard Chavair
By Simon Hepworth

~

"Good afternoon ladies and gentlemen, and all you scallies and slappers on a stag and hen weekend. Welcome aboard this inaugural Chavair flight from Liverpool to Ibiza. Your pilots today are Wayne and Daz, with their mate Baz leaning over from the jump seat urging them to go a bit faster. Your cabin staff are Shazza, Courtney and Kylie, who shouldn't be flying as she's up the duff again but wants her attendance bonus. Please ensure that all your Kwik Save carrier bags are safely stowed in the overhead lockers or shoved under the seat in front of you. Those passengers who have sat in the emergency exit rows thinking you will be able to get off of the plane first or who want the extra legroom so you can sprawl out admiring your white Kappa trainers will need to ensure that all items of hand baggage and spare trackies are stowed in the overhead lockers for take-off and again for landing, including when we divert to Barcelona to kick off the drunk ASBO-holder in Row 6. Please ensure that items you try to place in the overhead lockers such as baby buggies, bottles of Duty Free White Lightning, tamazipan and ghetto blasters are stowed securely as they could fall out and injure yourself or someone else. If you require any assistance at this time please do not hesitate to contact a member of Ambulance-Chasing Lawyers 4 U who will shortly pass through the cabin to hand out claim forms and business cards. You should now make sure that your seatbelt is fastened in preparation for departure. In the interest of safety and good taste your I-pod should be turned down to less than 120 decibels whilst the aircraft is on the ground. The use of electronic equipment (that's anything that requires batteries) is not permitted whilst the fasten seatbelt signs are illuminated so please take off your Securicor tags now. Mobile phones must now be switched off and remain switched off for the duration of the flight, even if you have only just lifted them from the Carphone Warehouse shop in the terminal building. We shall now take you through our safety procedures and equipment on board this Boeing 737-300GTi aircraft what Wayne has Twocked off the apron. In the seat pocket in front of you, you will find a safety instruction card, unless the last passenger nicked it to flog on E-bay. Please take time to look at the pictures and avoid dribbling as you move your lips while trying to read the words on it. It highlights important safety information such as escape routes, lifejackets and the sprinkler system that will hose you down if you try to have a crafty smoke in the toilets. It also shows the bracing position which must be adopted in an emergency landing to protect your medallions, sovs, and unnecessarily large hoop earrings. Emergency exits are located on both sides of the aircraft; they are clearly marked and are being pointed out to you now. Unlike other emergency situations that you might be more used to, you will not be able to do one out of the window. There are two doors at the rear of the cabin, (please note, these are not the ones marked 'Toilet'), two over-wing exits for those of you weighing less than twenty stone, and two doors at the front. Please take a moment now to locate your nearest exit, which might be behind you. To help you find your way, additional lighting is provided in the aisle at floor level so you can crawl out on your hands and knees, bit like going home on Saturday night. If the cabin air supply fails, cans like these will automatically be presented from the panel above your head. When the can appears, extinguish your cigarette (shame though it is to waste your last one), place it over your mouth and drink normally. Do make sure your own can is empty before helping yourself to others. A designer lifejacket is located in a pocket beneath your seat. For those of you who are unable to swim, you have left it a bit late to learn. Place the lifejacket over your head and secure it to your shell suit by means of this tape. Do not inflate your lifejacket until you are well outside the aircraft. You will know you are outside the aircraft as you will be very wet, especially those of you weighed down by too much fake gold jewellery from Argos. At this time your seatbelts should be fastened. Extension belts are available for those who are in possession of loyalty cards from Burger King. We will shortly be commencing your inflight service. This evening we will be giving you an opportunity to choose from our wide selection of bling, tax-free Lambrini and a range of snide Liverpool, Man U and England shirts. By the way we have anti-tampering alarms on all our trolleys that spray you with Burberry check dye should you try to rob from it! On board today we have on offer a choice of Super-sized Big Mac meals, chicken tikka masala or kebabs. We accept UK sterling or Euros as well as major credit cards which must be in your own name. You will find in the seat pocket a price list and full details of outlets and fences for your tax-free goods. Finally, on behalf of all of us at Chavair, may we thank you for flying with us today. We hope that you enjoy your flight and we look forward to seeing you when your licence is revoked and you are recalled to prison in a few days' time".

Author's note: This was originally written and performed as a sketch for a 'Wings' ceremony for cabin crew of a leading low cost airline. No one thought it was excessively ironic.

*

The Rider
By Ray Gregory:
~

Sitting at right angles to the southbound carriageway, as per instructions from on high, it was merely another day patrolling the M6 motorway just north of Shap in Cumbria. There wasn't a lot of traffic for the time of year, mid-summer and for a change the sun was shining. The motorway patrol officer was half way through his day shift. Not a lot had happened just a couple of routine stop checks, a bit of process - that's reporting drivers for offences for those not familiar with police jargon - so just watching the traffic trundle south.

The officer was just about to tootle off and have a run north when he saw a motorcycle travelling south, not a high powered job, but a 250cc Yamaha, doing about 50' with just the rider: you know that feeling you get when you just think something is worth a second look? Well this just seemed to be one of those times.

Pulling out behind the Yamaha the motorway patrol officer followed it south. A quick PNC check came back with nothing, but hey still worth a look, so he pulled alongside and waved the rider over onto the hard shoulder.

Without hesitation the rider nodded and moved onto the hard shoulder and stopped with the patrol officer stopping behind him. The officer found the rider to be a young Scottish lad, no more than eighteen. He was travelling south to visit friends and it was his first time on the motorway. The rider seemed nervous so he was asked to sit in the police vehicle whilst his details were checked.

He got into the Police car and sat in the front passenger seat. The officer could smell something on him. At first he thought it was just his leather jacket, but no it was something else. Yes, the faint smell of cannabis.

When asked him if he had any drugs on him the rider gave the stock reply, "No, don't use it."

The officer - being a trusting sort and believing every word - promptly suggested, "In that case just turn out your pockets for me."

The rider emptied his pockets. There was nothing but the officer was still not happy,

"Ok, let me just check then. Out of the car."

The policeman went through his jacket pockets and bingo, on the inside was a small quantity of the said substance, wrapped in foil. Lo and behold in his bag was another small amount. The young gent didn't know what to say his face and reaction said it all. Deflated balloon springs to mind.

The rider was arrested for possession but the policeman now had a slight dilemma: how to get him and his bike back to Penrith police station. There was not motorcyclist available to recover the rider's bike and requesting a recovery would take time, not to mention the cost, so plan "B" sprung to mind.

The police officer took possession of his rucksack, and other items and instructed him to travel down to the next interchange, leave the motorway then re-join it northbound. The officer would be following him and said, "Bear this in mind, young man. My car is a 3000cc Senator, with a top speed of over 100mph. Your bike is a 250cc Yamaha, which is not the fastest thing on two wheels, so it's a no contest. Plus I have all your stuff. Do you understand what I'm saying?"

The rider nodded, got on the bike and set off South with the police patrol car close behind.

Sure enough at the next interchange the rider turned off as instructed, than headed back north again with the officer in close attendance. Approaching Penrith the patrol car again went alongside the rider and pointed him towards the exit slip road where he was stopped again on the hard shoulder. The officer again gave him further instructions this time for him to follow the patrol car into town then to the Police Station. The rider again nodded and followed the patrol car like some well drilled sheep dog until they finally arrived at the Police Station. The prisoner, bike and drugs had all been safely delivered into the charge of the Sergeant.

It goes to show, that with a little bit of guile, and cunning, together with some well-chosen words, one can achieve almost anything.........

*

Mother Nature
By Dave Miller

~

Mother natures a wonderful thing
She gives us birds that fly and sing
She gives us trees, flowers and grass
The clouds in the sky that drift right past.
Alas she has a darker side
A fury, a passion that can't be denied.
Storms of snow hail and rain
Some with a fury that causes pain.
Earthquakes, tsunami floods as well
Mother Nature can bring us Hell.
But then the gentle side prevails
As high over our head she sails
New life born from her womb
As an older life moves to tomb
Mother Nature can be meek and mild
As families welcome a new born child.

*

Grass, the Green stuff
By Dave Miller
~

Ah! The smell of new mown grass
Bring back memories of a time long past,
Photo with my mother as a small child
A summer's day, so warm so mild.
The green-keeper, mower at the ready
Cutting straight lines, so long so steady.
The smell and aroma linger on
Well after the mowers gone
Rolling around in the soft green grass
Sticks to your feet like Elastoplast!
Piling it high in a great high heap
Then running and jumping, one giant leap
Into the grass, with its sweet sweet smell
It saved my bones whenever I fell.
Cows love to chew it oh yes they do
By magic they change its colour for me and you
Green to white and bottle it well
Green green grass, that lovely smell.

*

By Their Rules (An excerpt)
By Roger Price

~

Prologue

The look of terror on the man's face was a sight to stretch the imagination. A look few will have seen before, but for those watching, John Burrows knew most would never forget it. He wouldn't.

He saw the man's blank eyes stare back at his tormentor, the faintest glimmer of hope flashed across them, but in an instance faded, as they lost all colour once more.

Transfixed, he watched as the man he knew as Billy, pleaded in his thick Mancunian accent, "Please Boss, I don't know who's telling you this," adding. "I've not spoken to no one."

Blood and sweat combined on Billy's forehead, he blinked as the pink mixture ran onto his cheek in a stream of bloodied teardrops. The fluid oozing from a wound that didn't appear too severe, but for the fact it was now where his severed left ear was stapled to the top of his brow.

John Burrows had to look away for a moment's respite. Billy was only a small man of slight build, but he appeared gaunter than usual, and looked older than his thirty years. Burrows could see the light reflecting off his perspiration covered head, accentuating his baldness, and his complexion, which was turning grey. His breathing now coming in short rasps.

Ropes bound Billy securely to a wooden kitchen chair, which was screwed to the concrete floor with angled hinges of some kind. The room was obviously no kitchen. The only illumination came from a single low-wattage electric lamp overhead. No natural light was apparent, and the wall visible behind Billy was of plain brick, an old warehouse of some kind. Only Billy was clearly visible. His tormentor stood in front of him, in his personal space, at an ever-threatening proximity.

"I'm going to take a leak now," the tormentor said. "And when I come back, I'm going to ask you one more time, one last time, the name of the filth you've been talking to. If you don't tell me, I'm going to start cutting off other bits, until you do."

"No, please no."

The tormentor, who appeared to be in his late thirties, was a colossus of intimidating proportions. He turned and walked away, still holding in his huge, gloved hand, the bloodied staple-gun he'd used on Billy.

John Burrows stayed in the room to witness the one and only glimpse of the tormentor's face. He knew it didn't actually matter that he saw it, but it was vital that everyone else in the room did.

He looked back towards Billy on hearing him shout, "Ok, ok Boss, it was John Burrows, but honestly, he made me talk to him. I was going to tell you, straight up. But in any case, I only fed him shit."

Billy then looked down as if to avoid his tormentor's attention, should he turn back towards him. He appeared to know how shallow his excuse sounded. A dark wet patch visibly spread across his trousers. He sighed, and seemed resigned as to his fate. He appeared feeble. He looked spent.

Burrows turned to watch the remaining people in the room, as they all gasped, whilst viewing the video footage. He hoped it was the last time he'd have to watch those scenes replayed, unless they visited him in his dreams. They hadn't until now, but who knew what the future held?

Billy's admission had gone unanswered, the film continued, showing Billy tied to the chair, alone and unmoving, with his head down, his breathing heavy.

A few minutes later, came the sound of a door bursting open, followed by the sight of several uniformed police officers rushing into the room, and onto the images.

"Don't worry mate, you're safe now," the lead officer said to Billy. "You're safe now," he repeated.

"Thank God," he replied, "but be careful, Shonbo is still here, he just went for a leak."

"Don't worry, this place is now swarming with police, we'll get him if we haven't already."

However, Burrow knew they hadn't caught him, not until days later. How he slipped the police cordon remained unresolved. The loss of forensic evidence caused by the delay in his arrest had been significant. This had always troubled him.

The video ended, and the lights in the room came back on. He heard sighs of relief from the two rows of jurors who'd been watching the grisly show.

His Honour, the Judge, turned to face them. "You have endured an extremely unpleasant few minutes watching that police video evidence, for which the court is grateful to you, and also, for your rapt attention. I feel that before we continue with this case, now may be a suitable time to break for lunch."

And with that, a voice bellowed from the back of the room, "All rise in Her Majesty's Crown Court, and provide your attendance at two-fifteen."

As all who were in attendance slowly made their way out of the room, Burrows kept his gaze on Shonbo Cabilla: the man in the dock. He stood there grinning—as if to himself, rather than anyone else. Prison officers led him, handcuffed, still smiling, down the stairs to the court cells. Several of the jury members glanced at him as they shuffled their way out of court, and back towards the jury room.

Burrows could see that the grinning Cabilla in the dock looked different to the tormentor on the film. He had dyed his hair blonde, grown a black moustache and beard, and was wearing spectacles. The tormentor on the video had been clean-shaven, bald, and with no glasses. But the huge bulk and ethnicity were the same; he couldn't hide that.

Burrows hadn't wanted to remain in the courtroom to hear his name called out by Billy on the video footage, but he knew he was an experienced detective sergeant, and no one in the courtroom knew who he was. He also knew, he wouldn't have shown a reaction to hearing his name; he was confident in his training and expertise, to know how not to react. But he also knew he'd taken a huge risk sidling into the rear of the court in the first place. He couldn't stop his name being bandied about, not that anyone in the courtroom knew what Burrows looked like. He had just wanted to see Cabilla in the dock, and note the jury's reaction to the video. Surprised, at how he'd altered his appearance, Cabilla in the dock and the tormentor on the film, were obviously the same as far as Burrows was concerned. He just hoped the jury saw that too.

Burrows was an informant handler, amongst other skills, and Billy, or Billy the Kid as he knew him, had been the informant, or Covert Human Intelligence Source to give him his official title— CHIS for short—in Cabilla's case. Normally, he used an alias when handling an informant, but that was pointless in Billy's case, as they knew each other well. He had nicked Billy several times in the past, before he'd moved to a different covert role. Normal operating procedure would not have recommended he take the role of lead informant handler in Billy's case, but these had not been normal circumstances; he knew Billy well, and Billy trusted him, a relationship his bosses wanted to exploit for the greater good, anything to bring Cabilla down.

Burrows liked Minshull Street Crown Court for its charm; it was the oldest of the crown courts in Manchester, built in the late 1800s. Consequently, it was ornate with dark wood panels and hand-carved adornments, relating back to when it had been an Assizes court, used for the quarterly sessions, which had been the forerunner to the modern day crown courts. It retained that charisma from those early days with its décor more than paying respect to Italian gothic architecture—a character which the newer purpose-built crown courts lacked. But he knew it was built in a different age, and was a small building compared to the main Crown Square court building, which was located just over a mile away. He had read up on the Minshull street building's history, the intricacies of design fascinated him when compared to modern architecture.

However, as soon as Burrows walked out of court number one, he felt the confines of the building, and knew he could not hang about without drawing unwanted attention to himself.

Once outside, he turned his mobile telephone back on, and rang his boss Detective Chief Inspector Frank Briers, who picked up on the third ring.

"Are you out, John?"

"Yes, I didn't stay long, just watched the video, and then the Judge adjourned for lunch."

"Good, I was never that happy with you showing your face in there in the first place," Briers said.

"Is there any news on Billy the Kid?" Burrows asked, more in hope than in expectation.

"Sorry John, we've been searching everywhere but to no avail," Briers said, adding. "As to how he got out of the safe house in the first place? Well, that's a question we'll have to deal with later, and more worryingly, whether he had help. If he did, we've no idea how they knew where to find him. Billy himself didn't even know which town he was being housed in, let alone the address."

"I think he had help getting away all right, if help is the right word—and if it is Cabilla's men who have him—then both he, and the trial are probably sunk," Burrows said.

He felt an uncomfortable pause before Briers spoke again; they agreed to meet for lunch at a nearby bistro café. Burrows cut the connection and headed down Minshull Street, generally towards Piccadilly Gardens and the city centre.

As he headed off on foot to meet his boss, he couldn't help musing over how the trial was progressing, or not, as the case may be. He knew without Billy giving 'live' evidence to validate what appeared on the film, the video evidence on its own was of limited value, and challengeable by Cabilla's defence team.

It had taken him eighteen months to get Shonbo Cabilla to trial, and that was further than any other law enforcement agency had managed. He knew how far Shonbo Cabilla's reach could be, though until now he had prided himself on being a member of the Serious and Organised Crime Agency, the modern day 'untouchables' in his mind. But after Billy the Kid's disappearance, he was no longer so sure. He was getting a bad feeling about things.

Then he felt spots of rain on his face as the Manchester weather closed in.

...

Chapter One
Twelve Months Later

Shonbo Cabilla sat in the back of the black BMW saloon. Den Mackey, his right hand man, was on the front passenger seat next to the driver, who was hired help. Although, Mackey weighed around eighteen stone and was over six feet tall, Cabilla was slightly taller and larger than he was. He was also a year older at thirty-one. It added to his feeling of superiority over Mackey, he enjoyed that.

They'd been in the car parked up for over an hour, hidden in the shadows on the industrial estate with a view of the entrance to it. Cabilla had to agree to himself that Mackey had picked the venue well. The estate was located off a major urban thoroughfare in north London, adjacent to a large retail park. It was dark, and all the units within it were closed, probably had been for hours. Weak street lighting, sporadically spaced, only partly lit the empty parking area; ideal, he thought.

"You did remember to change the number plates didn't you dickhead?" Mackey asked the driver. Cabilla knew he was asking the question more out of something to say, rather than really expecting that the driver hadn't changed the plates.

"Of course I have, what you take me for?" the driver replied.

Mackey just grunted. Cabilla knew Mackey liked harassing the hired help, especially in front of him. He also knew the registration plates on their car related to the exact same model, age, and colour, as a different BMW parked up on a driveway at its owner's address in east London, whereas the BMW they were in, was stolen from south of the river Thames.

"That wagon is half an hour late and it'll be light in an hour—I'm beginning to wonder if someone is dicking with us," Cabilla said, before adding. "You set this up Den, you vouched for these Turkish bastards, this had better not be a rip?"

Cabilla noticed how Mackey's face abruptly lost some of its swagger, and he started to look pressured.

"Honest Boss, this firm comes highly recommended. Don't forget, our man rang us from Dover, so we know the wagon has cleared customs, there must be a hold up on the way into London," Mackey said.

"Perhaps," he answered, without looking at Mackey. If this was a rip-off, he would make someone pay dearly.

Ten minutes later, Cabilla heard the articulated wagon before he saw it. It drove past their secreted BMW, and onto the deserted industrial estate. The BMW driver was about to start the car engine when Cabilla put his huge hand on the man's shoulder, stopping him.

"Wait until I tell you, idiot; the wagon driver was told to park the wagon in the centre of the car park, and then to walk around the lorry a full circle, as if he's checking it, just to show us everything's all right."

"Sorry Boss, I didn't know," the BMW driver said.

"You weren't supposed to, you're just hired help," Mackey added.

Cabilla watched as a full five minutes passed. The wagon driver seemed motionless in the cab of the vehicle. Engine and lights turned off. Just sat there doing nothing.

"I don't like this; something's wrong, we need to make a call," Cabilla said. He told the BMW driver to start the engine, but keep the lights turned off. Then slowly drive out of the exit from the industrial estate, and down the urban dual carriageway for about half a mile, to where he knew a public telephone box was. He wouldn't risk using his mobile; when they got to a telephone box, he'd get Mackey to ring his contact to see what the hell was going on.

The BMW crawled a few feet within its secluded space, towards the exit road, when Cabilla heard the sound of revving car engines approaching fast from both sides out of the shadows. The first car braked hard to a halt, right in front of them, blocking their forward path, forming a letter T out of both their vehicles. An instant later, a second car approached from their right, from within the industrial estate, braking hard as its driver spun the steering wheel and forced the car into a J turn. It came to a stop next to the BMW, side on. Their car was blocked; a wall behind and to the left, and one car alongside them, with the other across their front.

Cabilla paused for a moment to think, and then shouted at the BMW driver. "Backwards, then ram the bastards."

The BMW only had a few feet of reversing room before the rear wall, but Cabilla hoped it would give them enough momentum for going forward again.

As the BMW driver slammed the gear into reverse, the drivers from both blocking vehicles were out of their cars and leaning over the roofs, pointing towards the BMW.

"Armed police, stay where you are," they shouted in unison.

Cabilla realised it wasn't their fingers they were pointing. He fell back into his seat as his driver started to accelerate, his foot clearly flooring the pedal.

"Ram the bastards, quickly," he shouted.

The BMW shot forward, and smashed into the front blocking car's passenger side with such force, that the officer who'd been leaning over the roof from the drivers' side, was knocked from view by his own car. The impact rocked Cabilla sideways, bashing the side of his head against the grab-handle above his door.

He swore as the BMW forced its way through the gap it had created, and as soon as it was clear onto the exit road, Cabilla told the driver to stop. The rear of the BMW was now facing back towards the two plain police cars. He looked out of the rear window to see officers clambering out of their vehicles. Some were running to help their stricken colleague, and some were turning their attention towards the idling BMW.

"I'll draw their attention, and you open up," Cabilla said to Mackey as he turned forward again. He then opened the car door, and slowly got out. Standing up square, he cautiously walked towards the two police cars, his hands above his head as he shouted, "Don't shoot, I'm unarmed."

Cabilla knew all the attention would be on him; as he walked towards the officers he veered wide to his left—away from the BMW. He'd effectively told Mackey, back in the car, to get out of the BMW quietly, whilst he drew the cops' focus.

He reckoned they were each approximately forty-five degrees to the police vehicles, when he heard Mackey open fire from the passenger side of the BMW. In the split-second that followed, all attention was now drawn from Cabilla towards Mackey—the hitherto unseen assailant now shooting at them with automatic fire.

During that moment, Cabilla drew his own MAC 10 machine pistol, and opened fire on the outmanoeuvred cops.

He knew the MAC 10 was a crude and inaccurate weapon at anything other than close distance, but it was able to 'spray' 1000 rounds a minute on fully automatic—'Spray and Pray'—as it had been nicknamed by various criminal gangs.

Seconds later, it was all over. Eight cops lay dead. It took less time than Cabilla would have expected. Not that he'd killed eight cops before, and all slaughtered without firing a single shot in reply.

The night air was thick with the smell of cordite and muzzle gases, which he watched rise and swirl into the downward gaze from the lamp standards. It left an eerie yellow hue, which Cabilla thought had a Jack the Ripper quality in the absolute silence that followed. Both men stood for a moment; Cabilla looked down on their handiwork as he inhaled the acrid aroma. Mackey moved forward, saying he'd check that no one was moving; nobody was. Cabilla returned to the BMW and Mackey followed, both throwing their weapons into the boot. He knew the barrels would be too hot to put back into their coats.

He then watched Mackey turn around to glance at the lorry, before looking at Cabilla, who understood the unspoken question.

"We haven't got time," Cabilla said. "We'll have to leave the gear. By the time we get the heroin out of the concealments, this place will be full of more filth. But don't worry Den, some fucker is gonna pay for this."

As they both climbed aboard the BMW, Cabilla could see the searching look in the driver's eyes in the rear view mirror. He broke the temporary silence. "We don't like witnesses. Do we Den?"

"No Boss, we don't."

"But they barely got a glimpse of us," the BMW driver said.

"A glimpse is all it takes to put you on trial, as I know to my cost, so shut the fuck up and get us out of here."

***

The undercover officer was in the wagon's driving seat when the shooting started. Though, the entrance to the estate was a hundred metres away, the continuous muzzle flashes were plain to see in the door mirrors. He could clearly see what was happening, and knew it wasn't part of the script. He was unarmed, and knew there was nothing he could realistically do to help. He decided it was plainly unwise to hang around in the wagon, in case the shooting headed his way. So he climbed out of the cab, and ran to a privet-hedge that boarded the tarmac parking area. No sooner had he buried himself into the hedge, the shooting stopped, and was shortly followed by the sound of a car being driven away at speed with tyres screeching. The undercover officer slowly emerged from the hedge, thereafter the full horror of what had happened extended before him. There were bodies and blood everywhere. He rushed over to the men, his finger pushing number 999 on his mobile as he ran.

Arriving, it was all too obvious they appeared beyond help. He wasn't medically trained, but that didn't matter; it wouldn't have been of any use. Then he heard a muffled sound. He looked down towards the noise and by the driver's door of one of the cars—the one that had been rammed from the other side—there was a man about his age, no more than thirty. A fellow officer, lying on his back, clearly badly injured. The man was holding his left side, and blood was coming from numerous wounds to his legs, oozing from him at a steady pace. The current pulsed, at a slowing, rhythmic speed. It throbbed like a heartbeat. As he took in the horror of all that was apparent, mixed with the smell of cordite that caught the back of his throat, he vomited.

The stricken man looked up at him from where he lay. His lips were moving but his voice was weak, the man kept mouthing the same shape repeatedly, but with little audible sound. The undercover officer wiped his mouth, and then lent over the man, turning his head to one side so that his ear was close to the man's face. With what was clearly a huge effort, the weakened officer raised up a little to meet him, and said one word loud enough for him to distinguish, "Cabilla."

And after that ultimate exertion, he fell back onto the tarmac, and the undercover officer could only watch as the blackness consumed him.

Chapter Two
Three Months Later

John Burrows was dozing in his armchair, bathed by shards of afternoon sun as the rays sliced their way through the semi-closed venetian blind covering his front room window. He succumbed, and was drifting into the haze-like state that was neither fully asleep, nor fully awake. Then abrupt banging on his front door brought him around with a jolt. Now that he had the time to take a siesta, he rarely managed it, he thought to himself as he climbed to his feet, and the mists in his head cleared.

Bang, bang, bang. The pounding resounded in rapid time.

Burrows shouted, "Alright, you impatient sod, I'm coming." When he reached the door, he opened it, and continued. "With a knock like that you should apply to join the cops."

"Hello John," the male caller replied as he came into view. "I see retirement hasn't done anything to improve your temperament."

"Well bugger me, if it isn't Frank Briers, the best governor I ever worked for. I didn't think I'd see you again Frank, you must really be in the soft stuff to come and dig me out," he said.

"Firstly, I'll decline your kind offer of sodomy, if it's all the same. Secondly, I'm not in the soft stuff as you put it, and thirdly, you can cut the fake platitudes. I'm here to make you an offer, though I'm not sure I could put up with your cheek again."

Burrows clasped Brier's outstretched hand with both of his, and shook it warmly, having enjoyed their opening banter. He invited Briers inside, and made some tea after Briers turned down the offer of anything stronger. He led the way into the living room, and noticed Briers seemingly take in the room as he entered. It was average size, with a three-piece suite and a 1980's retro glass coffee table he'd bought from a local charity shop. It was mostly clean and tidy though he knew it could do with a wipe down. The sun

143

streaming through the blinds bringing the floating dust into sharp focus, only emphasised the point.

He had not seen Briers since the trial of Shonbo Cabilla at Manchester Crown Court some fifteen months ago. After the disappearance of the witness Billy the Kid, defending counsel had argued that the man in the video was not Shonbo. Without a 'live' witness to give evidence, and identify Cabilla as his attacker, the case was doomed. He knew it was generally a fundamental right in English Law that an accused person had the right to face his or her accuser. Cabilla's barrister had all the ammunition he needed to cast doubt in the jury's minds, and that was all he had to do, job done. Cabilla had been acquitted. These events flooded his mind on seeing his old boss again.

Neither he, nor Briers had returned to court to watch the collapse of the case, and the following day Briers had disappeared from the squad office. Having been seconded down to London on some assignment, as he recalled. Burrows had taken the collapse of the case personally. A thing he knew he should never do, but it was difficult not to, he had put all his energies into the investigation, and it was a hard knock for even a case-hardened veteran like himself to take. It wasn't long afterwards that he decided to retire, or 'put his ticket in' as it was known in police circles. He'd done his thirty years and had had some great times, especially latterly with the Serious and Organised Crime Agency. He'd been with SOCA since its inception in 2006, having transferred directly from the National Crime Squad, which it replaced. It was now being reconstituted into the National Crime Agency. Similar thing, but with a new name, though many said it would be comparable to the old national crime squad, but only time would tell. He didn't have the energy to be part of another political re-shuffle. Having made his decision, he left a month later, and his only regret was that Briers couldn't make his retirement do. They spoke on the phone but Briers had been stuck in London, the job getting in the way again. So after all that, it was nice to see Briers once more.

Pleasantries and small talk out of the way, he asked Briers what his 'offer' entailed.

"I'm not sure where to start, but since I last saw you I have been working on a prototype, working deep inside the Home Office, and answering only to the Home Secretary Bill Dwyers. I've been promoted to detective superintendent for my troubles, and the prototype has been put into place for an operational trial," Briers said.

"Has this prototype got a name?" Burrows asked.

"Yes," Briers replied. "The special projects unit or SPU for short."

"So how does this affect me, a retired detective sergeant?"

"There is only so much I can tell you before you decide to hear more, and you'll have to re-sign the Official Secrets Act to hear what I have to say, but basically John, I'm offering you a job. But a very different job to anything you've done before."

Briers told him that when he had first been seconded to the Home Office, after the collapse of the Manchester trial, it had been swift and with no notice. This was why he had been there one moment, and then gone the next. He explained that he had no choice in the matter, and the speed was for operational security reasons. The pre-arranged cover story being that he was doing some crime-related policy study for the Home Office. But the truth was far more solemn.

"You've got my full attention Frank."

"That'll be a first."

Burrows listened, as Briers went on to explain how the whole concept of the SPU was something the Prime Minister David Greg, and the Home Secretary had been considering in private for some time. Apparently, they were only too aware that a certain number of criminals were becoming too hard to deal with. This was notwithstanding SOCA, MI5, and all the other law enforcement agencies working flat out within the rules, to bring the worst of the worst to justice. But, it was working within those rules that had become the problem. Briers carried on, saying that they'd realised things had only got worse since the Human Rights Act, which as he reminded Burrows, had banned most of the covert measures used by the police. Although, to redress the balance Government had brought out the Regulation of Investigatory Powers Act, which made it lawful again to conduct covert tactics such as surveillance, and planting listening devices, but Parliament had added very strict caveats into the law, which had not been present in the mere guidelines they had used to work by. Briers continued, highlighting the unfairness of the balance, and how the scales of justice were permanently tipped towards the bad guys.

"Frank, I know all this. Will you get to the point mate?" Burrows said, noticing that Briers had not lost his ability to drag a sentence out. Even if he had put on a few pounds, and gained more grey hair since last they'd met.

Appearing undeterred, Briers continued, explaining how the PM had reacted when briefed about the collapse of the Cabilla trial in Manchester. It was after that, that the executive was brought into being, or commissioned, as Briers put it. He explained that the prototype involved an executive committee of three people; the home secretary, the director of public prosecutions and the head of the serious and organised crime agency—which had become the national crime agency. Their job was to sit in committee ad hoc when required, and evaluate the greatest threats to communities by criminals who continue to escape justice. He added, the executive had no chairperson, but all three had to agree on the level of threat, and that 'executive' action should be taken. Then the home secretary would report back to the prime minister for final approval.

"If I understand you correctly Frank, what you're saying is when the bad guys are above the law, then the law goes out the window?"

"That sort of sums it up, though I wouldn't quite put it like that."

Briers then got up out of his chair bringing about a natural break in the briefing as he walked over to the window and put two fingers between the slats of the blind, widening them to provide a view into the garden.

Briers now had his back to Burrows who was still in his armchair. He watched Briers as he walked to the window, his back straight, immaculately turned out in his dark blue light wool suit. The sun was still shining through the blinds and to some degree hid Briers by his own silhouette. It seemed to add to his presence. Burrows broke the silence, "Ok Frank, I'm getting the picture, and I'm comfortable with it, so let's move on."

Briers walked back to the sofa, and opened his briefcase, he sat down as he passed Burrows a piece of paper. Briers explained to him that this was a copy of the official secrets act, to cover the outline he had received so far. Burrows signed it, and handed it back to Briers who continued; going on to explain that over the last few months the executive had been receiving trial intelligence assessments, which amounted to pretend reports, containing pretend threats. They practised their decision-making, and the projected outcomes from those decisions.

"What are the criteria which the executive run by?" Burrows asked.

"The threat has to be one that endangers the interests of the UK, its citizens and community cohesion. Normal investigative techniques within the law, either have failed, or are extremely unlikely to succeed. That established; the executive has to answer yes to two questions."

Briers paused, apparently in thought, before continuing, "First, is it in the public interest to take executive action? And if they all answer yes to that, then they ask themselves, is it against the public interest not to take executive action?"

Burrows raised his eyebrows, but before he could speak, Briers continued. "The difference between the two may sound too subtle, or even daft. But the test in that subtlety is to ensure we don't leave more damage behind after the action we take, weighed against the harm removed."

"Ok, I've got all that, so what's the upshot? And where do I fit in?"

Before Briers answered, he offered him a second piece of paper, similar to the first but entitled, 'Briefing Part Two'. He took it, read and signed it, and Briers continued.

"Something happened recently, something really bad. The PM went ballistic, and using some hitherto virtually unknown constitutional process, he has activated the executive, and they have considered their first real threat."

Burrows sat up straighter, his interest further heightened. "Don't tell me, I'm guessing they have given it two yesses?"

"They have indeed, or a Yankee, Yankee as it's known as. The PM has already technically agreed the decision, and will ratify it shortly, so the job is now ready to be operationalized. We're looking to recruit a two person team John, and we want you to be the lead operative, what do you say?"

He didn't reply straight away, he was slightly taken aback; he wasn't expecting to be offered an operational role. He could see where the conversation was going, sure enough, but he just assumed they wanted him for some sort of backroom advisory position.

"Who's the target? And what are the objectives?"

"Sorry John," replied Briers, shaking his head, "you've got all you're getting unless you sign up. But if you do join us, it will be on a contract by contract basis, job by job, so to speak."

Briers then gathered his papers together into his case, and stood up to leave.

"When do you need an answer by?" Burrows asked.

"I'm afraid, I can only give you forty-eight hours, things are progressing and becoming time-urgent."

Burrows just nodded, and then showed Briers out of his house and they said their goodbyes. He watched him drive off, and then went to the drinks cabinet in the dining room, grabbed a bottle of Scotch whiskey, and headed back to the lounge. He collapsed into his armchair. He had some serious thinking to do.

Chapter Three

Burrows woke the following morning with a bad headache, and an arid mouth, which made his tongue feel twice its normal size. His bedroom faced west so didn't get the morning sun, which always made getting up that bit harder. He'd bought the cottage ten years ago after his divorce. When they first parted, he decided he needed a new direction, and transferred from Manchester CID to the National Crime Squad at their Lancashire Branch Office. The divorce became Absolute a couple of months later, and whilst he was looking around for a house to buy, he had been approached by Briers for the first time. Frank Briers was a detective inspector who was clearly going places, whilst Burrows was a crusty old career detective sergeant, and proud of it, but both seemed to get along ok.

Because of his array of covert skills, Briers suggested he buy a house in the Home Counties near to London. He said that the 'firm' – their name for the national crime squad – would pay for a rented flat in the north west of England and he could use both addresses depending where in the country he was deployed. It was clear the bosses wanted him to remain as part of the Lancashire Branch Office due to his knowledge and experience of the worst that the North West had to offer – criminal-wise. However, as he was a fully trained undercover officer amongst his many covert skills, and as importantly, not known in London, he knew he would be an excellent asset at the crime squad's disposal. Briers explained to him at the time, being unknown in London wasn't just about not being recognised by the bad guys, but by the good guys as well. Some of the good guys weren't all that good.

So for the last ten years he had divided his time between Manchester and the North West, and London and the South East. But since he had bought his two-bedroomed cottage in Thame in Oxfordshire, he had settled there and it seemed like a good place to retire. He was divorced, and he and Kath had never had children, which had been one of the many causes of friction between them. Both his parents had passed away, and he had as many friends in Oxfordshire as he did in the North West, probably more.

He walked into the bathroom for a drink of water, and took stock of himself in the mirror over the washbasin. Apart from the hung-over look, he was still in pretty good shape, save for a couple of inches around his waist. But at fifty years of age, he guessed he was allowed that. In fact, only a few weeks before he left the cops he had passed a physical and his handgun requalification. Maybe that's why Briers had offered him the job; he had only been gone a few months so was still fairly current and fresh, yet as far as anyone in the job was concerned, he was history. He could see the sense in the cover his situation provided.

By early afternoon, he was still undecided what to do, sure, he fancied the job; sure, he liked the idea of really sticking it to the real bad guys, but did he need all the renewed hassle once again. He decided to go for a walk as it might help him think. He headed down East Street towards Kingsey Road and the outskirts of Thame. As pretty as this historic market town was, he wanted some open spaces to help him ponder.

***

Cabilla looked at the screen on his mobile phone to see who was calling him, even though he was careful who had this particular mobile phone number, he always checked nonetheless. If he didn't know the caller, he didn't answer. He pressed the green icon to accept the call, and put the phone to his ear without speaking.

"It's me," the caller said.

Cabilla recognised the male caller's cockney accent, so he responded. "Go on."

"It's still well hot down here, and they're still digging around; but before you go off on one, there's no problem. Suspecting and knowing are two different things, and they can't prove shit."

"And it better stay that way, all the money I'm paying you," Cabilla said.

"For which I'm truly grateful," the caller replied.

"Just ring me if there are any developments, yeah?"

"Yeah, will do."

And with that, Cabilla ended the call, and turned on his bar stool to face Mackey before speaking. "The Runt says they're still pissing blind."

"That's good news boss," Mackey answered.

Cabilla drained the remains of his pint glass before adding. "I can't stand that Runt, the moment we don't need him anymore I'm going to 'off' the bastard."

Cabilla stood and laughed, as did Mackey, before following him out of the pub. He squinted as they entered the bright spring Manchester sunshine.

....

Thank you, you've been reading an excerpt of 'By Their Rules' by Roger Price.

*

The Fragile Peace
By Paul Anthony

~

The dark grey Land Rover crept slowly through the Galliagh estate back towards Madams Bank Road, the River Foyle and the Strand Road police station. On the south side of the Foyle lived the Protestants and on the north side, lived the Catholics. The two seldom met. The sprawling city was divided as much by the river as by religion, politics, culture and the upbringing of its citizens. To the Protestants it was Londonderry and to the Catholics it was Derry.

Here, religion, beliefs and aspirations were determined by examining which side of the street you walked on. Occasionally, you could find a few streets in which the Catholics and the Protestants lived together. You could tell which was which. The Protestants painted their kerbstones red, white and blue, for the monarchy; the Catholics favoured the colours of the tricolour, green, white and orange. They rarely spoke to each other and sought comfort in their own respective communities: North and south, Catholic and Protestant. They were poles apart.

The occupants of the Land Rover wore the dark green uniform of the Royal Ulster Constabulary. They were both in their mid-twenties, married with young children, and Protestants. The driver was Gordon, named after his father, and his passenger was Brian. They were doing an ordinary job in an extraordinary city.

Swinging lazily into the Shantallow estate, the vehicle trundled slowly through the quiet streets of the Republican camp. It was dark, early evening and the air was damp. It was just starting to get a little breezy as the tide turned on the coast, bringing with it a fresh bout of weather.

Hidden, frightened faces behind partially drawn curtains moved back from the windows, lest they be seen by the policemen. Who wanted to solicit a wave or an acknowledgement from the police in this land? After all, it was a Protestant police force, wasn't it? Run by the 'Brits' in London?

The Land Rover drew to a halt and Brian peered cautiously through the bullet-proof windscreen. The armoured bodywork of the vehicle creaked and sighed as its weight was thrown forward when the brakes were applied. The army personnel carrier following the Land Rover also stopped and a patrol swiftly clambered from the rear passenger compartment onto the nearby footpath.

Rifles and submachine guns were brandished at the faceless buildings and the hostile streets. Apprehensive eyes searched the rooftops and high rise windows looking for the unusual, the out-of-the-ordinary, the suspicious.

The troops were young men, drawn mainly from the Home Counties and the south of England. To the Irish they spoke with a strange English accent. To some, the army was a friend. To others, it was the enemy. In some quarters it was preferable not to take sides at all and have as little to do with the army as possible. They had been there since August, 1969. The troops were nervous.

'What's going on? Why have we stopped?' shouted the army sergeant moving his fingers to release the safety catch on his assault rifle as he raised it across his chest in readiness.

Sitting on the crown of the road in the middle of Shantallow were a group of children. Aged about twelve, they wore short trousers, long-sleeved grey pullovers and scuffed, worn-out shoes. They were children at play, positioned across the road, as pearls on a rope.

The Land Rover was prevented from continuing its journey.

One of the children sang a gentle haunting song, 'God made the land and God made the sea. To be sure, I hope He shines down on me.'

Removing his cap, Gordon leaned out of the Land Rover and shouted, 'Clear off! Get off the road, will yer?'

Mumbling something softly to his partner about Catholic kids, Gordon reached into the rear compartment for his weapon.

He favoured a habit of never leaving the vehicle without his gun. As he was about to get out of the Land Rover he heard the faint sound of an old Irish melody drifting towards him again.

'God made the land and God made the sea. To be sure, I hope He shines down on me.'

The young child singing bathed in light from a nearby street lamp and remained seated cross-legged on the road, apparently oblivious to the policeman. The other children slowly moved from the roadway to the footpath.

The Land Rover idled about forty yards from them, its headlights illuminating the scene.

The engine continued to tick over. Gordon gently pressed the accelerator with the gear stick in neutral whilst his hands rested firmly on the steering wheel.

From the window of a high rise building overlooking the street, a middle-aged man in a long black coat put down his binoculars and pressed the transmit button of his walkie-talkie radio. The man spoke quietly, 'Now!'

It was all over in a matter of seconds.

On the wasteland, approximately fifty yards from the Land Rover, two young volunteers hoisted a home-made mortar tube out of a battered old blue suitcase and aimed it slightly above the roof of the Land Rover.

The taller of the two laid his walkie-talkie radio to one side and rested the mortar tube on his shoulder, whilst the other youth loaded it. He pulled the trigger.

There was a loud explosion and in less than a second a shell pierced the air and collided with the front offside of the Land Rover. The vehicle erupted into a ball of fire as the impact of the lethal home-made device lifted it off the ground and spun it round so that it turned at a right angle to its original axis.

The two young occupants of the Land Rover were heard screaming in the face of death when they were thrown about like peas in a drum.

A cloud of black smoke climbed the sky, billowing upwards in a horrible spiral.

The man in the long black coat stepped away from the window and pocketed his radio. As he walked quietly out of the room that had been seized only hours before for the 'hit' a motor bike rode off at high speed.

Simultaneously, a door opened nearby and an anxious mother gathered up her twelve-year-old son and took him indoors.

The voice of the twelve-year-old asked, 'Did Ah do alright, Ma? Did Ah do what you wanted, Ma? Did ya like ma song, Ma?'

His mother listened for the sound of approaching footsteps and men running. She heard nothing. She held the child closely, saying, 'Hush, Liam Connelly, will yer now? It's late. Now, go yerself ta bed before yer da' gets home.'

She guided the child up the stairs, whispering, 'Off to sleep with you now. To be sure, your uncle Padraigh will be upon us tomorrow, so he will, and he'll be wanting to hear about yer schooling. Off wid yer now while I make yer father's dinner. Don't you go waking yer sister up at this time of night or yer father'll have something to be saying.'

The smile of satisfaction on his mother's face was enough for Liam. He knew he'd done well. If Ma was pleased, all would be well in the world.

A telephone rang in a remote cottage situated between Dundalk and Dublin in the Republic of Eire. The Irish voice answering it belonged to Seamus Kelty, 'Yes?'

From the comfort of his home on the Creggan estate, in Londonderry, a man wearing a long black coat spoke, 'You have a party of two booked in for the fishing on the river at the weekend now. Unfortunately, they aren't going to be making it, that's for sure. Could you be cancelling the two rods?'

Seamus Kelty smiled and eased himself back into his chair, savouring the moment of triumph. He replied, 'Thank you.'

Kelty often received such calls; he replaced the telephone on the cradle end considered how well things had gone that night.

Damien Devenney also cut the connection. He slid his black overcoat from his shoulders, stoked the fire and sat back in the leather armchair, allowing himself the distinct pleasure of small glass of Jameson Irish whiskey before turning in for the night. Damien only drank Jameson when a good job had been successfully completed or when he toasted the dead. It was a smooth drink. His throat tingled, ever so slightly, as it flowed down his gullet. It was the only slight discomfort he endured that night. He relished the drink.

Liam climbed the stairs to his bed, passing the tricolour and the framed print of the 1914 Proclamation that declared the Easter Uprising and took pride of place in the family hallway. He crept passed his sister Shelagh's room, noting she was sound asleep.

Mother Connelly turned to the lounge curtains and drew them even tighter across the front window, not wanting to look towards the burning Land Rover.

A good job done for the cause tonight, she thought. Our Liam! Only twelve, but he will do alright one day.

Settling down for the night, she pulled the bolt across the front door. Her husband, Declan, would be a while before coming home from his work at the Fruit of the Loom factory.

The door closed on the carnage outside in the street as the air gradually filled with the sound of screaming men, hastily given orders and distant sirens rushing to the scene through the Brandywell and Pennyburn.

Within the hour a crowd of teenagers gathered, inspired by older, unseen men. They threw stones at the police; the fire brigade and the ambulance service, as they tended to the burning Land Rover and the latest casualties to be written in the history of 'The Troubles'.

Baton rounds were fired to disperse the crowd.

Another young woman had been widowed at an early age. Another young boy would grow up in a harsh land with only a crumpled photograph and a hazy memory of a father he never really knew.

In the coming weeks the Royal Ulster Constabulary ceremonially buried one dead colleague, the policeman Gordon, and medically discharged another due to the extensive injuries sustained in the attack.

Another name was added to the Book of Remembrance displayed in the foyer of the RUC police headquarters at Knock, in Belfast.

After a time, a burnt-out stolen Honda motor cycle was found dumped in a field near the road to Letterkenny, over the border. The army carried out a series of early morning raids, searching for arms, explosives and the latest homemade mortar device. Big black army issue boots kicked in soft wooden doors, causing more work for local council repair men. The prime suspects were rounded up, held in the police cells and interrogated at great length. The police followed up with extensive enquiries in the area and learnt nothing of importance.

Nobody saw anything. Nobody knew anything. No one wanted to help anyway. It was a land of frightened people.

The RUC put their trusty informants - 'touts' - to work and in due course were close to discovering who pulled the trigger. But by then it was far too late, since the evidence was long gone and the young offenders more than likely elsewhere.

It was only a short drive to the border and the sanctuary of the Republic until the heat and furore died down and things returned to normal.

Until the next time.

The jewel in the Irish Sea called Ireland had been mercilessly desecrated yet again by another mindless murder, another act of inhuman insanity, and another act of alleged political self-determination.

This is Shantallow, Londonderry, November, 1970: The birthplace of 'The Troubles', the home of the Provisional Irish Republican Army.

≈

It was one of those nights when the damp autumn air carried your breath in a misty cloud that disappeared into the atmosphere as soon as you'd said your piece. The sky was black save for a few stars that were fighting to get through the darkened clouds that you knew were there, although you couldn't quite see them.

The adults dug their hands deeper into their pockets and shuffled their feet to keep the cold out. Neck scarves were pulled in closer in a fervent battle to keep warm. Mothers inspected their offspring's Wellington boots, wondering how to prevent the children from running into the house and depositing mud all over the carpets.

The ladies stepped gingerly over the small pools of water that lay here and there in the local farmer's field whilst men folk walked with an air of resigned authority, carrying their tea flasks and sandwiches underneath their arms. The damp and the mud both had to be endured in the name of family life. It was a family night: The night when magic is made by striking a match and introducing it to the blue touch paper.

They approached the bonfire excitedly looking eagerly into the sky to see yet another rocket, from a rival bonfire far away, explode harmlessly into the heavens.

Clutching the box of fireworks tightly to his side, Billy knew Dad would let them off as soon as the farmer, Mr Lindsay, got the bonfire going and Mum would pretend to be frightened by the noise and the sparks as usual. In the distance, hidden in the dark and mysterious shadow of the fellside, the church clock tower struck seven and farmer Lindsay, with proud ceremony, stepped forward.

'Stand back everybody. Here we go!'

Tilting his flat cap onto the side of his head, Lindsay took a match from his waistcoat pocket and walked towards the bonfire. He took a long taper and lit the huge bonfire that dominated the centre of the field.

Slowly the flames climbed towards the top of the bonfire where Guy Fawkes sat resplendent in cast-off jacket and trousers stuffed with old straw. Lindsay walked round the bonfire, inserting the taper at carefully selected points to make sure that the fire took a firm hold.

This was his field and he had lit the bonfire every year since the end of the Second World War. As a village elder it was a big responsibility to make sure the bonfire was a success. Farmer Lindsay set his cap yet again and motioned with his arms to the assembled villagers that they best hadn't come too close just yet. It was his moment.

The evening rolled on. The night birds sought sanctuary in far-off trees as the cold breeze whispered the embers through the air and the smoke swirled round and round as it spiralled upwards to the stars. Gasps and cries of delight echoed across the field as the rich smell of fireworks began to fill people's nostrils and more and more pyrotechnical wizardry launched into the autumn heavens. The bonfire crackled and roared as it reached a climax. Flames reached out to devour old wood and dead leaves that Lindsay and the village elders were piling on.

Playing with a sparkler, Billy made circles in the air like the conductor of an orchestra. A crackerjack detonated, by kind permission of Lindsay, who was ever-present, organising and jollying the assembly.

Billy jumped as the crackerjack danced a dance of fire. The firework box lay at his feet.

Father leaned forward and collected the box saying, 'Come on, Billy Boyd, our turn now.'

Mrs Boyd smiled quietly as she pondered on how quickly Billy had grown and watched him walk beside his father to the area of the field where the men folk were letting off the fireworks.

The field was swelling now with most of the villagers gathered at the annual pilgrimage. A large trestle table had been erected by Lindsay and a variety of Roman candles and coloured cascades were displayed to the gathering.

A fiery Catherine wheel spun endlessly round from a pole embedded in the soft earth. The sparks lit up the arena as the fire warmed the congregation. A rocket aimed for the moon, only to explode in a fountain of coloured sparks that showered the scene as it plummeted into a neighbouring field.

Mrs Boyd directed Billy to the sky, not wanting him to miss the unfolding spectacle.

A police minivan trundled slowly along the lane which bordered one side of the field. Its driver carefully motioned the steering wheel from left to right as he negotiated the potholes in the rough track.

Billy could see the van approaching and made out the shape of the blue light mounted on the roof of the minivan. He knew one day he too would be a policeman.

The driver parked at the gateway to the field and got out of the van. He waved in acknowledgement at Lindsay and walked towards the bonfire with a big smile on his face. 'You've a good turnout again, Lindsay. It's to be hoped them beasts of yours are all safely in the barn?' he said, easing himself out of his overcoat.

Lindsay replied, 'That they are, Johnny me lad. How goes it with you this night? Making yer rounds on bonfire night is no place for an old codger like you. Will the police not give you a night off?'

The village bobby laughed, removed a box of fireworks from inside his tunic pocket, and handed them to Lindsay. 'You'll be needing these soon when you run out, Lindsay. Best make sure the kids have a good time tonight.'

'Thank you kindly, Johnny me lad. There's tea over there if you've time to keep the cold out.'

Lindsay motioned towards a small card table on which a collection of tea flasks and coffee cups were receiving the avid attention of the villagers.

Nodding to Lindsay, the policeman joined the throng. He placed his helmet on the table, helped himself to a mug of tea, and was immediately buttonholed by the vicar who decided it was a good moment to discuss the recent outbreak of petty vandalism at the church hall.

On the other side of the bonfire, Billy set up his fireworks on the trestle. 'We've been doing about Guy Fawkes at school this week. Dad!'

'Oh! And what do you remember about Guy Fawkes?' enquired his father, as Billy's mother bent forward to listen to the answer.

Billy thought for a while before responding with, 'Well, he planted a big bomb under the Houses of Parliament hundreds of years ago but the coppers caught him. We have bonfires now every November the fifth to celebrate.' Billy lined up his Roman candles, like soldiers waiting to go forward to do their duty.

His father laughed, 'Well, that's not quite the whole story, but it's near enough for this time of night, I expect.' Raising his head to the skies, he saw smoke hanging in the air since the breeze had dropped. It reminded him of his younger days when he had been a sergeant in the Second World War in France. He recalled how the RAF bombed the way ahead for his infantry platoon when they marched on Germany. Now he wore the regimental badge on the breast pocket of his blazer to remind him of those who died.

He sought out his wife's eyes. Ann Boyd was a nurse who had fallen in love with the dashing young sergeant. She had no regrets about the marriage and neither had he.

William Boyd looked into his child's eyes and wondered what future his son would have.

A rocket dropped towards the River Eden.

In the distance Saddleback could be seen rising above the land. The Eden sprang to earth just above Kirkby Stephen and meandered lazily through the county before it dissected Carlisle and spilled into the Solway Firth. Across the Solway and beyond the Isle of Man lay Ireland, not more than a couple of hour's journey from the Cumbrian coast.

The table was engulfed by fire.

The Roman candle sitting right in front of Billy ignited without warning as a rogue rocket from a distant bonfire plunged downwards, landing on Lindsay's trestle and causing instantaneous havoc. It landed in Billy's box and was still warm enough to ignite the contents.

A cacophony of sound and a flash of light followed as fireworks exploded at will. Sparks flew across the table and people shielded their faces with hasty arms. Those nearest turned and ran away from the developing scene.

Lindsay, and the policeman, together tried to push the trestle over onto the soft earth in an attempt to defuse the situation. A rocket launched itself from the table on a horizontal flight path, miraculously cutting through the crowds without claiming a victim.

The vicar dropped his cup of tea in the excitement and took control. 'Calm now! Calm!' he cried, raising his arms as if to prevent the turn of events.

Billy screamed, holding his hands to his face where the firework singed his eyebrows.

'Water. Quickly!' shouted his father.

Mr Boyd's arms enveloped his son, lifting him up cautiously as Mrs Boyd and the vicar rushed in, carefully dabbing his eyebrows.

The vicar became over-excited and dropped the water container.

Mrs Boyd held her son closely and cuddled him into her bosom. She comforted him as she inspected his angelic face to make sure there was no permanent damage. 'No harm done, Billy, just an accident, not to worry. You'll be alright. It's just singed your eyebrows. They'll grow back,' said his mother tenderly.

Within minutes, normality returned. The fuss and the excitement that epitomised Guy Fawkes Night subsided. It was over for another year.

It was November the fifth, 1970, and young Billy Boyd, aged twelve, had experienced his first contact with an explosive substance.

Thank you for reading chapter one of Paul Anthony's first book – The Fragile Peace: written in 1994 and published in 1996

*

Moonlight Shadows
By Paul Anthony

~

Here's an extract from my personal favourite 'Moonlight Shadows'.... You'll need a passport for this international chase thriller.... We catch up with the non-stop intrigue and action far away from the murder scene....

~

Kamakura, Kanagawa Prefecture: The Archipelago of Japan.

Once the moonlight shadows slipped away, a new dawn steadily tumbled over the 'Land of the Rising Sun'.

Maureen McCluskey smiled appreciatively when the first distinct rays of sunshine penetrated the skyscrapers of the thriving bustling city that was her home, Kamakura: a city with a population of about 200,000 situated on the archipelago of Japan, in the Pacific Ocean, and located approximately thirty miles south of Tokyo.

A holidaymaker from England travelled to visit Maureen.

On a scheduled flight, he'd flown into Narita International Airport, Tokyo, stayed overnight in Yokohama, and now made his way to meet her. More importantly, she was making her way to meet him.

Conscious of the sun slowly rising and bearing down on the streets, Maureen heralded the new day as a unique opportunity to celebrate. It was the tenth anniversary of her residence in the town she'd made her home. Gradually, carefully, and as dawn grew into the fullness of day, she strode through the streets to the rendezvous.

Maureen had settled well from the outset and taken residence in a reasonably well appointed apartment close to the town centre. She found useful employment and bought herself a second hand semi-reliable car with which to tour Japan. Over the years, she learned to speak the language despite, generally, keeping herself to herself. In time, she made friends, particularly at work.

Now she enjoyed pals who were Japanese, Chinese, American, Spanish, English, Dutch and German. Most of her mates shared one thing in common: they were all whizz kids, computer geeks, and slightly bizarre brainy people. Some of her friends wondered how she had survived financially in the beginning but Maureen reminded them of the inheritance her uncle bequeathed her some years ago. Of course, she hadn't been stupid, she declared. No, she explained, an annuity had been bought with the inheritance and a comfortable amount deposited into her account every month. Maureen met most of her friends at work. And work was an electronics company specialising in making computer software for a global market. From small beginnings, she gained both respect and knowledge as she progressively climbed the career ladder.

Of course, that's why he was visiting her from England today. Maureen had found something useful, something she knew the man would be interested in.

Dressed in a dark fur-trimmed blouson, dark trousers and flat heeled knee-length boots, Maureen was single and into her late thirties. Her light brown hair was fairly long but rested easily on her narrow shoulders. Tall, slim, and self-assured, Maureen was, in her own quiet way, a self-disciplinarian. If she had a weakness, it would be a propensity to be occasionally naive.

There was a faint bluish mist ahead but the phenomenon held no fear for her. Kamakura was located not too far from the coast so a touch of adverse visibility now and again wasn't unusual.

Approaching the mist-shrouded Kotoku-in Temple, Maureen evoked memories of her real home and the reason she had specifically asked to meet the man who had flown from England to see her. Chuckling to herself, she read the notice at the entrance to the grounds. The words seemed so appropriate to her appointment and read:

'Stranger, whosoever thou art and whatsoever be thy creed, when thou enterest this sanctuary remember thou treadest upon ground hallowed by the worship of ages. This is the Temple of Buddha and the gate of the eternal, and should be entered with reverence.'

When Maureen approached the ubiquitous outdoor bronze statue of the Great Buddha of Kamakura, she reflected that in Dublin, her birthplace, almost everyone was Catholic. Here in Japan, virtually all and sundry were Buddhist, and she'd decided it was time to leave the sanctuary. She was homesick. Her mother needed her and she wanted to return to the banks of the Liffey and the Emerald Isle. Maureen wanted to go home now.

Early morning tourists were filtering into the area, marvelling at the Great Buddha, touching it, prodding it, photographing it, and just enjoying its presence, its religious significance.

'According to the handbook, the Great Buddha of Kamakura is over forty feet tall and weighs over ninety three tons,' said a man's voice.

Maureen identified his voice, hadn't heard it for a decade, but recognised it immediately, and assumed he'd shadowed her for a while before approaching her from behind. He's probably followed me for the last twenty minutes at least, she decided.

Replying unhesitatingly, Maureen said, 'I didn't think you'd miss it standing that tall; the statue I mean.'

'Makes sense to meet in a place full of tourists,' said the voice.

'Are we alone, Dickey?' she asked.

'Alone as we need to be, Siofra,' he replied.

'Is anyone following me, Dickey?'

'No, should there be?' he asked.

Siofra glanced casually over her shoulder and caught sight of him standing quite close. It was Dickey: the man she called the Baron. He was dressed in a brown leather three quarter length jacket that was belted but unbuckled. His belt hung loosely from the waist loops and the two ends trailed away below four dark brown buttons that might occasionally fasten his coat. The fourth button was looser than the others and about to become a nuisance. She watched him smooth his dark swept back hair as he fingered the lowest button. It was made of horn, coloured dark brown, and complimented the soft leather he wore. A tan open-necked shirt lay beneath the jacket and his sharply creased coffee coloured slacks looked down on highly polished brown lace up shoes.

'I thought you'd be pleased to see me,' she said. 'Instead, I see you're browned off, Dickey.'

'I often dress in brown. It's one of my favourite colours. Do you like my jacket, Siofra?'

'No, I don't. Funny that though, Dickey, I've waited ten years for someone to call me Siofra and when they do they can't even pronounce it correctly. She-Fra, say it.'

But who is the Baron? Why has he travelled from London to see her? And why does Maureen have two names?

*

Luguvalium's Story:
By Paul Anthony

~

Dateline: AD 122: Luguvalium.

Alexander was a Syrian by birth, from Mesopotamia: the land lying between the rivers of the Tigris and Euphrates. His country had been under Roman rule since 64 BC. In the beginning Alexander's ancestors had settled on the north bank of 'al-furat' – the Euphrates, and made their home in Ar Raqqah. Alexander's predecessors learnt from their Roman masters. Indeed, a century earlier, before Jesus Christ was born, Gaius Julius Caesar built the bedrock of Roman Imperialism that was to last three hundred years. Not surprisingly, Alexander's broad family counted many who had served under Rome. When he reached maturity, when he finally determined upon his life, Alexander left his home and walked alone south through the Syrian Desert.

He walked as a boy and became a man. As Alexander grew, so did the Roman Empire. Emperor Claudius crossed the plains of Belgica and conquered the distant green island of Britannia. The Roman Empire spread across a continent: Baetica, Lusitania and Tarraconensis: south of the Pyrenees, fell. Aquitania, Narbonensis and Lugdunensis: in the plains of the Garonne, and the Loire, and the Seine, succumbed to the Roman Senate.

Alexander journeyed through barren plains in search of the riches he had dreamt of. Climbing Mount Hermon, he saw the Golan Heights and Damascus. It was in Damascus that Alexander enlisted with the Roman army under Emperor Trajan. He learnt of the Roman Gods, Fortuna, Jupiter and Mars, and abandoned his own religion in favour of the Roman icons. Alexander kept his own language but learnt the tongue of his fellow soldiers. Serving with distinction in Asia Minor and Germania, he was posted in AD 108 to Eboracum, Britannia, where the rivers of the Ouse and the Fosse meet. Alexander was respected by all around him. Tactics and strategy were his hallmarks but he was also a great fighter, valiant and bold in the family tradition. He gained promotion through the ranks to Chief Standard Bearer: 'Optio ad Spem'. He was a centurion: one of sixty centurions, each of whom commanded a 'century' of eighty men. His century was the first century of the second cohort of the Ninth Legion. He was a senior centurion and had been appointed 'primus pilus': the chief centurion of his legion. As primus pilus, Alexander commanded his legion in the absence of the Legate. Alexander was of proven bravery; a man who was a leader of fighting men, a man respected by his century and cohort, and feared by his enemies. Each cohort contained six centuries, or four hundred and eighty men. Alexander's century consisted of ten units of eight men. Each unit of eight men formed a 'contubernium' and they lived together in the same quarters. There were ten cohorts in the legion that was overseen by six 'tribunes'. Tribunes were Roman citizens who each regulated the lives of eight hundred men. In addition, two or three hundred civilian workers supported each legion. They were generally engineers, surveyors, musicians and clerks. A 'Legate' commanded the legion and was a man of Senatorial class. The Legate spoke in the Senate at Rome and was a politician, a man who might be Emperor, and Alexander's Legate was in overall command of the Ninth Legion.

The Legion had sworn to a man to be faithful to their Emperor, had sworn never to leave the line of battle except to save a comrade's life, and had sworn allegiance to Rome, for that was the way of Rome. The Roman army that conquered the known world had structure, discipline and strength. It was formidable. It thought it was invincible.

As primus pilus, Alexander obeyed orders and led his men north to green and desolate lands where no discernible border existed. Under his Standard of the Ninth Legion, Alexander camped on the banks of the River Eden, in the town of Luguvalium. Governor Petillius Cerialis had defeated local Brigante tribes and built a fort at Luguvalium in AD 71. Governor Agricola then reinforced that fort with turf and stronger defences nine years later. As one of the most northerly forts in the Empire, Luguvalium proved one of the most important commands in the region. Ever since, occasional bands of marauding Picts had raided the settlement, damaged its fort umpteen times, and enraged Rome. About AD 80, the Romans abandoned any attempt to expand north of Luguvalium and withdrew from the frontier to consolidate their holdings. They strengthened their troublesome border by building another fort on twenty acres of land, by the River Caldew.

It was summer and Alexander's Ninth Legion had ventured north towards the lands of the Picts, the north-westerly outpost of the Roman Empire. Once the year was through, Alexander expected to receive the Emperor's Diploma of Discharge and return to Rome to live in peace.

Tired by his journey from Eboracum, Alexander rested by the Eden as twilight hovered and sand martins, ducks and kingfishers played amongst rustling reeds. He feasted on deer and hare, caught in nearby fields, and washed down the last of their raisins and dates with a superior red wine from a clay goblet. Guarding the perimeter of the camp, his sentries occupied high ground on the banks of Stanwix, north of the river, where the Legion's surveyors plotted another fort. Further north, his scouts carried out reconnaissance and gathered military intelligence.

It had been a long week and a long hard march to these unfriendly lands. Fatigue became their final friend, a friend to be shunned with the welcome advent of rest. In coming days, the Ninth Legion would be joined by elements of the Second Augusta Legion, the Twentieth Valeria Victrix and the Sixth Legion. An important meeting on strategy was to be held. This meeting was to be held in council and was of such importance that all legions based in Britannia were to be represented. Many cohorts from these legions marched with celebrated pomp and grandeur to join the Ninth at Luguvalium. Once present, Rome's military leaders would discuss orders received from the Senate: a great work was to be undertaken. Luguvalium was proud to be chosen for the great council for it was the most important centre in the north. The Legion would provide escort and security for the momentous assembly. The Ninth's Legate was charged with ensuring that the council was not attacked by an errant band of Picts. Other legions would secure the surrounding countryside while their leaders spoke. Once the grand meeting was over and food had been eaten, and wines quaffed, the Ninth would return to Eboracum and prepare for their triumphant return to Rome. Their long tour of duty was nearly over; others would finish the project.

Alexander polished his Legion's Standard, proudly arranged his armour, attended his tunic, smoothed out his leather shorts, and cleaned his coveted weapons. Beside him, on a small wooden stool, sat his uncle's gift: the Tablet of Masada. It was Hussein's astonishing present to the centurion. The tablet was small and handy-sized, measuring nine inches by six inches by three inches, and when the sun caught the handicraft, it occasionally glinted. Alexander had carried the tablet with him since the days of his youth, fascinated by its image and strangely drawn to the mystical rock. The legacy had been handed down from Hussein – the Syrian archer – to a beloved sister and mother and then promised to son and nephew, Alexander. The tablet had accompanied Alexander, man and boy, through every battle and skirmish he had fought. From his desert home in Ar Raqqah, to Damascus, to Asia Minor, to Germania, and now Britannia, the tablet had been his keepsake. Once the tablet had probably saved his life when a Briton had lunged at his stomach with a knife. Now the tablet bore a dull impression where a Briton's blade had glanced from the stone missing Alexander's belly and saving him from certain death in the process. The tablet rested next to Alexander's vine wood staff: a staff that signified his rank. Alexander weighed his stone affectionately and placed the tablet in his bundle of blankets as he settled down to sleep. He felt tiredness in his legs and stiffness in his back. He felt black invade his eyelids as his mind drifted in fatigue and he fell into a dismal abyss of unconscious sleep.

Evening stars peeped out from behind far away clouds and sparkled over leather papilos as row upon row of the legion's campsite drifted into sleep. Luguvalium closed its eyes and relaxed.

They were strange men, these men from the army of Rome. They were international, in the way of Rome. It was an army formed from conquered countries, fed and watered and trained in the ways of Rome. They spoke with a sharp tongue, the men of the Ninth: mainly Hispanic. Yet those understanding people of Luguvalium had welcomed their arrival, perhaps mindful of constant incursions from the Picts. It was rumoured in Luguvalium market place – some mile or so from the campsite – that a Roman Governor, Aulus Platorius Nepos, would soon arrive. It was whispered Governor Nepos planned to build a vast wall running from the mouth of the Eden, across Britannia. The wall would stretch to the mouth of a giant river in the east, the Tyne. At the mouth of the Tyne, the wall would end. This wall would be broad enough and strong enough to carry a marching army at four abreast and would define the boundary of the Roman Empire; thus preventing the Picts from pillaging the Border countryside.

Market traders and craftsmen spoke of a great general called Hadrian who was travelling to them from a place named Frankfurt in far-off lands near the rivers of the Rhine and Main. General Hadrian had been ordered by the Senate to supervise the construction of a wall. It was just rumour, they said, and then they had all laughed heartily. They'd gossiped no end. Townsfolk had tittle-tattled and shilly-shallied constantly. It was just speculation, wasn't it? No one could possibly build a wall in the middle of nowhere, they'd cackled. In any case, how would they make such a wall meet in the middle? They would have to build it from either east to west or west to east. If they didn't, then east and west must compromise somewhere in the middle of the moors and arrange to meet half way. They'd giggled at the prospect of a thousand Roman slaves building a wall that failed to meet in the middle. Would they build their wall close to the Stanegate Road, the road running across the Tyne – Solway isthmus? In any event, what name would they give their wall, the wall of Nepos? Some said it would be called Hadrian's Dyke, and there had been laughter. Others named it Hadrian's Folly, and there had been sniggering. Who would man the wall? Where would the guards live? How would they exist in the cruel wintry lands between east and west? And what was known of those strange people from east Britannia? Did they not speak with an accent warped beyond recognition? There had been whooping laughter again. It was just rumour, wasn't it? Either way, the townsfolk of Luguvalium looked forward to many riches that would come from being a garrison of such importance....

The invaders were marching. Men had left their homes in the far north. They had gathered in huge numbers, walked due south, and flattened the ground before them. They had arrived.

North of the Eden, north of Stanwix, they assembled in a multitude during the night. Dangerous, hungry men with long unkempt hair, rugged faces and straggly untamed beards, had trudged through lowlands in search of riches. Their dress bore no resemblance to Roman uniforms. They originated from Caledonia: a distant country north of the Borderlands. They were Picts and wore heavy coloured robes to protect them from the cold. Their robes were a dull chequered garment skirting just above the knee. The kilt, as they called it, swished smoothly with a strong movement from the hips. The Picts carried axes, clubs, an occasional bow or a lethal slingshot. Yet they wore no particular armour to speak of. They had crossed high mountains, great rivers, and deep valleys before the lowlands greeted them and a fresh, salty smell of a nearby Firth invaded their nostrils.

The men of Caledonia – all twelve thousand of them – crept cautiously towards an unmarked border that carried no wall to hinder them.

'Duncan the Bold' led the Caledonian Picts. His tall, rugged frame dominated those around him as he ordered three captured Roman scouts to be put to death by the sword. Once Alexander's scouts had been tortured and interrogated, they were disposed of. They were butchered without a prayer. Duncan had neither time nor inclination to take prisoners now that the way was clear to strike south towards the River Eden and Luguvalium. The daring Caledonian planned to delight his eyes with a view of a settlement built on the southern flank of the Eden between the tributaries of the Petteril and Caldew. It was indeed a unique site maturing within the confines of three rivers. Its attraction was obvious since between the triad of bountiful rivers lay rich and luscious green lands. Luguvalium prospered from the wealth of fertile soils, unlike the rocky, heather-clad grounds of Caledonia. Once dawn broke, Duncan's Picts would storm across the wooden bridge, which divided the fields of Stanwix and Luguvalium.

Duncan led the invasion.

Cautiously, the multitude tramped over cold barren moors until they found a deserted broken fort that had seen better days. Silently, they looked down on rows of sleeping tents below. Duncan disciplined his men, gathered his clans' leaders about him, and planned his final assault.

The first welcome chink of piercing daylight broke through a grey night as Alexander turned in his slumbers. A frenzied hand shook the centurion's broad shoulder.

'Primus pilus! Primus pilus!' A hushed but pained voice invaded Alexander's ear. 'Primus pilus, waken up! Our scouts have not returned. The God, Jupiter, has abandoned us.'

Opening his eyes suddenly, Alexander rolled instinctively and grasped the hilt of his sword. 'What manner is this that you wake me in the dead of night, Julius?'

'The guards report our scouts have not returned. Men have been sighted in yonder fields of Stanwix,' replied Julius, a trusted legionary. His stifled voice was trembling with excitement.

'Then they are fickle and still tired from our long march, Julius. Their stupid eyes play ungodly tricks in this cold and desolate land. You worry too much, my friend.'

'No, Alexander! Men gather in the dark woods, north of the river.' Urgency rose in Julius's voice. 'We are in great danger, Primus pilus. Our perimeter guards heard noises and report many legions of fighting men nearby. They carry arms and march without precision to an old wooden fort.'

'Many legions! How many legions, Julius?'

'We are outnumbered two to one or more.'

Rising abruptly, reaching for his apparel, Alexander began to dress. Sheathing his sword, he said, 'Then the God, Fortuna, has warned us, my good friend. Raise our tribune quickly, Julius, then wake our centuries. We must defend this camp for we have no orders of retreat. This ground must be held for the Emperor.'

Julius ran swiftly from Alexander's papilo and hurriedly roused the second cohort, passing Alexander's order by word of mouth as night clouds moved casually to one side in deference to the onset of bullying daylight.

When he was dressed and armed with his vine wood staff, Alexander rushed to his Commander's side and, without pretension, woke his sleeping leader.

'My legate, rise quickly! A band of Picts threatens us.'

A balding man wallowed in uncertainty, clutched night attire to his prominent gut and rose to greet Alexander. Then he burped. The legate's baldhead shook in annoyance at Alexander's intrusion. He burped again. He was such an arrogant man.

'The guards?' he asked anxiously, wiping his mind clear of wicked dreams. 'Where are our guards, Alexander? Have them deal with this band of unruly rabble. Put them to the sword if need be.'

'The guards have roused me, my legate. Our scouts have not yet returned but our sentries report an army of men in the fields of Stanwix, near the old fort that lies in decay. We are outnumbered, two to one, by all accounts. I fear for our scouts, my noble leader. I have made arrangements for your tribune to be at your side since I fear the worse, my legate.'

'An army, you say?'

'It is surely an army of Picts, my legate, an army from the far reaches of Caledonia. Only the lands of Caledonia are yet to be brought to heel, to feel our sword, to see our Standards planted in their mother earth.'

'There is no time for a council of war,' mused the worried legate. 'No time for a sacrifice at the altar before battle.' Dressed hurriedly, he barked, 'Sound the alarm, Alexander. What manoeuvre do we need?'

'Defend the bridge, my legate,' advised Alexander boldly. 'It is the entrance to this town from Stanwix and the chosen route by which General Hadrian will forge north and defend Britannia's moors whilst our great wall is being built. The waters run deep there, too deep to charge across, my legate. So our enemy must use that bridge. He cannot wade those waters without loss. Unless…'

Pausing, Alexander drew his sword and scrawled the course of the river in soil at their feet… He mapped their camp… He etched the banks of Stanwix… He imprinted Luguvalium in the soil…

'Unless our enemy moves men downstream and seeks out shallow waters, if so, we may find ourselves under attack from all four sides. I know not my enemy nor his tactic but I know how I would use such an army. I would half my force and cross in the shallows. They will surround us for they have great numbers whilst we are only a legion strong. We must remain tight and mass together. We should not disperse our men. Hold tight, I say. We must hold this bridge even if Luguvalium is lost.'

'Damn them! They could be at our rear already!'

'It is true, my legate. I advise you to mass our legion in a square formation and block that bridge over the river. It is the key to everything.'

'A square formation you say, a strange manoeuvre, Alexander?'

'If we are attacked from the rear then our square will hold until relieved or until we stand no more. I say light our bonfire now. There is half a legion camped in a fort near the River Caldew. Our smoke will signal reinforcements to our side. We should also send a messenger to the Sixth by the shores of the great lake; the lake the Britons call Ullswater.'

The legate's face twisted. He looked down at the soil and etchings made by Alexander's blade and then turned and walked towards a small table resting in one corner of the papilo. Snatching a square of beeswax from the table, he began writing a message in the soft media. Once his letter was finished, the legate read it over in his mind. The beeswax was contained within a wooden frame. The frame folded over to hide the message and could be carried easily in a pocket or the palm of a hand. Satisfied, the legate balled his fist and punched the beeswax with the imprint of his ring. Then he folded the beeswax letter over and handed it to Alexander.

'You are correct, Alexander. See to it.'

The bald man poured water from a jug into a basin, patted his cheeks with water, and dried his hands with soft towelling. He drained the last mouthful of wine from a cup and felt its distaste on his tongue.

'We are five thousand strong, our enemy is ten or more, you say, Alexander. This is not just a band of marauding Picts out for quick plunder, my friend. This is an invasion of our lands... And soon, our great council... That's just what I needed. It is a nightmare, Alexander.'

Throwing down his towel, the legate then banished his wine cup to the floor as the first of his tribunes rushed into the tent.

'Where've you been, tribune? Sleep well, did you?'

'Sorry, I…'

'No matter,' scowled the legate, turning away from the tribune and facing Alexander. 'Primus pilus! This is a stab to the heart. Invasion! Such men have no honour, my friend. Do you not agree?'

'My noble legate sees our problem well,' replied Alexander. 'Our strength lies in our discipline and training. We can hold out against the enemy but we have no reserves with which to counter-attack and push these invaders into the wastelands of the north.'

'Primus pilus, Standard bearer of the Ninth Legion, prove again how well you defend the Ninth's Standard,' said the legate.

Alexander snapped to attention.

'Raise all my centurions, Primus pilus, I order you. Use all your noble training and pitch our Standard on that bridge. Defend the Standard and defend Rome. There must be no retreat, Primus pilus.' Thoughts of retreating from the chosen place of their great council caused a cold fear to ripple through the legate's body, thoughts of his tongue failing to find words of explanation in the Senate in Rome bit into his brain. A droplet of fear, perhaps dread, leaked from his balding head. Thoughts of political ruin caused panic to swell in his gut and manifest itself in a voice of hysteria. 'Alexander! There must be no surrender! There are no orders to surrender!

'Consider it done,' swore Alexander, strapping his legate into armour of gold. 'I will take my leave, oh noble legate.'

'Wait!' cried the elderly commander. The phobia of failure in the eyes of Rome raged in the legate's mind. 'Give my beeswax imprint to our messenger. The message in the writing tells the Legate of the Sixth to ride north with all haste to help repel the Caledonian invasion. You must send our best rider south to valley of the lakes. The Sixth Legion is resting by the lakeside on the way to the great council. They must relieve us if we are to hold Luguvalium but they must also send riders south to those who march to the council. The word of invasion must be passed. You must impress upon our messenger that we stand until the Sixth arrives. Each late minute means a Roman death.'

Nodding in agreement, Alexander pocketed the beeswax, clenched his fist across his heart in salute, and retired to his duties.

The cornua sounded. First one, and then a symphony of music followed as Roman trumpets sounded action stations and Alexander's cohorts mustered to the call.

Duncan heard the sound of a faint bugle and swore. The crucial element of surprise lost at the final bridge! 'We are discovered, my clansmen,' shouted the rugged Pict. 'I shall lead you over the bridge whilst many of our number practice subterfuge. Take strength from your sword; wield well your axes of desire. Forward! Let us take this battle forward. Attack, I say. Attack!'

A multitude of Picts rose up as one and scurried towards the Eden Bridge with Duncan's tall figure leading the way.

Rome responded with Alexander's second cohort soon in armour.

A horse was found; Julius was chosen; Alexander spoke.

'Ride to the land of the great lakes, south of the settlement known as Voreda.' Alexander handed over the beeswax impression. 'Deliver this. Ride towards the great mountains of Britannia that rise towards the grey clouds. Here you will find the lake the Britons call Ullswater.'

Julius pocketed the beeswax. He carried only a spear for protection as he leapt upon his horse: it was a beautiful white charger. With neither stirrup nor saddle, he tugged masterfully on his stallion's mane as he listened to Alexander's final instructions.

'No man rides faster than you, Julius. No man this day carries any greater obligation than you. You must ride as freely as the wind and use each ascent as an eagle soars in the sky. Feed not your steed nor fill your hungered belly. When climbing hills command your charger well and think not of tomorrow's gallop, for there may be no tomorrow for us. Do this, I command you, Julius.'

Sticking out his chest, shaking his spear with arrogant pride, Julius hollered, 'Better to die for Rome than surrender to a Pict! I ride for the Ninth, Alexander. I shall ride to Rome if needs be. I give you my word; I give you my honour, Alexander.'

Alexander saluted in final tribute as a single arrow dived from the sky and drilled into soil a mere yard from where they spoke. Thin shadows flattened across the earth as more arrows filled the skies and plummeted downwards in search of the unwary.

'This day I plant our Standard high, Julius,' revealed Alexander, ignoring the attack from above. 'This day we do not move. This day is our day. Fly like a bird south to the valley of the great lakes, some twenty leagues and five or more. Deliver the beeswax message but tell the men of the Sixth that our Standard is in danger. Bring back the Sixth and you will bring us back our lives. Go, Julius... Without you... We are doomed.'

The horse pranced and bucked in anticipation as Julius flaunted his spear defiantly in the air. Turning, Julius galloped south through the streets of Luguvalium as the sound of armour and leather, and swords and shields, rattled in his ear.

Alexander watched his main chance disappear up the incline towards Luguvalium's market place before switching his mind to the coming battle. Running to a bonfire in the middle of their camp, he quickly lit a taper and inserted the flame into the heart of the wooden edifice. He stood back and watched the smoke drift into the sky, growing in strength, billowing in confusion, signalling to men at a fort by the Caldew that they were under attack. It was a plea for help. Then the fire took hold, crackling and sizzling in its birth, in its infancy.

'Hurry!' instructed Alexander. 'Mars is with us. Gather your shields. Standard Bearers to the front.'

Anxious legionaries clambered from their tents, gladius and pilum: iron and ebony, clattering noisily in confusion as the might of the Ninth Legion listened to orders trumpeting across their bustling campsite.

In nearby fields, a deer ran and a fox scuttled to its lair. An oystercatcher dipped into the reeds and buried itself in a nest. The old grey river lapped at its banks as its course meandered slowly to the Solway Firth.

As Duncan's first foot made the wooden bridge across the river, Alexander's foremost cohort barred their way. Shields in front of their chests and pilum pointed forward, their manoeuvre resembled a porcupine under attack, for under attack they were. Clerks and surveyors ran to warn the townsfolk of Luguvalium amid an avalanche of arrows falling from the heavens. Kneeling on high ground on the north bank of the Eden, archers fired high into the air searching out their quarry in the enemy's campsite. A clerk fell, skewered from behind. A musician felt the flint drill through his neck, as his throat was rendered useless by an arrow from the sky. The Ninth Legion rushed into position bolstering their porcupine tactic by lining up behind their defences with majestic strength. Yet men continued to fall, pierced by the arrows of Caledonia.

Alexander ignored the first brief encounter on the bridge. The centurion, leader of men, bravest of the brave, strode amongst his legionaries. Oblivious to the enemy, turning his back against the Picts, his contempt for the aggressor was apparent to his cohorts before him. He mounted a pile of shields lying near the Eden Bridge and stood head and shoulders above his noble legion.

'Men of the Ninth,' and courage and leadership were stamped in his voice and the manner of his standing, 'Plant your Standards well for there are no orders for retreat. Hear me! No surrender, men of the Ninth.'

Turning to face his enemy on yonder banks of Stanwix, Alexander shook his vine wood staff and boomed scorn and terror across the broad divide. 'Their numbers will never exceed the power of Mars. This day we stand with honour for the glory of Rome.'

Alexander, Optio Ad Spem, seized the Legion's Standard in his mighty fist and sank it heavily into the centre of the Eden Bridge. He shouted aloud, 'Here we stand! Here we fight! For the glory of the Ninth!'

Lungs filled with air, chests bulged, and weapons of destruction rattled and shivered in the morning sun. Battle cries went up: a throaty cheer from inspired defenders, and a lusty roar from hungry invaders.

A rabble of Pict charged across the broad bridge throwing axes and spears high into a wall of Roman shields. Screams of agony penetrated the air as a handful of legionaries fell under an array of cutting blades. More centuries took their place as yard by yard the Ninth Legion strengthened their defences and inched their way to the centre of the Eden Bridge. Some held shields high above their heads to prevent injury from falling arrows while others carried shields to their front to deny thrusting blades. Their Standard dominated the structure as the legion gathered round their charge. Alexander knew that the Standard was the rallying point. No legion had ever lost its Standard outright. If taken, a legion would fight for years to regain its Standard. To the Standard they rallied, a symbol of attrition, a noble emblem of universal power.

In the hours that followed, blades cut, blood ran red, and the Ninth's Standard stood blood-stained but proud.

Hand to hand fighting endured with the sheer weight of numbers forcing a deluge of warring men into the centre of the mighty bridge. The biggest bridge in the north, crossing the widest river in Luguvalium, creaked and shook with the weight of fighting men. Screaming, brawling warriors battled for control of the wooden structure as three thousand Picts found shallow water two miles upstream near the confluence of the Petteril. They waded through waist high water, crossed the mainstream, and turned to strike at Alexander's campsite from the rear.

Julius was galloping towards Voreda, tugging his stallion's mare, riding for all he was worth. He wouldn't let them down. He would return, triumphant, to save his friends from slaughter. Julius would be there for his colleagues, once he'd gathered reinforcements.

At the crest of a hill to the south of Voreda, Ullswater finally came into view, bathing in an unexpected spell of sunshine. The towering fells of the land of the lakes sprouted above the grey-blue tranquil waters of Ullswater. With renewed vigour in his heart, Julius mastered his stallion towards the Sixth's camp.

Suddenly, there was a narrow stream and then the branch of a tree appeared without warning, but Julius's eyes were focused on the lake below. At the last second, he ducked, yet the weeping bough caught Julius on the side of the head and he reared on the stallion. Back on its hind legs, the stallion unfastened Julius and he fell to the ground. As Julius plunged to the earth, the beeswax message slipped from his robe…

Duncan the Bold hacked ferociously, sword in one hand and battle-axe in the other. Fearless in leadership, he discarded the thrusting, stabbing javelins before him and battered his way into a wall of Roman shields. He forced the defenders backwards on their heels with a swish of his tartan and a slice of his blade. Skewers of doom clouded the light as arrow and slingshot rained down on the Ninth Legion. Screams and cries of desperation ripped apart the morning as a mob of Picts pushed forward from the north while the Ninth defended with a colossal wall of imposing shields. As the second cohort took primary position in the defensive strategy, more cohorts rushed to the fray. The centurions rapidly deployed their men amid the trumpet calls and flashing blades of battle.

Alexander fingered the handle of his weapon, its killing edge encased within a leather sheath, withdrew his gladius and sought out a giant of a man to whom the Picts were rallying. The centurion cut down one attacker, trampled over the tartan of another, and slashed viciously at an approaching tribesman.

'Forward! Forward!' screamed Duncan, taking a spear in his hand. 'Luguvalium will be ours. Forward!' His spear thrust; its iron point to kill.

'Hold fast,' ordered Alexander, in control. 'More cohorts to the Standard! Shields on high! Fortuna has granted our respite. Hold fast.'

Eden Bridge was littered with wounded, dead, fighting, and dying men. From the banks of Stanwix thousands queued to battle on the bridge, and in Alexander's eyes, there could be no retreat to the safety of the narrow streets and meandering lanes of Luguvalium. The bridge had to be held. Indeed, there could be no retreat since there were no reserves to call upon; there could be no retreat since there were no orders to retreat.

The two men locked their eyes in mortal combat as Duncan slashed his way into a wall of Roman shields. Alexander attacked the giant Pict, flaying his pilum in one hand while his gladius searched for the enemy's chest. As Duncan's multitude pressed forward, Alexander felt his pilum slip away. He felt Duncan's blade cut deep into his arm. Blood spilled from the centurion's body. Alexander fell backwards into a row of leather shields, dropping his gladius, and gesticulating in majestic defence with his vine wood staff: his symbol of authority. The staff swished through the air cutting the invader deep in his face as Alexander tried to roll beneath his second cohort's shields.

A craggy face, seethed in blood, scarred, looked down into Alexander's deep brown eyes. Duncan yelled in victory as he buried his sword in Alexander's stomach. Duncan twisted his blade, rupturing the belly before continuing onward to hack at the second cohort's defences.

Duncan trampled boldly across Alexander's body. Seconds later, a quartet of revenging javelins were thrust out from a wall of shields and embedded deep in Duncan's chest. Heaving and pushing, their pilums stabbing and thrusting, Alexander's comrades took revenge on the Caledonian leader as Roman spears propelled the heathen's body backwards into a multitude of screaming Picts. A barbed curl at the end of a pilum drove deep into the heathen's chest. The pilum broke at its wooden neck and a barbed iron point remained embedded in the chest as its shaft broke and trailed the ground. Duncan's blood dripped from the barbed curl and life oozed from his chest. Duncan died on that bridge; his body cut to ribbons.

Alexander rolled from the woodwork, threw out his good arm in an attempt to grasp a stanchion, but fell with a final groan towards the river. In the final micro-seconds of his valiant life, Alexander mustered all his remaining strength and thundered, 'No surrender.' It was his final order.

With a splash, droplets of water raced into the air and the centurion sank towards unknown depths. With a gentle, unsoundly thud, he hit the bottom of the riverbed. His body cavorted, twisted, turned, and wrestled with the gently flowing reeds of the Eden as waters turned red with his fluid and the Tablet of Masada, the rock of Judea, sought escape from his blood-stained robe. Alexander's mind raced back to the banks of the Euphrates and a place in a desert where there was only peace and quiet and solitude. His mind raced back to Mount Hermon and the Golan Heights and Damascus. His mind raced back in time, curving and spinning in a whirlpool of anguish. There was blackness in the water, a chasm in his mind, and an abyss of unknown depth. Then there was nothing.

Minutes later, defiant to the last, Alexander's body floated to the surface in the finality of his death.

His mystical rock: the Tablet of Masada: his legacy, drowned without trace in the murky waters of the Eden. The rock buried itself in the muddy sands of the River Eden. The legacy of the Ninth rested in the sands of time, as all around fought Luguvalium for the glory of the Ninth.

Charging, warring Picts made Duncan's battle-plan succeed as all hell broke out in Luguvalium. Having crossed the Eden, the Caledonian Picts reaped havoc on the five thousand men of the

Ninth Legion. From all four asides, the Ninth found themselves under attack, falling back to the Standard and defending their honour as best they could.

Slingshots of slaughter, burning arrows of ruination, and the cold clash of steel, mingled with screams of injured, dying warriors as Luguvalium gave way to hordes of incorrigible Picts. Flames grew with a lick and then a lash and then took hold, burning and destroying everything in its path.

Hours later, in burning, sobbing, Luguvalium, the Standard of the Ninth was lost forever to the men of Caledonia. The Standard was seized from the bridge, never to be seen again. Yet by midday, Caledonia's marauding Picts were halved in number, held back from final victory by the disciplined, well-trained remnants of Alexander's bloodied second cohort, and a handful of men from the Caldew fort who had responded to a distress signal in the sky.

A cornua sounded in the distance…

The sound of cornua grew in the ear…

The sound of cornua grew in the ear and was accompanied by the thunder of horses' hooves…

Julius led the way, arrogantly shaking his spear, bleeding from the head, roaring revenge, galloping through the streets with the splendour of the Sixth Legion behind him. Yet his horse was broken, spent in its endeavour, and exhausted by the long gallop from Ullswater. The horse made the Market Square and promptly collapsed, stone dead.

Julius pulled himself from underneath his valiant steed as the Sixth Legion jogged into position. Limping from his fall, Julius took a shield from a dead centurion and joined the men who had journeyed from Ullswater.

Cornua sounded again. The Sixth Legion formed its battle lines.

The auxiliary infantry dominated the ground at the front of the legion. Each man stood a yard apart from his colleagues, but behind the auxiliaries, the Sixth Legion formed a wall of shields and gradually closed tightly together. Closer and closer they jostled until there was no daylight between their shields and no break in the line of shields. Eventually, they formed a shell of leather shields that was totally protected from an attack from either front or rear. They were a tortoise shell standing in waiting.

The cornua sounded and the legion stood in silence. Five thousand men heaved and panted in exertion from their journey, stood and inhaled the acrid air of Luguvalium, and stood in ordered readiness as they allowed the thumping of their hearts to subside.

The cornua sounded and the legion set off at a slow march from the Market Square. As the legion marched towards the Eden Bridge, the heat of the flames licked their shields, threatened their tunics, and warmed their faces. They saw the narrow lanes of Luguvalium on fire as they marched into a cauldron of burning hate.

The men of the Sixth Legion saw blood red fluid running down muddy gutters, yet still they held their pace at a slow march. They saw the injured, yet still they held their line and made no fissure in their shields. They could smell burning timbers and see burning flesh, yet still they made no move to help their fallen comrades. They heard the screams of fighting men and the cold clash of steel in a valley below, yet still they marched in slowness down the bank.

The cornua sounded and their march became a jog. Their metal gleamed, their Standard shone, their leather rubbed, and dancing robes swished with the speed of moving men. The cornua sounded and their march became a run. The cornua sounded and their run became a charge. Their run was held at line abreast and still there was no fracture in their wall of leather shields. The rumble of the half boot pounding on the ground drove fear into the heart of Caledonia. The mud splattered and the thunder of five thousand charging men echoed in the luscious green valley of the Eden. The cornua sounded again and the tightness of their shields fractured slightly and allowed a wall of pilum to spearhead the attack.

Suddenly, they were terrifying and formidable, and magnificent in their control. Awesome, they were a mass of charging men with shields and steel thrusting into battle. The tortoise shell exploded, erupted, turned into a raging porcupine as the Sixth Legion stormed towards the bridge.

The cornua sounded and the men of the Ninth reacted to the signal in the music. The Ninth split, abandoned the ground and ran to east and west. The Ninth ducked, dived for cover, opened up a gap, and threw the sucker punch. The porcupine of the Sixth Legion stormed into the space in a masterpiece of Roman tactics. One minute the Caledonian warriors were fighting a weakened, tired Ninth; the next they were looking into a wall of colossal shields and row upon row of thrusting pilum.

The dying Ninth closed behind the advancing Sixth.

With leather shields and sharpened sword, the Sixth pushed their aggressor back to the riverbank. A throat was cut and a chest was staved and a limb was sliced to the ground. There was a roar of battle, a smell of fear, and a sobbing cry of a dying man embracing the green valley of the Eden. To the west, in the lands of the Petteril and to the east, in the lands of the Caldew, the Caledonian threat was dispatched with military precision.

Leaderless, dumbfounded by the brave, illogical courage of such defenders, Caledonia fled in retreat to the safety of her heather-clad moors.

By evening time, a myriad of glowing flames lit up the heavens, scarlet tongues of fire acted as a beacon in the Borderlands; a flag to mark the fiercest battle in Britannia's Roman history.

The fires, by the rivers, in Luguvalium, were doused. The Sixth Legion held fast the northwest frontier of the Roman Empire.

When the Picts had gone and the dying had been gathered, Julius and the few remnants of an inspired Ninth Legion stood on that bridge. They had fought for their Standard on that bridge. They had died on that bridge that day.

The Eden ran red with the blood of man.

Within a year, Hadrian arrived in the Borderlands and sent an army across the Eden to occupy high ground at Stanwix. A fort named 'Petriana' was built on nine acres of land. From that day on Stanwix grew in prosperity and splendour. In the same year, work commenced on the great wall that the Romans had planned. A thousand strong cavalry regiment moved into the fort of Petriana and policed Hadrian's Wall and the rugged, unforgiving lands of the border.

But not that day in burning, violent, sorrowful Luguvalium! Not that day when the Standard was lost. No! Not that day. Thousands died that day. But no more the Ninth… Lost in the rivers of time…

~

Thank you for reading the opening pages of 'The Legacy of the Ninth: A full length thriller by Paul Anthony

…

*

Paper Trail
By Wayne Zurl

~

Sergeant Stanley Rose scrambled from behind his patrol car and moved clockwise toward the school's rear entrance. When he reached a white Toyota parked near the corner of the building, he rested an Ithaca pump shotgun over the hood, pointing it at the admin office window.

POs Junior Huskey and Harley Flatt scurried in the opposite direction until they found cover behind a Ford Fusion and a Chevy pickup. Junior carried a scoped Winchester model 70 and Harley an AR-15. Their khaki uniform shirts contrasted with the darker vehicles; their green trousers blended with the grass.

Bobby Crockett and I remained at the side of the school behind my unmarked Crown Victoria, no more than sixty feet from the building, carefully watching a young man hold the muzzle end of an AK-47 at the head of John Woolford, the assistant principal of the Lamar E. Shields Elementary School in Prospect, Tennessee, a small city generally said to be on the "peaceful side of the Smokies." In addition to carrying an assault rifle, the grips of two high-capacity semiautomatics protruded from the gunman's waistband. That much firepower turned a skinny kid into a formidable opponent.

I'm not a professional hostage negotiator, but I needed to establish contact and do something to keep the situation from swirling down the toilet. Using my cell phone, I called a landline in the school's office.

Woolford picked up. "Yes?"

"John, Sam Jenkins, Prospect PD. Can I speak to the man with the guns?"

On the other end I heard, "The police chief wants to speak with you."

The young man, who looked to be in his late teens or early twenties, was very thin and dressed all in black. After hearing the message, he pushed Woolford roughly into a chair and grabbed the phone.

"What?" he said.

I identified myself and began a dialogue. "Tell me what you want. What can I do to work this out?"

His nostrils flared as he sucked air in through his nose; he took no time to reply. "I already done what I came here for. I got nothin' more to say."

As he dropped the phone onto the desk, I yelled, "Wait!"

Without further ado, he calmly squeezed the trigger of the assault rifle. The muzzle flashed and recoiled slightly, the cracking report loud enough for us to hear outside the building as one 7.62 x 39 millimeter round travelled through John Woolford's head. The young man showed no emotion, no more feeling for another living thing than if he had cut the head off a fish.

For a moment afterwards, he looked out the window. His head turned thirty degrees to the right, then to the left, perhaps searching for the eyes of the last person with whom he spoke. Who knows what a homicidal individual thinks? I've met plenty and can never figure them out.

The silent radio broke squelch and Junior said, "I've got a shot."

"Standby," I said. "Let's see what he does."

The young gunman shrugged, turned the rifle, placing the muzzle between his lips, and put a bullet through the top of his head.

He collapsed out of my view and I keyed the transmit button on my small handheld radio again. "It looks like he ate the gun. Move in, but be careful."

I let out a long breath and shook my head. Could I chalk up yet another example of colossal waste to the collection I'd amassed over the years? What else would we find once we entered the school? The apparent is not always the sole factor in a can of worms like the one before us. But a few precautions were necessary before running headlong into the building.

The elementary school, named for our mayor's grandfather, occupied a small, one-story brick building with only six ways in or out.

Stan Rose, a tall black man, built like a professional wrestler, ran to the pair of double doors at the rear of the building.

My radio squawked. "Door's locked," Stan said. "Looks like he wrapped a chain between the bars."

"Junior," I said, "try another door. Harley, check the front."

The two officers acknowledged my transmission.

I turned to Bobby. "We'll take those two on this side."

Junior reported in first. "This one's chained, too."

"Same here in front," Harley said.

When I reached my pair of doors, I found them secured with a bicycle chain and padlock. But from one of the classrooms, a woman stepped into the hall; she must have heard me rattling the door. Four young children followed her; two girls held hands. The boys just stood there, one with tears on his cheek, both wide-eyed.

"Stan," I said, "get bolt cutters from your car and meet me at the side doors. And bring a windshield hammer. Junior, Bobby, Harley, keep circling the building. Check all doors and windows. Look for an accomplice or anyone who seems like they don't belong."

Moments later, Stanley jogged up to meet me, carrying an orange hammer especially designed to break safety glass and a bolt cutting tool more than two feet long.

"Stand back, the glass fragments may scatter," I yelled at the woman, but probably didn't need to. Everything had become quiet, but I was still cranked up.

I waited a moment. She turned, gathered the children together and stepped back almost twenty feet. Heads peeked from doorways. More children and adults stepped into the hall from other classrooms in the wing, many were crying, most stared dully, obviously in shock.

I swung the hammer, striking the upper half of the glass door in the center with the pointed end of the head. A small spider of cracks appeared, but I was far from accomplishing my goal. I tried again and saw a bit more progress. Additional cracks appeared, as did a small indentation.

"That might have done it," Stanley said. "Gimme a little room."

He swung the bolt cutters like a bat, putting all his 235 pounds behind the effort. The glass broke inward. Then he smashed the business end of the tool against the glass like a soldier driving the butt of his rifle into a Goliath-like opponent. After the third try, the glass disappeared from the metal door frame. A quick snip of the chain that secured the bars locking the doors together gave us entry. I tried to imagine what we'd find, what damage and horror the gunman left behind.

Stan used his radio to call the three other officers and coordinate with the sheriff's units and state troopers the county dispatcher sent to assist.

"Who needs first aid?" I asked the closest teacher.

Tears rolled down her check. "It's too late."

She shivered slightly and shook her head, probably never having experienced anything close to what happened moments before and the results she was forced to see. I felt sorry for her and wondered how many shrinks would work overtime to help these survivors sort out their mental anguish.

"Show me," I said.

I followed her while Stan and Harley Flatt, guns in hand, jogged down the hall to look for the shooter.

My other two cops herded the teachers and children into the blacktop parking area, twenty yards from the building. Car doors slammed and two uniformed deputies walked toward the crowd in the parking lot.

The teacher and I entered a first grade classroom. The smell of spilled blood hit me like the stink of low tide on the mud flats in the Great South Bay where I grew up. Immediately, I scanned the room. The body of a woman in her forties lie on the floor below the blackboard; blood stained her pale yellow blouse and a pool of maroon covered the floor around her. Off to one side lie more bodies—a younger woman and six children—all shot. The amount of blood appeared excessive, like the dark red contents of several gallon paint cans had been spilled on the floor and splattered on the walls. The putrid odor of the bodily releases that occur at a time of death could have gagged a maggot. No one gets paid enough to deal with something like that.

In the furthest corner, behind an overturned desk, a small boy and girl huddled together. I pushed my way through the scattered, tiny desks.

"Are you hurt?"

The boy shook his head and the girl whimpered, "No."

"I'm a policeman," I said softly. "No one will harm you."

They nodded, but looked at me with a thousand yard stare people their age shouldn't possess. Their smooth young faces displayed a mental pain one could only imagine. The girl's breathing sounded uneven and labored. The boy held her tightly—his way of protecting a friend.

"Everything's okay now," I said, knowing that was a convenient lie. "Let me help you up and you can go with this teacher."

The kids rose unsteadily to their feet. The woman bent to put her arm around the pair and ushered them into the hallway.

The older-looking dead woman, dark-haired, tall, and probably once attractive, who I assumed was the teacher, lay beneath the blackboard with two bullet wounds in her chest. A two inch stick of white chalk lay only a foot from her right hand. At the rear of the room, the second woman, petite, baby-faced, but perhaps in her late-twenties and probably a teacher's aide, had taken one round to the head. A portion of her skull was blown away, exposing blood-stained brain tissue. A halo of congealing blood surrounded the remainder of her head in a very unholy manner. The six children all suffered multiple gunshot wounds to various parts of their upper bodies. Everyone, of course, was dead. I assumed that Stanley would find the dead shooter in possession of a select-fire AK-47. It appeared that, for a reason perhaps known only to the gunman, he sprayed that corner of the classroom with a long burst of automatic fire. A semiautomatic weapon couldn't do as much fast and concentrated damage.

I walked into the hallway and found the teacher still holding the boy and girl and asked her to keep the children away from anyone else until I spoke with them.

Outside the building, I found Junior, Bobby, the two deputies, and a state trooper standing in a loose circle around the group of people they had moved from within the school. Teachers, children, two men wearing green janitor's uniforms, and three women who I knew worked in the admin office, milled uneasily in the parking lot like cattle waiting outside the slaughter house. I asked the trooper and deputies to set up an outer perimeter and keep anyone, especially the press, away from the school building.

"Bobby," I said, "call the sheriff's duty officer and ask for as much help as they can spare. Junior, call Bettye and have her round up as many of the off-duty guys as she can find and send them here." It was no time to worry about my overtime budget.

I trotted down the hallway to the administration office where I found Stanley holding the shooter's wallet. On the desk closest to the body, he had arranged two 9mm pistols, a Sig-Sauer P-225, and a Glock 17, along with two extra loaded magazines for each handgun, giving the shooter almost one hundred rounds of potent hollow points to use if he exhausted his complement of rifle ammunition. Next to them lay a civilian import, Russian-made Kalashnikov AK-47. The gunman had taped together three thirty-round magazines so, with only minimum effort, he could almost continuously fire ninety rounds of the high velocity ammo. And if that wasn't enough to do the damage he intended, three additional loaded rifle magazines were stored in a pouch still slung over his shoulder, something for the evidence technicians to remove after they took photographs.

"Who is he?" I asked.

"License says Lindell Merritt. He would have been twenty-one next month. Prospect address," Stan said.

"In addition to this man," I pointed to the body of the assistant principal, "I've got two dead women and six children in one of the classrooms."

"Son-of-a-bitch."

"You bet."

Spattered blood and other bodily materials covered the wall behind the chair where John Woolford sat when he died. The .30 caliber bullet entered his frontal lobe traveling at approximately 2,400 feet per second and exited the rear of his skull, taking blood, bone, and brain tissue along for the ride. A wider splatter pattern covered the ceiling above the gunman. His self-inflicted wound included a sizable loss of his skull. A sticky patch of gray and red matter clung to the fiber ceiling tile over his body.

"Call for crime scene units and the medical examiner?" I asked.

"Already have," Harley said.

I returned to the place where we had entered the building. Standing just outside the door where Stanley broke the glass, I found the teacher and two children.

"What's your name, miss?"

She appeared to be in her mid-thirties, blonde with some dark roots showing, and attractive in a clean-cut and pretty girl-next-door way.

"I'm Lucene Helmer. I teach second grade here."

"Did you see what happened?"

"No, sir. I was two doors away." Lucene acted calmer than only a few moments earlier. Perhaps tending to the two children occupied her mind and distracted her from the aftermath of the massacre she observed in the classroom. She'd be lucky if she could ever erase those images from her mind. But that's not reality. It's a good thing denial isn't only a river in Egypt.

I nodded and knelt on one knee to speak with the children. Even that close to the floor, I looked down at my two witnesses. The boy was blond and the girl had long dark hair.

"Hi," I said. "Remember me? I'm one of the policemen." The kids nodded. "I know you guys are upset. I am too. But did you see what happened?" I knew they did, and hoped they could talk about it.

The frail little girl began to cry silently. The boy nodded again.

I spoke to the girl first. "What's your name, sweetie?"

"Dora."

"Dora what?"

"Dora Plemmons."

"Thank you, Dora." I looked the boy in the eye. "And how about you, son?"

He pushed his shoulders back and lifted his chin. "Randy Glen Dillard, sir."

I rested a hand on his shoulder. "Good man, Randy." The boy was obviously shaken, but stood tall, took a deep breath, and did his best to act like a soldier.

"You guys think you can tell me what you saw?"

Dora sniffed and wiped a tear from her cheek before nodding. Randy looked like he was fighting back tears, but said, "Yes, sir."

"Dora, I'm guessing you could use a drink of water. Please go to the fountain with Ms. Helmer and I'll meet you ladies as soon as Randy and I finish talking."

I smiled at Lucene Helmer. "Would you mind?"

She forced a smile, nodded, and walked with Dora down the hall.

"Okay, partner," I said to Randy, "I'm sorry to lean on you, but you're the best help I've got right now. Go slow and tell me what you saw."

Controlling your emotions after a traumatic incident isn't easy, but if you don't have to talk about it, a person's survival mode kicks in and allows them to appear calm and collected. Asking the boy to recount the shooting brought everything back to reality for him, and with no small amount of difficulty, Randy Glen mustered up the strength to tell me that Lindell Merritt entered the classroom and withdrew the AK-47 from a large canvas bag. He confronted his mother, teacher Wynona Merritt, and after a brief conversation and argument, he leveled the gun and shot her twice.

The sound of gunfire and sight of Mrs. Merritt being killed scattered the students across the rear of the classroom. Off to the shooter's left, a group of kids huddled near Sarah Ledbetter, a twenty-six year-old teacher's aide, with one girl crying uncontrollably. Lindell Merritt pointed the rifle at them and yelled for the girl to shut up. His angry words, smoking assault rifle, and the body of their dead teacher lying only yards away—never a calming combination—only exacerbated the situation and the girl cried louder and a few other children joined in.

After a second attempt to quiet the students failed, the frustrated Merritt held down the trigger and sprayed the corner of the room with the remaining twenty-eight bullets in the magazine. When he finished killing Ms. Ledbetter and two boys and four girls, he ejected and reversed the magazine assembly, jammed a loaded clip into the port of the AK, and pulled and released the bolt to seat a new round. Then he quietly left the room without looking back and headed toward the administrative office where we assume he met Mr. Woolford.

Thirteen of the surviving students ran from the room after Merritt left, looking for the safety of a teacher and another classroom. Randy stayed with Dora, thinking the shooter wouldn't return to the scene of the killing; probably a wise choice on the kid's part.

I patted the small boy's shoulder. "Thanks, Randy, you're a good man. Now let's go find Ms. Helmer so I can speak with Dora."

I left Randy with the teacher and listened to virtually the same story from Dora Plemmons, who added that she and Randy remained in the room, too frightened to venture out, until Ms. Helmer and I walked into the classroom.

Finished speaking with my young witnesses, I decided to check on the remainder of the school population and stepped outside. The grounds appeared to be in a state of controlled chaos. Parents were driving up in all kinds of motor vehicles to look for their children. Television news crews and newspaper reporters and cameramen walked the perimeter looking for information and pictures. Helicopters from the TV stations hovered overhead and I saw the mayor's black Lincoln Navigator parked near Junior's police car. Three additional state troopers had arrived and the sheriff sent two crime scene units, three detectives, and four more deputies to assist. Then everyone's favorite, the morgue wagon, pulled in. Unfortunately, the medical examiner would need additional vehicles to transport all the bodies to the UT Forensics Lab for autopsies.

A sharp pain encompassed my entire head. I was hungry and wanted a drink, but had miles to go before I sorted out Prospect, Tennessee's worst nightmare.

<><><>

At early afternoon the next day, less than twenty-four hours after ten people died in an elementary school designed to shape lives, not lose them, I sat in my office with Stan Rose, Junior Huskey, Bobby John Crockett, Harlan Flatt, and my admin sergeant and den mother to the eleven other Prospect cops, Bettye Lambert. We needed to kick around the happenings of yesterday and see what more needed to be done. It was the kind of thing some of the nitwits I worked for in New York called a debriefing. I guess they used that phrase to sound more governmental.

I don't know what happens in the germ-laden cubicles of a room filled with telemarketers or in a post office when workers are subjected to a horrific incident, but I know good cops. They don't demonstrate their emotions, they internalize them. They may take an extra drink the night after or snap at the kid for leaving his bicycle in the driveway, but they don't do things like that at work. The five officers around me appeared stolid, stoic, professional—anything but unglued from the events of the day before and the horror imprinted on their memory chips.

Bobby said, "Couple teachers said Mrs. Merritt claimed ta be havin' problems with her son. Biggest thing bein' he wasn't takin' his meds faithfully."

"What were the meds for?" I asked.

"They thought he was bi-polar or somethin'."

"What kind of background did you get on the shooter?" I asked Bettye.

"He was charged as a juvenile with killing a neighbor's puppy when he was nine."

She pressed her lips together and shook her head; Bettye's telltale sign of annoyance and frustration.

"Family court said he had to visit a psychologist and after six sessions, the records were sealed. At seventeen, he got picked up by Blount County with an ounce of marijuana. His lawyer requested youthful offender status, pled him out to misdemeanor possession seventh, and asked the court to hold the verdict in abeyance. Lindell stayed out of trouble for six months and the record was expunged. That's all for a criminal history. Couple of traffic tickets and he was suspended from high school once for fighting." She paused and took a sip of coffee.

"That's it?" I asked.

"I checked a little further and found out his mother talked him into a voluntary committal at Peninsula Psychiatric almost three years ago. He spent twenty-one days and walked out with a couple of prescriptions."

"How'd you get that information? Peninsula isn't famous for giving out confidential records without a release or court order."

"I know someone and told her we'd not be using it officially. Don't ask who."

I shrugged. "Far be it from me to ask another cop to divulge her informant. How about the mother?"

"Clean record all around. Divorced ten years," Junior said. "Broke up mostly because of the kid. Father wanted him to get more mental he'p, mother said he was doin' okay with his meds. He's workin' on oil rigs down in Loosiana. Off shore right now, but he said he'd come back soon as possible. Her parents moved to Florida and both his are deceased. Said he'd call her family."

"And now the big problem," I said. "What do you know about the guns?"

"TBI says the Glock was a legitimate purchase from that big dealer on Broadway in Maryville," Stan said. "Mrs. Merritt bought it for home protection. The Sig was sold to a lawyer from Knoxville more than twenty years ago by a gun shop no longer in business. Former owner told TBI after five or six years he lost interest and sold it at a gun show at the convention center. That buyer's ID is unknown and where it's been since then is anyone's guess. The AK was imported prior to the first assault weapon ban and sold to a dealer in Harriman. He's outta business, too, so since assault rifles are not subject to a pre-purchase records search, ATF will have to hand check those old store records for the first buyer."

"You take the guns to TBI for processing?"

"I did," Harley said. "First thing this mornin'. Bill Werner, the firearms examiner, says he'll give them priority and see what he can tell us."

201

"Three guns and two of them have virtually no paper trail," I said. "Makes you wonder where they've been."

"Sure does," Stanley said. "That AK started life as a legal semi-automatic, but somebody altered it with one of those drop-in sears and made it full-auto."

"Those semi-autos are all legal," Harley said, "but there's at least a dozen mail-order places who advertise in the Shotgun News sellin' conversion kits, silencers, ten-inch illegal barrels, and any other part you'd ever need. For a few bucks and with a set of instructions, anyone can rock an' roll."

Harley knows his firearms.

Bettye tossed her pad onto my desktop. "That is a damn shame. Those parts should be just as illegal as a machine gun. And how do you suppose that young man got those two undocumented guns?"

"You're right about the parts," I said. "If you need a federal permit to own an automatic weapon, the conversion kits should be regulated and illegal to ship to buyers in states that totally ban machinegun ownership."

Bettye shook her head, made that annoyed face again, and walked over to the counter where Mr. Coffee sat.

Only a slight display of emotion, which women aren't afraid to show, but something we macho guys wouldn't dare.

When she got to the counter, Bettye turned around. "I shouldn't keep drinkin' this coffee, but I'm so mad I don't know what else to do."

"There's always a bottle of scotch in here." I tapped the bottom desk drawer with my toe.

The guys laughed. Bettye didn't. She was one of the prettiest blondes I'd ever met. Her hazel eyes were usually bright and happy. Today, they looked dark and somber. She wasn't in the mood for a joke.

"That's all I need." She returned to her seat and gave me a look mothers reserve for bad children.

I gave her my repentant little boy smile and shrugged. "Back to your question about Lindell Merritt buying undocumented weapons. They're as common as slingshots in states that don't require a permit for a handgun. And assault rifles have never been controlled. Buy one from a dealer and when you get tired of it, sell it to whoever has the cash, no paperwork needed."

"And Tennessee only requires a permit to carry a handgun concealed," she said.

"Sure. If a civilian buys a handgun from a dealer, the dealer has to get approval from the TBI, which only does a record check for convictions and committals to a state mental facility."

"So our boy with a sealed juvie record, expunged criminal conviction, and time in a private mental hospital would have been approved," Stanley said.

"Afraid so," I said.

"More guns are sold outta the trunks o' cars in the parkin' lot at a gun show than bought off the tables inside," Harley said.

"Yeah," Bobby added, "most people don't want their guns on paper. And it's all legal."

"They think Big Brother will come and take 'em away," Junior said.

"That's also ridiculous," Bettye said.

"That's the casual sale rule," I said. "Don't want a pistol any longer? Sell it to someone who does. If you're not a gun dealer, it's simpler than selling a car."

Stanley said, "My neighbor had a big .357 he used to take hunting that he didn't want anymore. Asked me if he needed to tell anyone when he sold it. I told him no, but he'd be crazy not to get ID and keep a record of the one who bought it. I mean what happens if this buyer offs his mother-in-law with the gun signed out to you and you don't remember who you sold it to?"

"Did he take your advice?" Bettye asked.

"Hell no. Said the buyer would have backed out if he had to give his ID."

"Everything we're talking about is part of that Brady Bill," I said, "a federal law that's about as potent as a ninety-year-old man with prostate problems."

Junior laughed.

"That law's a joke," Bobby said.

<><><>

At 9:30 the next morning, Bettye buzzed my phone.

"Bill Werner from TBI firearms for you."

I thanked her and she transferred the call.

"Sam, I've got a two out of three jackpot for you."

"Why do you state cops always complicate my life?"

"Better than making no impact at all."

"What's my jackpot?"

"The Glock is clean, but you probably knew that. Only the owner obviously didn't safeguard it properly."

"Assuming she didn't buy it for her former mental patient son, that's an understatement. What's next?"

"It gets more interesting. The Sig, originally bought by a Knoxville lawyer, test fired as a gun used to wound a Roane County deputy six years ago."

"Lovely. I wonder if my guy was their shooter."

"I checked. Their description isn't even close. But they'd like to hear what you find out after you track these things down."

"I'll give them what I get. How about the AK?"

"Another problem. It comes up as stolen during a house burglary in Anderson County. But there's a glitch here. Somehow the transfer of data from Anderson County to NCIC failed. There's a state record of the stolen gun, but the info never made it to the national computer, or it got deleted and drifted off into the ether."

"I hate computers."

"You're just old and cranky." He chuckled. "But I did call around to a few local places that deal in and repair those kinds of guns. That AK showed up in a Knoxville gun shop for repair three years ago."

"And this gun shop has a name for that owner?"

"Yes, and it's not your shooter."

<><><>

I began my investigation tracking the life of those firearms with the closest and probably most cooperative subject, a retired Marine Corps gunnery sergeant who owned a firearms store in nearby Maryville. Sarge Greene's Armory occupied a former IGA food market in a non-affluent section of town.

I walked through the front door to find enough firepower to equip half an infantry battalion. Wall racks filled with sporting rifles, shotguns, surplus military rifles, modern assault rifles; more used long guns than you could fit in the bed of an average pickup truck surrounded me. No less than ninety linear feet of double-shelved, glass-fronted display cases loaded with every form of handgun, swept across more than half the perimeter of the showroom, separating the sales personnel from the customer. The sound of muffled gunshots filtered up from the well-advertised twenty-five yard range set up in the basement. I spoke with the owner, Leonard Greene, a man in his early fifties, who stood a hefty six-one and had an all-around military look about him—the kind of guy Aldo Ray made a fortune portraying in the movies.

He flipped through a thick ledger until he found the page we needed.

"Sold that one before we went computerized," he said. "Here ya go, Wynona Merritt. Bought a Glock 17 on June 10th, three years ago. I remember her now. Nice lookin' woman. Said she wanted home protection."

"You sell lots of pistols, Gunny. Why do you remember her?"

"B'sides bein' good-lookin', she seemed ta know jest what she wanted. Specified a Glock 9mm. Said her son suggested gettin' an all double action weapon. I had a new 17 in stock."

I had to be careful with my next question. I didn't want him to think I suspected him of agreeing to a "straw-man" purchase, a sale he'd be obligated to deny. "You think she was buying it for her kid? Like a birthday present or . . . coming of age gift?"

"Had no reason to believe that. I remember sellin' her a cleanin' kit and some ammo. I'll pull the sales receipt and we'll see exactly what."

He rummaged around in a file cabinet for a few minutes and came back to the counter with several pages stapled together.

"Look here, sir, she also bought two boxes of reloads ta practice with and a box of factory hollow points. Also paid for a half hour of instruction and an hour of range time."

"Know if she took any safety classes?"

"Not from us. Didn't say she had or wanted a concealed carry permit. Buzz, over there," he pointed to a short and stocky young man with a crew cut matching his own helping another customer, "he's one of my instructors. NRA certified. He showed her the ropes. Would've talked basic safety, shown her how to load the weapon, clean it, and talked her through shootin' a few rounds."

"And that's it?"

"Don't ever remember seein' her again."

"No more range time? Ammo sales? Ever bring her son here to shoot?"

"I'd have ta check on that, but I don't think so. Hang on another minute, sir. I'll ask Buzz if he knows anymore."

After a few moments, he came back with Buzz in tow.

"I'm trying to learn anything I can about this woman," I said. "She was the victim of a homicide. Do you remember something about her after she bought the Glock and you gave her instructions?"

"No, sir," Buzz said. "I remember this woman. She had a hunnert rounds o' practice ammo, but only shot about thirty. She didn't stay on the range for the full hour she paid for, either."

<><><>

From Maryville, I drove to the law office of Roland Farley in Knoxville's old town. Originally from a little jerkwater burgh in Missouri's Ozark region, Morrow was a dapper fifty-six, working out of a two-hundred-year-old, three-story mansion overlooking the Tennessee River.

"The Sig-Sauer distributor says they sold this gun to Dutch Valley Firearms. That business has changed hands and names three times over the years, but the Tennessee Bureau of Investigation has your name on file. Am I correct in assuming you're the original buyer?"

"Yeah, like I told the TBI agent on the phone, I got it new in the box. The shop was on Cedar Bluff, just north of the Interstate."

"Did you want it for personal protection?"

He laughed. "No. I didn't know how to use a gun. If I tried to protect myself, I'm afraid the bad guy would have taken the gun from me, stuck it up my ass, and pulled the trigger."

I smiled at his honesty. "I wish more gun buyers would consider that possibility."

"I bought it because my neighbor was a shooter. Nice guy. We used to socialize with him and his wife. He said if I owned a gun we could go to the Oak Ridge shooting complex. He suggested the Sig because the Navy SEALS were using them."

"And you didn't stay interested in the shooting hobby?"

"I was never very good at it, and my neighbor moved to Florida. So, I sold the gun."

"To whom?"

"I don't know."

That surprised me. I thought a lawyer would be sharper, more conscious of liabilities. "I beg your pardon?"

He shook his head. "I never got his name. I took it to a gun show at the convention center. Two cops checked to see it wasn't loaded and then used an electrician's plastic tie to hold the slide open and sent me into the hall. You ever been to a gun show?"

"Sure."

"Then you know how crowded it can be, and how many people walking around are trying to sell guns. I stopped at a few tables with signs saying that they'd buy, but those dealers wouldn't even pay half of what it was worth. The gun was like new, with the box, papers and an extra magazine."

"And what happened next?"

"Some guy stopped me in the aisle and asked if the gun was for sale. He looked it over and finally offered me four hundred bucks."

"And you took it, no questions asked?"

"I looked up the rules before I got there and also spoke to one of the cops who confirmed there was no paperwork necessary for a sale between two private individuals."

"Would have been a good idea to know who bought the gun. Your name's attached to it and now who knows where it's been?"

"I guess you're right, but I just wanted to sell it and get out."

"Did you know your gun was used to shoot a cop?"

I had no doubt attorney Roland Farley practiced keeping a poker face at the appropriate moments, but my remark jolted his cool demeanor.

"Good Lord, no. Was he killed?"

"He lived, but you see how getting a buyer's name would be helpful?"

"Of course. I'm sorry. I didn't know."

"That happened a long time ago, but the case was initiated and the statute of limitations won't apply. I'll be forwarding my information to Roane County. You'll probably hear from one of their detectives shortly."

"I'll cooperate fully."

He didn't have a chance to regain his composure when I hit him with another guilt trip.

"The problem didn't stop there."

I explained the school shooting and showed him a photo of Lindell Merritt. "This person would have been very young when you sold the gun, but have you ever seen him?"

"On the news yesterday. I can't believe he had my gun with him."

"I've learned that strange occurrences can be more the rule than the exception. Remember what the gun buyer looked like?"

He provided a good physical description.

"Thanks for your time, counselor."

"I'm sorry I ever sold that damn thing."

<><><>

So far, I had visited a gun shop owner who did all the right things and his legally sold merchandise ended up in the hands of a fruitcake. A damn shame, but not something to spend time fretting about. Then I met an outwardly successful and intelligent attorney who, like a moron, cared more about getting four hundred bucks for a gun in which he lost interest than keeping it out of the hands of an illicit buyer. Something like that only refreshed my belief in the old adage, 'You meet all kinds.'

My third stop took me to a store called Knoxville Arms Depot and Grundy's Custom Shop on Kingston Pike in central Knoxville. The store wasn't as large as Leonard Greene's, but it was loaded with military surplus rifles and pistols, modern paramilitary assault rifles and shotguns, and rows of cases holding hundreds of new and used handguns. Military recruiting posters and enlarged photos of American GIs hung on all the walls. It looked like a hangout for the wannabe mercenary and armchair soldier of fortune.

The manager was in his late-thirties, had a shaved head and close-cropped Vandyke beard and mustache, and wore a big Desert Eagle semi-auto holstered on his right hip.

He took me into the backroom workshop to chat with the gunsmith, an older, paunchy-looking man with curly gray hair, who stared at me over a pair of narrow reading glasses.

I explained the reason for my visit and asked for any information he could provide on my murder weapon or the man who dropped it off for repair.

"You know, of course," he said, "we're not responsible for anything a gun owner does with a weapon we fix or modify. They sign a document relieving us of any liability."

Tell that to the families of the dead teachers and students.

"I assume you only do legitimate repairs and legal modifications?"

"Of course."

"This AK had been altered to select fire. I hope you don't make those conversions."

"We do not." He sounded indignant. "Never have, never will. I'd lose my license."

I wanted to believe him, but wondered what he'd do for a friend.

"What work did you do on that gun?"

"Hang on a minute, I'll get the books."

I hung in there and he dug out his ledger.

"Says here he complained about jamming and stove piping. That means . . ."

"I know what it means."

He nodded. "I checked and cleaned the bolt and extractor and polished the throat and port area, making sure there were no burrs or rough spots. Some of these imports coming out of the old Warsaw Pact countries in the early nineties weren't as well made as the real military versions."

I wondered how many real ones came through his door.

"Just cranked out to keep us Americans armed and dangerous?" It wasn't exactly a question.

"Afraid so."

Before I left, he handed me a business card. From it I read,
O.L. Grundy
Master Gunsmith
Repairs~Modifications~Appraisals
Buy~Sell~Trade

Grundy provided me with the name and address of then fifty-year-old Eltone Seebold, a resident of North Knoxville.

I found the small, one-story post-war home unoccupied, but a neighbor said I could locate Eunice Seebold working at a nearby beauty shop. When I found her, I started a conversation.

"My husband died two years ago in a wreck on Rutledge Pike," she said. "Damn motorcycle. I hated when he'd go off on it."

Eunice was a middle-aged blonde wearing enough makeup to fill the dents on a battered old car.

"Sorry for your loss," I said.

"Thanks, but he'd been drinkin'. Damn motorcycle and a damn fool."

I shrugged. "Happens, doesn't it? What did you do with his gun?"

"Ya mean guns. Eltone had a bunch. His brother Alvis took 'em all and sold 'em for me."

"Where can I find Alvis?"

<><><>

I drove to a diesel engine repair shop on Asheville Highway in East Knoxville and found Alvis Seebold bent over the fender of a Dodge pickup, working on a Cummins engine. When I tapped him on the shoulder, he flinched and almost knocked himself out on the hood of the truck.

Alvis shook off the effects of his self-inflicted bruise and wiped his hands on a clean rag while I identified myself.

"I need to talk to you about your brother's AK-47."

Alvis's expression made him look like I just demanded to know who shot JFK. "Man, I ain't got that one no more."

"I know. It turned up in a shooting."

He shook his head quickly. "Don't know nuthin' about that."

"The gun is listed as stolen. You know where Eltone got it?"

Alvis frowned. "My brother weren't no thief. Had him a good job. Didn't need ta steal nuthin'."

I wasn't looking for a brotherly endorsement, I needed a name.

"Where did he get the gun?" I repeated.

"Believe it was from some guy at work."

"I need to be sure." I sighed and added, "Any idea who?"

"Got a good deal on it from one of them Mexicans who worked on his roofin' crew."

That narrowed it down to just under half a million people.

"When was that?"

"Not sure. It's been a while. Eltone's been dead more'n two years now."

"He owned a roofing business?"

"Was a foreman for Dowdle Brothers Roofin'."

"I need to track down that AK. Can you help?"

"I kin try."

I hoped to get results from his renewed enthusiasm.

"How many guns did Eltone have?" I asked.

"Oh, lemme see."

He kept wiping his hands. I didn't think they'd ever get any cleaner.

"The AK ya know about, a Chi-neez SKS, same caliber, a Marlin lever action deer rifle, a Remin'ton bolt action thirty-ought-six, couple o' 12 gauge shotguns, and I guess two revolvers and two automatics."

"That's a lot of firepower."

"We used ta go huntin' and shootin' a lot."

"You sell all the guns?"

"Kept me the Remin'ton and a side-by-side 12 gauge. Paid Eunice what they's worth, though, didn't keep nuthin' without payin' fer 'em."

Hell of a guy.

"I understand. What happened to the rest?"

"Sold 'em."

"To a dealer?"

"Naw, dealers won't pay nuthin'. I took 'em to a gun show at the Expo Center. Cain't remember 'xactly when. Some time jest after Eltone died, I s'ppose. With two promoters in town, they's havin' almost a show a month back then. I trolled around inside awhile, sold a couple, then set out in the parkin' lot with the tailgate down and sold the rest fer cash money."

Alvis was a prime example of a jerk and the cause of frustration an investigator deals with all too often. I already knew the answer, and I had nothing to lose but my sanity, so I asked a stupid question. "Get names from the buyers?"

"Sure, Andrew Jackson, U-lysses Grant, Abe Lincoln. Like I said, the sales was fer cash money. But I do know one man who bought a couple pieces."

"Would one of those pieces be the AK-47?"

"Matter o' fact, it would."

As I get older my patience doesn't get any greater, but I really try. "Lucky me. Who's that?"

"I ain't gonna git him in no trouble, am I?"

I felt no obligation to tell Alvis the truth. "No, of course not. He didn't do the shooting. I'm just trying to trace the guns that have no paper trail."

"Man's name is Cecil Brogdan."

"Why do you remember him?"

"I done bought guns from him before. Sold him some, too. Cecil's always good fer cash."

"But he's not a dealer?"

"Not exactly."

"You mean he's unlicensed, but dabbles in gun sales?"

"Ol' Cecil's been a gun trader long as I kin r'member. Handles good stuff. Prices are always right. Ain't afraid ta pay fer a gun neither."

All things considered, it was easy to pry information from Alvis. "You mean he doesn't try to rip anyone off? Doesn't need big profits?"

"Right. He's happy ta make a few bucks and turn the stuff over quick-like. Ol' Cecil's an honest man."

Actually, the Bureau of Alcohol, Tobacco, Firearms, and Explosives might question Cecil's honesty, since profiting from the sale of guns without a federal and state license is a crime. But I didn't bother to mention that to Alvis.

"Sounds like a good guy. Where can I find Cecil?"

"Don't know where he lives at. Knoxville somewhere, I suspect. Try any gun show. He hits 'em all."

"He pay for tables and set up?"

"Naw, Cecil don't want his name on nuthin'. He jest walks around with a few pieces lookin' fer buyers."

"Thanks for your help, Mr. Seebold." Spending all that quality time with Alvis had given me a tension headache. "You're a fine American."

He smiled like a happy baboon. A gold tooth twinkled from his upper left quadrant.

<><><>

I called the most knowledgeable gunslinger I knew, Police Officer Harlan Flatt.

"Who do you know who could lead me to a casual gun dealer named Cecil Brogdan?"

"Hell, boss, I know Cecil. He's been around fer years."

"You know where he lives or works?"

"No. I don't socialize with him. Jest been seein' him buyin' and sellin' guns for a long time. He makes about every gun show 'tween Lexington and Chattanooga. Maybe more."

"Who would know where to find him?"

Harley thought for a long moment. "Best guy ta ask—leastwise a guy who'll give ya a straight answer —is Dickey Hollowell. He's a retired Knox County deputy and used ta be president of the Smoky Mountain Gun Collectin' Society."

Dickey and I sat in his living room in a post-World War Two home in the North Knoxville community of Fountain City.

"You have a big collection?" I asked Hollowell, a medium-sized man with a gray buzz cut and bi-focal glasses.

"Yeah. Been collectin' old Colts for more 'an forty years. I love these antiques—Single Action Armies, Bisleys, Lightnin's, cap and ball Armies and Navies—you name it. If it's an old west Colt, I'll buy it."

"Ever buy guns from Cecil Brogdan?"

"Not many. He's usually selling modern stuff. He likes his Smith & Wessons. Not too knowledgeable about antiques. But occasionally he'll run across an old gun and he calls me first."

"Think he'd help me track down an AK-47 that once passed through his hands?"

"Gun from the school shootin'?"

"That's the one."

"Cecil in trouble?"

"Probably not over this, unless he altered the gun to shoot full auto."

"I can't speak for Cecil, but figger he's not the type who does that. He can tinker with guns, but he's not a smith."

"Doesn't seem necessary to have much knowledge to install a drop-in sear and get full auto capability out of one of these imports. They provide full instructions. Not much more than installing a light bulb."

"Still, getting' caught with a machine gun could be federal hard time. I doubt Cecil would risk it when he can make a quick profit and move on."

"Profiting from gun sales without a license is a federal crime."

"Yeah, but everybody does it."

Dickey Hollowell told me I might find Cecil Brogdan working at a commercial plumbing supply store in the industrial area of the old city. It was getting late, so I decided to continue my fool's errand the next morning.

<><><>

At 9 a.m., I sat in my shiny gray unmarked Ford outside Volunteer Wholesale Plumbing and Supply at the corner of McCalla and Bertrand. But before going inside to roust Cecil Brogdan, I called my friend Ned 'The Fed' Greznik at the BATF&E office on Locust Street.

"You interested in an unlicensed guy who's been dealing in guns for decades?"

"Maybe. Who are we talking about?"

"Guy named Cecil Brogdan."

He laughed. "We've known about Cecil since before I got here. Why are you looking at him?"

"At one point he owned the AK-47 used to kill ten people at my school shooting."

"That sucks."

"Tell me about it."

"Trouble is," he said, "more than fifty percent of the part-time gun dealers in the U.S. are operating without a federal license. Everybody and his brother want to make a few bucks buying and selling guns. They troll gun shows, set up at weekly flea markets in every backcountry town in the south, and say they're just disposing of their collection."

"So what about Cecil? I'm sitting outside his job right now."

"We've tried to buy guns from him dozens of times. Every time a new agent comes into the office, we try again. We know what he's doing, but he knows us or he can smell a cop across a crowded gun show and always says and does the right thing."

"There's got to be somebody who can score a gun from this guy."

"I'm sure there is, but I need multiple sales from an unlicensed individual to establish an ongoing criminal enterprise and make a case. It would take too much time and money only to get a smalltime dealer."

"You gotta be kiddin'."

"It's the same as most of the drug dealers out there. The narcs know who's selling, but knowing and making a case are two different things."

"So, after I talk to him, you have no interest?"

"Unfortunately not."

"The AK was altered to full auto."

"If you can prove Cecil altered it and sold it that way, yeah. If you don't want him in state court, we'll take him for that."

"I'd have an easier time solving the Lindberg kidnapping."

"Sorry. But from what we know of Cecil Brogdan, he probably didn't mess with an automatic weapon."

"That's what I hear, too."

"Look, Sam, don't spin your wheels too much. For a couple months after your shooting, the public and the politicians will act outraged and call for tighter gun control. Three months from now, after the pro gun lobbies start chanting about the Second Amendment and the politicians envision votes going down the drain, their plans for more regulation fade away."

"Hard to believe most states don't care about keeping a paper trail on handguns and assault weapons."

"I agree," Greznik said, "but prior to the Brady Bill, you could walk into a gun dealer or pawn shop in most states and legitimately buy a handgun with nothing more than a driver's license proving you were a resident."

"I know. In New York, I used to arrest people all the time with a trunk full of guns that came from the Carolinas. Local skells who had friends or relatives down south would take a drive and stock up on handguns. Even if they bought retail from pawn brokers or real gun dealers where the friend or relative acted as their straw man, they'd pick up Saturday night specials they could sell on any street corner for ridiculous prices and make a fortune. New York kids seemed to need a gun so they'd have more juice than the other kids on the block."

"Unless every state requires a permit to buy handguns, and I'd even toss assault rifles into that restriction, and outlaw these casual sales, we're pissing in the wind. You don't have to ban guns, you just have to make sure they're only sold to people qualified to own them—honest citizens, not criminals and head cases."

After Greznik thoroughly ruined my morning, I walked into the plumbing supply store. Dressed in my Harris Tweed sport jacket, I doubted that anyone thought I'd come to buy pipe fittings. But no one gave me a hard time and Cecil Brogdan wasn't difficult to find.

"You ever hear your car backfire and stall and you just know it's not going to start again, Cecil?" I asked, somewhat cryptically.

"I don't understand what ya mean."

Cecil was pushing sixty, thin and clean cut with short gray hair.

"I've got you in possession of the AK-47 that killed ten people at the elementary school in Prospect."

His eyes bugged out and he stammered before making his next statement.

"I didn't kill nobody."

Lack of common sense always amazes me. "If you sold that gun to Lindell Merritt, you idiot, I'm going to give your name to every spouse or parent of a victim. Ever hear of a wrongful death suit?'

He nodded slowly.

"I hope you don't own much because after their lawyers get finished with you, you'll be living in a cardboard box."

"Whoa, officer. That's got nuthin' ta do with me."

Cecil sounded troubled . . . and sincere. Sometimes a little nudge works wonders.

"How so?"

"Cause I didn't sell that gun to no head case who shot up your grammar school."

"And how can you be so sure?"

"Cause I saw that kid's pitcher on the news. He weren't my buyer. It ain't that long ago and that's the only AK I ever owned and turned over. I sold it to some Cherokee guy."

"What Cherokee guy? What's his name?"

Cecil began blinking like a camera on motor drive. His Adam's apple jiggled up and down and he tried his best to moisten the cotton in his mouth with saliva. Classic signs of someone getting exasperated. I should have prepared myself to do CPR on the man.

"How in hell should I know?" he squawked. "I was walkin' through a gun show at the Jacob Building with a fer sale sign stuck in the muzzle o' that gun and this Indian stopped me and bought it."

"How do you know he was a Cherokee?" I knew I'd love his answer.

"Cherokee, Chickasaw, how's I supposed ta know what kinda Indian he was? Looked like he posed for the back o' the buffalo nickel. Coulda been an Apache, for all I know."

"How old was this Indian?"

"Way over the age limit. I don't sell no guns ta no kids."

219

I wasn't getting anywhere with Cecil, so I tried a new line of questioning.

"Okay, listen. Let's forget about the AK for now. The shooter also had a Sig-Sauer 9mm that the original buyer sold at a Knoxville gun show. It's been a while, but the seller gave me a good description of the guy who bought it. If I tell you what he looked like, would you tell me if you know him from the local gun shows?"

"Why would I do that?"

"Because then I won't call my friend at ATF and tell him I have you handling a gun used in multiple murders."

True or not, that grabbed his attention, so I softened up a little.

"And I've got three dead teachers and six dead children not much older than babies lying in the morgue," I said. "Somebody has to stick up for them."

Cecil didn't answer right away.

"Most people in this area claim to be good Christians. How about you, Cecil?" I asked, trying to pry the right thing from him.

He remained silent for another long moment.

"Okay," he said, reluctantly, "what's he look like?"

"This description is a little old, but maybe six foot, medium build, salt and pepper hair pulled back into a ponytail, Fu Manchu mustache. Wore a gold earring made like the base end of a bullet. Had a primer and said .38 Special on it."

"Needed a shave most o' the time?"

"He did that day."

Cecil sighed, looking like he'd rather do anything other than give up a brother gun dealer.

"Zell Wakeman."

Perhaps Zell Wakeman was a light at the end of my tunnel, an actual player who really did something I could substantiate and tie him to my shooter. "How do I find Zell?"

"Don't know where he's at now. Ain't seen him around for more 'an a year. Heard he got him a job down in Atlanta or Birmin'ham. Chattanooga, maybe. I'm not sure where."

Another cold trail. And I was moving from the realm of an investigation pertinent to my case to just being plain nosey. If I found Zell Wakeman and he was stupid enough to admit he sold a handgun to an underage buyer, if in fact he did, I could charge him with an offense. But maybe Wakeman never met Lindell Merritt and he sold the Sig to someone else. Without seeing a documented history on the ownership of that gun, I could envision it being in the possession of many other people. Nonetheless, Merritt had been twenty years old when he died and even if I could tie Wakeman to him, Wakeman's lawyer would stall their court appearance for months to let the emotions of the moment pass. By that time, I doubted anyone would care. A sad state of affairs, but painfully true.

The Sig was used to shoot a police officer, so I wanted to help Roane County further their efforts by passing along the information. But that was their case, not mine. And all this was eclipsed by the hour and my mayor not wanting me to work overtime.

<><><>

At 4:45, I walked back into Prospect PD, tired of interviewing witlings and seeing no satisfying conclusion to a frustrating few days. At least my little neat and orderly police department provided a respite from the lunacy of the outside world. I dropped into the chair next to Bettye Lambert's desk like a paratrooper hitting a drop zone with ninety pounds of combat gear attached to him. I let out a sigh.

"Darlin', you look frazzled," she said.

"You ain't just whistlin' Dixie, Blondie."

"What's the matter, hit a brick wall?"

"Ever hear about the man shoveling sand against the tide?"

"You've mentioned that before, but didn't call it sand."

I chuckled. Bettye has a good memory.

"Three adults, six kids, and one deranged bastard who woke up one morning, didn't take his meds, and decided to kill his mother, all died and I doubt anyone can do anything about it."

"Couldn't find anything?"

"I found a lot, but I also learned that we're going to need more than ten lost lives to make any common sense changes."

"What do you mean?"

"Everybody is selling guns—handguns, assault weapons, sporting guns, you name it. If they can make a buck, they sell it. But neither the cops nor the feds can or want to expend much energy to control who gets an off-the-books firearm that's almost untraceable."

"Sounds like a long story. Want me to make coffee?"

"I want something stronger than coffee."

"From the bottom drawer?"

"Where else?"

"It's almost five o'clock. I'll switch the radio and phone over to county 9-1-1."

"I'll meet you in my office."

A few minutes later, Bettye walked into my room, took off her gun belt, and laid it on the center of my desk. Her khaki shirt and green uniform pants fit like they were tailor-made, but I knew she bought off the rack.

I dropped my feet from the desktop, spun my chair to the right, and took a bottle of Glenfiddich and two clean glasses from the bottom drawer and set them on the blotter.

"Ice?" I asked.

"Please, and a little water."

I stepped over to the mini-fridge and fixed two drinks. I walked back, sat in the guest chair facing her, and took a pull on the three fingers of scotch I'd poured for myself.

"Tell me," she said.

"I've spent two days chasing down these guns and just got more and more frustrated."

Her expression softened. "I'm sorry."

"Any felon, mentally screwed-up weirdo, terrorist, or person looking to kill his mother-in-law with a virtually untraceable handgun can buy one easier than finding a bottle of good whisky in one of the dry counties in this state."

"I don't know what to say."

"It'll take more than you and me to make sense out of this."

I shook my head and drained another half of the scotch sitting in my glass. Bettye took a tiny sip of hers.

"Have you got any more leads to follow?"

"Sure, two doozies. The Sig was last seen in possession of a guy named Zell Wakeman who may have relocated to Atlanta or Birmingham or Chattanooga, or Upper Volta for all I know. The last recorded owner of the stolen AK-47 may have gotten it from an unidentified Mexican who, years ago, worked on a roofing crew out of North Knoxville. And the brother of the dead guy who bought it from the Mexican, sold it to a guy who sold it to an unknown Native American who could have been a Cherokee or Navajo or Eskimo for all anyone knows."

Bettye took a turn shaking her head. "Lord have mercy. Is it even worth tryin' anythin' more?"

"The Sig was used to shoot a cop, so I'll tell Roane County what I learned and, since this Wakeman may have gone out of state, they can ask the FBI for help. I am not going to jump through any more hoops to find a mysterious Mexican and an Indian who may have followed the letter of the law in obtaining and disposing of the assault rifle."

I finished my drink and poured a second. "Want any more while I've got this open?"

She shook her head and showed me her mostly full glass. Her shoulder-length hair swayed from side to side. "I've got a long way to go with this. And do you think you should go easy with that? You still have to drive home."

"Yeah, you're right. I'll sip this one."

She blinked a few times and smiled slightly. After a long moment of looking into my eyes over the rim of her glass, she asked, "You doing okay with this?"

"I've run across some frustrating stuff in my life, but this tops it all."

"I didn't mean your investigation. I meant after the massacre at the school."

I smiled at her thoughtfulness. "Thanks for asking. I'm no worse than anyone else. Maybe better. If I let this kind of stuff bother me, I'd be a candidate for a straight jacket."

"You're a piece of work, Sam Jenkins."

My mother also called me by both names when I annoyed her. I like when Bettye does it.

I grinned like the village idiot. "Did you tell all the guys involved that I want them to visit our girl at dial-a-shrink?"

"I did. Want me to make an appointment with Peggy for you, too?"

"When I get finished."

"Promise?"

"Don't nag."

"I'll use my gun."

"I give up."

"You'd never surrender. You're just being nice."

I shrugged, took another gulp of scotch, and realized it hadn't left any effect on me. I rattled the cubes in the glass. The second drink was almost gone; must have evaporated in the low humidity.

"I can't imagine what it was like to see those six dead children," she said. "I feel so sorry for anyone there."

"Yeah, dead kids are different. The first homicide I ever handled were twins strangled with a pair of pantyhose. They were only five weeks old."

"Oh, Lord have mercy. I'm so sorry."

"The woman's husband was a soldier getting ready to go overseas. She'd been suffering with post-partum depression and one day . . . just decided she needed to kill her babies."

We sat in silence for a few moments. Bettye wiped a single tear from her cheek and took another sip of scotch. I didn't refill my glass.

"The mayor called down while you were out" she said. "The city council held an emergency meeting and decided they want to allocate funds to hire two full-time and one part-time armed security guard to cover the middle and elementary schools."

I rolled my eyes.

"I don't know how I feel about that," she said.

"Neither do I. It's something to do, but I'm not sure it's the right thing. They don't pay the teachers an honest wage, how much do they intend to pay these security experts?"

"Ten dollars an hour."

I went to the side of my desk and started banging numbers into a calculator.

"Four hundred dollars a week and they're off all summer." I reached a bottom line. "That's an annual salary below the poverty level."

"Who can afford to take a job like that?" she asked. "Certainly not someone qualified to take on an armed man."

I returned to the guest chair, crossed my legs, and folded my arms over my chest. I'm sure she could read my body language. "I know who'll apply, old Jesse Fart who owns a gun and collects a pension or anyone who wants to supplement their Social Security income. They'd be lucky to get a retired cop."

"Would a single guard help in a case like ours?"

"The people who commit these atrocities may be mentally unstable, but they're not stupid. And they seem to know their guns and tactics. If I wanted to kill specific people in a building with an armed guard, I'd take out the guard first. And no one can tell me they couldn't. After that, the gunman is right back to where we were when a teacher called 9-1-1. Either we kill him after he does the damage or he takes his own life."

"The mayor said he'd like you to train the guards."

I sat up straight and laughed. "Oh, sure, give me a week and I turn them into a combat-ready fighting machine. Ronnie needs psychiatric help."

She chuckled.

"I'll call Ralph Oliveri at the FBI and see if he can send me their statistics on how many bank guards are killed during the armed robberies they were hired to prevent."

"I never thought of that," she said.

"Here's an even more sobering question. Ever think how it would feel if one of your kids were murdered?"

Bettye's eyes opened much wider. "Not until this happened."

"Neither did the parents of those six children. And what will those mothers and fathers think when, after the fever cools down, those who can change things for the better are no longer enthused about formulating a workable, common sense plan to keep something like this from happening again?"

"Two people like us will ask the same questions."

Smart woman.

*

Carpathia
By Scott Whitmore

~

After retiring from the U.S. Navy I decided to try my hand at writing a novel, but struggled a bit getting started — what to write about? I did so many things in the military — supply and logistics, operations and scheduling, force security, and being an instructor — but nothing about my service struck a chord. At the time I was working at a newspaper as a sportswriter covering motorsports, so the idea of centering the story around an old-time cross-country endurance race came to mind. But there needed to be something more, I thought. As a kid I enjoyed munching popcorn and watching "creature feature" monster movies on Saturday nights, so I decided to try and recreate a bit of that. The result was Carpathia. — Scott Whitmore…

Prologue

The dream was crystal clear and always the same: a reflection of the events as they occurred that stopped just short of the unthinkable, heart-shattering conclusion.

At first he woke up screaming and wet with sweat, but after several years and hundreds of nights reliving what happened while asleep he stopped thinking of it as a nightmare.

Amanda is in the middle of a stone bridge, standing in the pool of light provided by a gas lantern hanging from a pole and gently rocking in the breeze off the river below. Overhead are the lights of an airship, one of the very first upon these shores.

Two carriages stand at either end of the bridge, the one to the north having screeched to a halt just moments before. For a brief moment the only sounds are the breeze, the panting of the foam-flecked horses and the putter of the airship.

One man jumps down from the north carriage; three men from the other — two from the coachman's seat and the third from the passenger compartment. Both groups move toward the center of the bridge, heading for the lone figure in the pool of light that is Amanda.

The bridge is arched, and as he climbs the gentle slope the solitary man can see just the upper half of the three other men. Two of the figures drop from view and then just as suddenly two black shapes, close to the stones of the bridge, crest the rise and approach him at a dead run on four legs, passing Amanda without pausing.

In the feeble light he can see they are wolves, but larger than any seen in nature.

He has anticipated this and prepared accordingly. As the wolves approach the man reaches into a coat pocket with his left hand while his right finds the hilt of the short sword hanging by a belt around his waist. The wolves are almost on him and in one motion he waves his left hand upwards, spreading a fine mist of powder into their path while stepping to one side.

The front legs of both animals collapse when they run through the powder, sending them snout-first into the cobblestones but propelled forward by the momentum of their hind quarters. The man knows the wolfsbane won't kill the creatures, but it provides a tactical advantage. He runs several paces to where the wolves lie sprawled on the stones, panting and snarling; the sword flashes twice, three, four times in the dim light and the man looks down at the now headless wolves at his feet.

The man turns to resume the climb to the apex of the bridge, but he can see the third figure, a man with glowing red eyes, has reached Amanda. He slips one hand around her waist and the other clamps onto her wrist, turning and guiding her away from the light to the opposite end of the bridge.

"There are many more where they came from, you know," a voice whispers in the man's ear as he begins to run toward the two figures disappearing into the darkness. "You are a clever boy, but I have lived far too long to let a boy get the best of me."

The man reaches the top of the bridge and as he crosses the circle of light something strikes his back, sending him tumbling. From his hands and knees the man sees a rope ladder gliding toward the two figures below.

The man looks up, sees the lights of the airship hovering over the bridge and through the pounding of blood in his ears he hears the wheezing of pumps and motors. From his knees the man watches as the red-eyed figure below him pulls Amanda close and climbs the first few rungs of the ladder. The airship quickly climbs, and they are gone — she is gone — into the night.

Amanda was gone.

Chapter 1

The tarnished brass bell over the door leading into the store gave a hollow tinkle when Jameson pushed it open. He stepped across the threshold into the dimly lit emporium, his boots softly pushing sawdust over and into the edges of the worn but uneven floor boards.

The two people in the store — the shopkeeper wearing a flowing floor-length shirt, small vest, baggy pants and brimless cap, a similar attire worn by many of a certain faith in the Black Sea town of Constanta, and a customer dressed much as Jameson was in a dark suit, coat and hat — turned toward the door from their places at the counter. The shopkeeper's eyes caught and held Jameson's for a few seconds then he turned back to his customer, repeating the various prices for whatever gadget or gizmo they were bargaining over. Jameson walked among the aisles of shelves as he waited for their business to be done.

The shelves were piled with all manner of goods, from cooking utensils to tools to clothing. Combined with the low ceiling and dim lighting, the clutter gave the store's interior a cramped, stuffy feel. Near the front by tall and dusty windows, Jameson found a section of medical supplies and equipment, with modern and ancient remedies sitting side-by-side. Next to leather pouches of herbs for headaches were glass jars filled with a butter-colored cream for use on steam burns.

Jameson looked through the dirty windows down to the harbor and thought the store was an accurate reflection of recent events in the town, which had started hundreds of years ago as a trading stop serving the tribes of the seacoast and mountainous interior as well as nomads of the nearby steppe. The natural harbor had been dredged and enlarged and four long wharves lined with steam-powered gantry cranes built to service the steam- and sail-powered ships that continuously called at the port. Goods flowed from Constanta north to Russia, making Romania significant enough that the Russian Tsar hand-picked the King from his own family after the country broke free from the Ottoman Empire.

As Jameson watched a massive airship lazily circled above, disappearing from view behind him over the town to the north and reappearing to the south. A smallish temporary landing field had been laid out north of the harbor, with docking pylons and rudimentary passenger and cargo facilities. Indeed, that was how Jameson had arrived a day previously. A larger, permanent aviation servicing facility was under construction on ground to the south that had until recently been marshland.

Warehouses of various sizes, built to accommodate the harbor and aviation field, stood between both and a north-south railroad line ran parallel to the sea coast. The harbor, airfield and storage sites were connected by lanes paved with brick and thick steam pipes strung along on head-high braces. Other than a brick lane from the harbor that became a cobblestone road through the town and then on to a rutted track, there was nothing running westward. And that, Jameson reflected, was the reason for it all — the stated reason, he corrected himself with the hint of a smile.

In the corner of the window was the shadow of a poster pasted to the outside, and even though he couldn't see through the dark square Jameson knew exactly what it said as he had seen the same poster many times over the past year.

> Crown Prince Stefan of Romania Announces
> The Greatest Scientific Endeavor of the Century!
> A Race of Endurance and Power Without Rival!
> From Constanta to Bucharest via Bacau,
> Targu-Mures and Pitesti!
> For Self-Propelled Ground Machines!
> Grand Prize: 20,000 English Pounds Sterling
> (or equivalent)!
> And a Royal Commission for
> Manufacture Of The Winning Vehicle!
> 15 August 1882

Russia's interest in Romania was centered on the port of Constanta and having a bulwark against the tottering Ottomans but the King and his ambitious son the Crown Prince were not so limited in their thinking. Crown Prince Stefan had traveled to other European nations, taking in the sights and seeing with keen interest the development of their industries, and he convinced his father that the "Race of Endurance and Power without Rival" would be the first step toward Romania joining the ranks of the Great Powers.

Over the water, the airship turned and began another circuit. A tricolor flag could be seen snapping in the wind behind the gondola hanging down from the gasbag. Jameson heard steps shuffling through the sawdust and then the bell over the door. He turned to the shopkeeper, who motioned him to the counter with a lazy wave of his hand.

"I have some news of interest to you," the shopkeeper said with a lopsided grin that displayed uneven and dirty teeth. "Two more groups have arrived for the expedition, making four in all."

"Four? Hmmm." Jameson nodded. "Good, Imare, good. Where are these latest two from, do you know? Did you get any names?"

"France and America. No names; my source did not have direct access to the passengers. A Count and a cowboy … well, the American group includes a cowboy but the leader appears to be just a commoner."

"That's all they have there, Imare," Jameson said with a tight smile. He reached into his waistcoat and laid some golden coins on the counter. "Thank you. I imagine this concludes our arrangement. I doubt additional groups will arrive before the start. In fact, these latest two will be hard pressed to get ready in time for the start."

The shopkeeper studied Jameson for a moment. Imare had met many men from many countries in his day, and Jameson seemed unremarkable in comparison. The man's accent was English, but it was not quite the same English as the shopkeeper had heard in the past. Jameson was tall and of average build, his clothes clean but not expensive, and his brown hair cut short and pushed back from his face, which was thin and clean shaven. Imare found Jameson's age hard to determine; he was obviously no longer a young man, but there was no gray hair and he had just a few wrinkles around his hazel eyes. He smiled frequently, but Imare noticed the gesture did not include Jameson's eyes, which seemed to miss nothing.

"Indeed, they are hard at work in the warehouses set aside for them, but I am told the progress of each has been satisfactory." Imare used a fingertip to move one of the coins on the counter, tracing a figure eight pattern. He looked up, showing his dirty teeth. "One cannot help but wonder what interests you so greatly about these groups that you seek help from a poor shopkeeper such as I, and not address your questions to government officials."

Jameson took the hint and pulled a few more coins from his pocket. He could easily ignore Imare's veiled threat, knowing he would likely leave the city before any action could be taken, but why take the chance? Placing the coins on the counter, he returned the shopkeeper's smile.

"Tell me, Imare, have you ever traveled beyond Constanta, into the countryside or to the mountains?"

"What? No, no, my good friend. Such a man as myself, a simple shopkeeper born in Izmir, would be lost outside of a city." Imare swept the coins up from the counter and into a pocket in his vest. "The people of the mountains here are very different, very unusual. Their ways are ... not what I am used to. I would fear for my life to move amongst them."

Jameson nodded gravely and placed a finger alongside his nose. Using the same finger, he pointed at the shopkeeper, whose eyes went wide at the gesture, a sign of caution used by the "people of the mountains" he so recently expressed fear of.

With a quick nod Jameson turned on his heel and walked out. He stood outside the store for a moment, looking up. The airship was still circling, which seemed unusual. The passenger ship that carried him to Constanta had gone straight to the temporary landing dock.

The day was bright, sunny and hot, and the skies were clear. A blast of steam erupted from an overflow valve on one of the gantry cranes in the harbor, temporarily drowning out the screeching of gulls common to most seaports. His hotel was just minutes from the shop, but Jameson took a half hour to cover the distance. He was deep in thought over the newly obtained information, which presented an opportunity he hadn't considered before.

Four groups, the three from Europe that he expected, and the Americans who he hadn't....

Thank you for reading an excerpt from the full length novel 'Carpathia' by Scott Whitmore.

Nights
By Ray Gregory

~

He goes out the door, the cold air bites; it's going to be a long cold night.

Tramping the streets, shaking hands with door knobs, keeping everything right.

Torch in your hand, checking dark nooks and crannies keeping well out of sight, on this cold frosty night.

You hide in a doorway, and have a quick fag; these bloody nights shifts they can be a drag, could do with a brew, or a quick pint would do, round the back of the ale house I knock on the door.

Come on you landlord you know why I'm here, get me a pint of your fine ale house beer.

I step inside, slump in a chair, the roaring log fire that gives me good cheer, feet up on the chair a pint in my hand, have a hot pie old lad, I hear someone say it will set you up well when you go on your way.

I sit for a while, then bid my farewell, then back to the beat, boy this policing is hell.

Shaking hands with door knobs, I check all my beat, till its brew time again and get me some heat.

No pint next time, or hot pie for me, but a cold curled up buttie, and a mug of stewed tea, then back to the beat shaking door knobs for me.

*

Breakwater
By Paul Anthony

~

Corbera d'Ebre, Catalonia, Spain
November, 1938

Dawn shuffled lazily from behind Catalonia's rolling mountains when the sun rose silently to cast its energising rays on a valley below. A sudden shaft of light boldly settled on the rippling water, sparkled on its surface, and gradually extended its reach to a group of soldiers advancing across the River Ebro from Corbera.

Enrico led his troops across a narrow wooden bridge straddling the waterway. They walked in single file towards the distant bank trying to ignore the scars of their tired bloody war. Gory, prostrate, a headless corpse lay sprawled in the centre of the bridge with its lower limbs dangling in muddy water. The uniform was dishevelled, torn, and unrecognisable. Deftly guiding his boot, Enrico slid the remains from the crossing. There was a gentle, almost inaudible splash, when the carcass entered the dark slimy water and slid graciously beneath the surface.

The horror of war surrounded them. It was everywhere. Even the stench of death and decay defeated the smell of fresh morning dew rising from nearby meadowland.

Tall, lean, with a week's growth of facial hair, yellowing teeth, and bad breath, Captain Enrico De La Cruz hauled his thirty year old frame towards the Nationalist enemy. His old friend, Sergeant Javier Rodriguez, stuck close to the leader of his unit in the Republic's Fifth Army Corps.

The two weary comrades had grown up together on the streets of Valencia and had fought hard to halt the Nationalist advance towards their home. Today they were part of a counter attack calculated to drive Franco's army from their heartland.

'It's going to be another hot one,' suggested Javier smoothing his ragged moustache. 'It'll be over thirty five degrees by midday.'

'By noon we will have slit our enemy's throat and pushed those Nationalists back a dozen miles or more,' chuckled Enrico.

Pausing for a moment, Javier knelt down and scooped river water into his canteen.

'The river is foul you fool,' snapped Enrico. 'Didn't you see the last one I committed to the depths? Are you stupid, Javier?'

'No, I am thirsty and so are our men,' countered the sergeant.

'Then we'll find clean water on the other side, you idiot. The number of dead rises every day. Pour it away. That's an order.'

Javier glared at his friend, mockingly raised the canteen to his lips, grimaced, and then reluctantly tipped its contents into the Ebro.

'Damn you, Enrico,' griped Javier.

'Get in line, Sergeant Rodriguez, and don't let our men see you acting like a spoilt child. It is a war we fight and if we have to struggle with an empty belly and dry lips then so be it.'

Slinging the canteen across his shoulders Javier stood to one side and ushered his troops forward with a cynical, 'For Spain, my friends, one last push for clean water!'

Ignoring Javier's cynicism Enrico snapped, 'Move the men through quickly. The opposition will never know what hit them. Quickly now, Javier! We can't dawdle here.'

Enrico raised a pair of binoculars and scanned the ridge across the river. His face was smeared with soil and his uniform was pitted with dirt. Yet somehow he stood dominant on the narrow bridge as if Captain Enrico De La Cruz was meant to be the saviour of the Republic.

There was a movement on the opposite bank when Enrico focused his binoculars and zoomed in on his nemesis.

An artillery shell whistled over the column of men and landed harmlessly in the river. As Enrico followed its flight the sound of a machine gun unexpectedly broke the relative peace of the morning and took out three men in their Republican line.

Unnerved, panicking soldiers ran for cover.

'Charge!' shouted Enrico. 'Forward!'

'Charge! You heard the captain,' screamed Javier.

Machine gun fire raked their narrow bridge and cut down more men as another shell flew overhead.

'They were waiting for us,' exploded Javier.

In the face of overwhelming firepower, distraught soldiers took flight and withdrew towards Corbera. Amidst the panic and confusion, others tried to dash across the bridge to engage the enemy but were mown down and slaughtered in their stride.

Another artillery shell whistled overhead and splashed into the river nearby.

'Captain! They'll have our range soon,' advised Javier.

'Forward!' implored Enrico. 'Charge our enemy!'

A salvo of mortar bombs exploded in the ranks blowing the narrow bridge sky high and destroying any immediate chance of further attack. Then a hail of heavy duty machine gun bullets flew over their heads, slammed into a stand of trees on the river bank.

Abandoning their position, Enrico and Javier ran towards Corbera yelling, 'Mortar! Mortar!'

More than five hundred men ran for their lives. They dived into the undergrowth, hid behind walls and rubble, dashed into abandoned farm buildings and outhouses, and dug into the ground for cover.

Finally, the enemy's artillery found their range and more shells exploded killing and maiming a dozen men.

Leading the main body of troops, Enrico and Javier headed towards the church on the hill. With bullets flying and ricocheting from its masonry the men hit the ground and scrambled to safety.

Enrico and Javier crawled into a bomb crater close to the church.

'Radio for our anti-aircraft artillery,' ordered Enrico as he withdrew his pistol and returned fire. 'Tell them to aim for the big guns and fire flashes on the other side of the river bank.'

Pointing skywards, Javier cried, 'What about him?'

An aircraft cruised low, released its bombs, and swiftly banked to the left as its machine guns opened up on troops below.

There was an almighty explosion when the aircraft's projectiles hit the side of the church. A huge cloud of debris rose as mayhem and destruction tore into the Fifth Army Corps and halted their counter offensive.

'Where are our tanks?' bawled Javier as he flipped onto his belly and unleashed his rifle on the enemy position.

'They were promised in July,' replied Enrico.

'Yeah and it's now November. We still have no tanks or aircraft to speak of,' protested Javier.

'They're coming,' countered Enrico. 'I dream every night that they are coming. I dream that one day we will defeat our enemy. The Mexicans will not let us down.'

More shells landed and heavy machine gun fire peppered their Republican lines as Javier ducked low and scuttled backwards into the bomb crater. 'Your dream is a nightmare, Enrico. We should retreat further,' he suggested.

Reloading, Enrico fired wildly over the crater's rim before announcing, 'The General's orders are to shoot any man who tries to retreat or surrender, sergeant. We have to hold this ground and wait for reinforcements.'

'You'd shoot your own men?' probed Javier, unsure.

'Javier, we have to obey orders,' responded Enrico.

Snarling, Javier disputed, 'What reinforcements are you on about, Enrico? We have a handful of anti-aircraft guns, half a dozen mortars, and a pathetic array of machine guns.'

'Yes, Javier, my friend, but we have brave men. We have warriors who have hearts bigger than lions. Men who will fight to the end if need be.'

'They'll need to if you're going to shoot them all when they retreat,' suggested Javier.

Crawling to the rim of the crater, Enrico took a look through his binoculars and remarked, 'The enemy haven't crossed yet. Our braves will stand and fight once this barrage has settled down.'

'But it's not enough,' argued Javier. 'We need more than guts and courage, Enrico. We've got all the heroes you could wish for. We need arms and ammunition, aircraft and tanks. Give me a bullet and I'll give you a body!'

Javier stood, defiant, and fired towards Franco's Nationalist army before ducking down again and reloading.

'Fool,' remarked Enrico. 'Make your bullets count, Javier.'

Minutes later, the artillery assault stopped.

'It's gone quiet,' said Enrico.

'They're coming,' yelled Javier to his fellow troops. 'Stand by everyone. They'll counter attack. Pick out your targets. Make every shot count.'

Checking his grenades, Javier snapped, 'We need more than luck now, Enrico.'

'The Mexicans won't let us down,' remarked Enrico.

Javier crawled across the bomb crater, shook Enrico by the arm, and demanded, 'You and your dreams. How long does this war last in your dreams, Enrico.'

'Who knows? Another year maybe, but if we get a hundred aircraft and a hundred tanks we can fight forever, my friend.'

'What if they overrun us, Enrico?'

'Valencia will fall and Barcelona will be our last stand.'

Lining up his grenades on the crater's rim, Javier remarked, 'If we don't win this one, Enrico, all is lost unless our friends help.'

Enrico broke his pistol, reloaded it, grabbed a nearby rifle and shouted, 'Then I shall die here on this land, in this earth, within this soil. For this is my Spain. Here! This is my country.'

Two German dive bombers sporting Nationalist emblems on their wings flew across the river as a barrage of heavy machine gun opened up from the Nationalist ranks. They circled, swooped low, and opened up with machine gun fire strafing the Republic's positions Enrico's Republican's had no answer to airborne artillery.

Moments later, a unit of troops began assembling a pontoon bridge destined to provide a platform for a counter attack across the Ebro.

Eventually, the machine gun fire stopped and more than a thousand men of the Nationalist army charged across the bridge.

As the counter attack got under way, Enrico's men dug in intending to hold their ground.

A shot rang out and penetrated Enrico's skull. He fell backwards into the crater. His body twitched in its final throes as he sprawled across the dirt.

'Enrico!' screamed Javier. 'No! No! It cannot be.'

High above the town, a solitary Junker dive bomber discharged a shell from its belly. The missile whistled downwards and exploded in the centre of Corbera.

'No, not my friend, Enrico,' wept Javier holding his comrade's body close to his. 'No, please, Lord. Stop the killing. Wake Enrico from his dream, Lord. Please, God…. Stop the noise…. Stop the killing…. Wake Enrico from his dream.'

More shots rang out and a grenade exploded close by as Javier cuddled close the body of his friend.

The church in the hill stood lonely and defiant as the battle exploded and the River Ebro flowed casually by, awash with the blood of man…

Thank you – you've been reading an excerpt from Chapter One of 'Breakwater' – a full length novel by Paul Anthony.

*

Gotcha!
By the Boss's Snout

~

The Boss's Snout: Gotcha at last!

Station Sergeant: Who me? What are you talking about?

The Boss's Snout: You! Gotcha at last. The boss will be pleased.

Station Sergeant: Have you really and how do you explain that?

The Boss's Snout: It's taken me a full book and years to identify you but today I got you.

Station Sergeant: Really? Well done. And I had you down as the leader of the Home Office Hit Squad.

The Boss's Snout: Which one?

Station Sergeant: The one that clones the top brass.

The Boss's Snout: You can't prove that.

Station Sergeant: Well, it's been such a long time since one broke the mould.

The Boss's Snout: Well, the game's up…. You Station Sergeant are that well known Spanish undercover officer …SERGIO TENNSTATA…

Station Sergeant: Don't be stupid. That makes me an anagram. I don't even exist. But then again, I suppose it's a starter for ten….

The Boss's Snout: I'm rumbled…. Who are you then? Go on, you can tell me….

~

THE END….. NEARLY

The Doors Ajar!
By Ray Gregory

~

Have you heard that call?

"Come on old lad, it's time for bed. It's 6 o'clock and you need your rest".

Sitting here against the wall, watching daytime TV, adverts, soaps and all.

You've done your bit I hear you say, so sit back and relax it's the end of the day. Don't worry, old lad we will keep you well fed. Now drink up your cocoa it's time for your bed.

I take it all in and ponder a while, say to myself, "No, that's not my style."

Looking across the room see the door that's not closed, but merely ajar, I think, "What the hell." Cannot stay here all day, must get to those places so far away.

Kick off your slippers, go grab your shoes, pack up your bags go take in the views. Passport ready, my taxi awaits lets go old friends our aircraft awaits.

Life is for living not mooching around, staring at walls, well that's not for me.

See that door, it's not closed but merely ajar, so off I must go to places afar.

Sun on my back, a beer in my hand, I take in the sights of this far away land,

"Ah this is for me, sun surf and sand no worries you see, you will understand!"

So come on old friends you have done of your best, but life is for living don't lay down to rest, look at that door…

… It's not closed but ajar…

*

THE END

~

PLEASE ACCEPT OUR INVITATION TO....
...MEET THE AUTHORS...

~

Meg Johnston

~

A retired Orthopaedic Nursing Sister, Meg Johnston is the pseudonym of a published author of 'children's fantasy'. Born and bred in Cumbria, Meg has been married to a now retired Cumbrian police officer for 42 years. They have two sons, one daughter, two gorgeous grandsons, and three beautiful granddaughters. Meg has been part of the Paul Anthony Associates editorial team for over two decades, is an avid reader, especially of science fiction/fantasy, and a recent convert to 'electronic reading'.

http://paulanthonys.blogspot.co.uk/2011/12/the-paul-anthony-book-shop.html

*

Dave "Dusty" Miller.

~

Dave 'Dusty' Miller left home at 15 and became an Apprentice in the Army in Carlisle, 350 miles from his home in Southend. Following training he became a Craftsman in the Royal Electrical Mechanical Engineers. (REME). Posted to Germany he spent more time playing basketball but managed military exercises in Libya and in 1967 was deployed to the area at the time of the first Israeli-Egyptian 6 day war. Dave served for short periods in Malta, Naples and Germany before returning home to get married.

Married for 47 years, he and his wife have 2 children and 4 grandchildren. (3 boys and one girl). They are all involved in sports to a high standard playing for their schools as well as County in Football and Rugby and Cricket, (and that includes his granddaughter).

Dave joined Cumbria Constabulary in 1970 and was involved in many sections. He was a Beat officer, Traffic officer,

Village bobby, Tactical Support Group officer, Firearms officer, Control room operator, and Van driver. He was.involved in policing the Miners' strike, the Toxteth riots in Liverpool, and numerous murder enquiries throughout the county. He carried out Youth work within the police service and was a drill instructor with the Cadet Force. In later years he worked with Social Services, children support, and residential care.

Dave 'Dusty' Miller took up writing as a means of dealing with bouts of depression. Woken through the night having started writing in his dreams!!!.

He is currently working on his life story "Boy left home and returned a Man" He has been encouraged by other writers during a very varied life.

*

Ray Gregory
~

Ray served over 30 years from 1966 to 1998 as a police officer in Cumbria. He likens his journey from Hearbeat to Star Trek and has worked in Uniform in the Lakes, then as a Village Bobby, moving to the Traffic Department, and finally taking the post as a Rural Sergeant covering an area stretching from the edge of the National Park to the Solway Coast. Ray ran a Charity for 5 years taking medical aid including ambulances to Iasi in Romania. (He is an honorary member of the City of Isai ambulance service) Ray worked for a tour Company on retiring from Cumbria Police - his last trip being to Lourdes, before returning to work for the Police in Communications. He finally hung up his headset in 2012. Now happily retired, but not letting the grass grow under his feet, travel is the new drug - particularly the Greek Islands with his wife Isabel. They have four grandchildren and his hobbies include travel and photography.

*

Edward Lightfoot

~

Edward Lightfoot was born in Carlisle in 1974. Leaving Caldew School in 1990 he firstly worked as an Insurance Broker before joining the administration team in Carlisle Police Station. He subsequently took his admin skills and joined the Royal Air Force in 1999 as a Personnel Administrator. The next 9 years Edward saw service in the UK, Germany, USA and The Gulf. . He left the RAF in 2008 and fulfilled a life-long ambition (following in his father's footsteps) and joined Cumbria Constabulary as a Police Officer. Edward lives locally with his wife, Sharron, and three daughters Aimee, Alex, and Paige.

*

Ian Bruce

~

Ian Bruce is the pseudonym of a man born in Liverpool in 1960. He grew up in North Wales, East Fife, Aberdeenshire and County .Durham. It was quite a journey following his father's career with H.M. Customs and Excise. Ian's childhood memories form a massive part of his scene setting when writing. From his first school, which was Welsh speaking, his memories include 'helping' his granddad shoe horses, delivering milk, and race pigeons., and catching fish, crabs and lobsters in an old ship's lifeboat.

Ian had the privilege to meet his great great aunt who only spoke Gaelic and had been evicted from her croft in the Highland Clearances. He has lived on country estates, been aboard trawlers, sat on the baker's van on its rounds, poached for brown trout, taken part in excavations of Roman sites and was lucky enough to live in houses with lots of books, quite a childhood.

Adulthood brought qualifications in hotel,catering and institutional management, near ruin in the miners' strike, and latterly thirty years in the police where he will end his career as a country sergeant in Cumbria. Ian lives in Scotland in a house built in 1740 with his lovely wife. They have three great grown up children and

Ian is looking forward to having enough time to write seriously in retirement.

*

Wayne Zurl

~

Wayne Zurl grew up on Long Island and retired after twenty years with the Suffolk County Police Department, one of the largest municipal law enforcement agencies in New York and the United States. For thirteen of those years he served as a section commander supervising investigators. He is a graduate of State University of New York, Empire State College and served on active duty in the US Army during the Vietnam War and later in the reserves. Zurl left New York to live in the foothills of the Great Smoky Mountains of Tennessee with his wife, Barbara.

Twenty of his Sam Jenkins mysteries have been produced as audio books and simultaneously published as eBooks. Ten of these novelettes are available in print under the titles of A MURDER IN KNOXVILLE and Other Smoky Mountain Mysteries and REENACTING A MURDER and Other Smoky Mountain Mysteries. Zurl has won Eric Hoffer and Indie Book Awards and has been named as a finalist for a Montaigne Medal and First Horizon Book Award. His full-length novels are: A NEW PROSPECT, A LEPRECHAUN'S LAMENT, HEROES & LOVERS, and PIGEON RIVER BLUES.

For more information on Wayne's Sam Jenkins mystery series see www.waynezurlbooks.net. You can read excerpts, reviews and endorsements, interviews, coming events, and see photos of the area where the stories take place.

You can find put more about Wayne at the following links:
Author website: http://www.waynezurlbooks.net
Twitter: http://www.twitter.com/#!/waynezurl
Facebook: http://www.facebook.com/waynezurl
Amazon author page:
http://www.amazon.com/author/waynezurl

Roger Price

~

Roger A Price is a retired Detective Inspector from Lancashire Constabulary who has been in charge of a covert unit, which received national acclaim for its successes in engaging those who openly sold Class A drugs.

Prior to this, Roger was in charge of the Criminal Investigation Department. at Preston, having first led a dedicated informant unit.

He also worked on murders, drugs squads, and the regional and national crime squads, often in covert roles across the UK, Europe and the Far East, receiving several commendations.

Now writing crime thrillers, Roger uses his previous professional experiences to add gritty realism.

Author Website: www.rogerapriceauthor.com
Twitter: https://twitter.com/RAPriceAuthor
Facebook: www.facebook.com/pages/Roger-A-Price-Author-Page/548720605149036?focus_composer=true&ref_type=bookmark
Amazon UK: http://www.amazon.co.uk/Their-Rules-Roger-Price-ebook/dp/B00HQLSRR4/ref=sr_1_1?ie=UTF8&qid=1404152728&sr=8-1&keywords=by+their+rules
Amazon US: http://www.amazon.com/By-Their-Rules-Roger-Price/dp/1843867540/ref=cm_cr_pr_pb_i

*

Simon Hepworth

~

Simon Hepworth is a former Cumbrian police officer now serving in the West Yorkshire Constabulary. And, in his spare time, he is a freelance writer and author. For a number of years Simon had a regular column in Police Review. His latest work, 'Late Shift', is a police-based novel which combines the genres of crime thriller with the paranormal, mixing in some good old-fashioned cynicism and humour for good measure.

Simon's other work includes the non-fictional 'Striking Through Clouds': the day-to-day operational diary of 514 Squadron, an RAF bomber unit in World War Two. He is currently writing a follow-up narrative history of 514 Squadron and its crews, 'Nothing Can Stop Us', along with another paranormal novel, 'Dead Reckoning'.

Simon lives in Leeds with his partner, Mandy, and son, William.

Amazon UK:

http://www.amazon.co.uk/Simon-Hepworth/e/B00E2UMTWG

*

Mike McNeff

~

Mike McNeff is a retired police officer and lawyer who always wanted to write novels. So when he retired that's just what he started doing. His novels draw from his American law enforcement experiences which included working on SWAT and training with Special Forces. They also reflect his obsession with history and current events.

Mike has worked as a state trooper, a deputy sheriff and a city police officer. He's been a prosecutor, police legal advisor, defense lawyer and a civil trial lawyer, using each experience to learn great lessons about life.

Mike is married with four children and seven grandchildren. In addition to writing, he does volunteer work and spends time teaching folks about firearms and shooting. He enjoys hiking, biking, fishing and playing guitar. Mike lives on an island off the coast of Washington State.

His books can be found on Amazon at http://bit.ly/1kUw97G and Barnes and Noble at http://bit.ly/1kUvSld

*

Scott Whitmore
~

Our 'special guest writer' Scott Whitmore was born and raised in the American Midwest. Scott enlisted in the U.S. Navy in 1982 and was later commissioned as an officer. After retiring from military service he joined the sports staff at The Herald, a daily newspaper located in Everett, Washington. In 2009 his feature story about a young Everett sprint car racer was awarded third place in the annual writing contest held by the National Motorsports Press Association. Scott left The Herald in 2009 to begin working as a freelance writer. In addition to his novels, he has written for various sports and motorsports magazines and blogs, and his article on NASCAR driver Danica Patrick was included in the August 2011 New York Yankees Magazine as part of a special issue celebrating women in sports. Apart from his writing abilities, Scott is renown for his unfaltering support of authors and, as an avid reader himself, runs a website highlighting book reviews from all over the world. You can discover more about Scott at http://scottwhitmorewriter.wordpress.com/

*

Paul Anthony

~

Paul Anthony is the pseudonym of a man born in Southport, Lancashire. He wrote his first novel in 1994 whilst a serving officer in Cumbria Constabulary and was advised to publish it under a pseudonym. Following publication in 1996 Paul went on to develop his love of writing and subsequently evolved into what he describes as 'an independent publisher'. He has now written and published over a dozen full length novels but he has also written television scripts, screenplays and film scripts as an individual or with the award winning scriptwriter, Nick Gordon.

Paul has been a featured author both at the Frankfurt Book Fair in Germany, and the 'Books Without Borders' Book Fair in New York.

Married with three children and five grandchildren he lives in the Eden Valley, Cumbria.

http://paulanthonys.blogspot.co.uk/2011/12/the-paul-anthony-book-shop.html

*

Printed in Great Britain
by Amazon